The Summer
SPRINGSTEEN'S SONGS
Saved Me

BARBARA QUINN

To Tassimo espresso and green tea

Do you believe in rock n' roll?
Don McClean/American Pie

CHAPTER ONE

Badlands

T HE SIGHS FROM MY SUPPOSED-TO-BE-EMPTY bedroom grow into moans, and my pulse thuds in my temples.
I know the dark place might suck me in if I'm not careful, but I
can't stop myself from looking.

I peer through the half-open door. My husband crouches
naked on the bed with his face buried between long, shapely
legs. Gorgeous, oddly-familiar legs.

"Oooh, oooh," groans the owner of the silky limbs.

"Mmm, mmmmm," answers Jerome. His rear wags from side
to side. The two bald spots in the center of his butt cheeks stare
at me, and my skin tingles the way it did when I drew too close
to the sparklers little Benjamin played with on the fourth of July.

The bed creaks. After twenty-six years the thing still makes
the same noise. A chill winds its way up my back, and pain
sears beneath my ribcage. My breaths rush in and out.

How can he? What the hell? In our bed. Today of all days.

Darkness grows, and flames erupt behind my eyelids. In a red
fury, I howl and charge. I whoop again and bear down on the
startled couple.

With a jolt, the name of the owner of the legs explodes into my mind.

Mandy.

I know Mandy. Sort of.

Jerome's personal trainer. Mandy Malone.

I slip on the area rug and lose my balance. Oh, yes. I know Mandy. At the gym Christmas party Mandy's hips sported a short, pink thing that appeared to be more like a headband than a skirt. The Christmas party was where I saw those legs before.

Mandy jumps out of bed and pulls the covers around her. She cowers in the corner.

I'm not proud of what I do next.

I grab a red high heel from the floor and climb to my feet. Taking aim, I hurl the shoe, but Jerome rolls away and the stiletto lands on the pillow. I reach for one of Jerome's wing tips resting annoyingly on the floor beside a pair of red panties and matching bustier. I launch the shoe, and the ever-athletic creep dodges and leaps from the bed. A pink rubber phallus lands with a *thunk*, and a yowl bursts from deep within me. "Sex toys. You're using sex toys." My hands grasp the floor lamp and level it like a spear.

"Sof, cut it out." Jerome's voice quavers, and he holds his hands over his privates.

Yanking the plug from the wall, I swing the lamp in a circle with no idea of what I'm doing, acting on instinct. I run towards him, but Jerome darts out of the way. The lamp smashes into the headboard, shattering bulbs and sending the pole flying from my hands. Shards of glass cover the bed and floor.

A tiny red mini-skirt and pink tank top catch my attention. My God, she must shop in the children's department. And what an awful color combination.

"Sof, this isn't doing anyone any good. Can we talk?" He's bobbing and weaving now, waiting for the next assault.

"Talk? Talk? What's there to talk about?" My brain sizzles, and my thoughts stab mercilessly. I seize his belt from the floor and hurl it, grazing the top of his head. "Do you remember when we bought this bed?"

No answer leaves his lips.

"I do." I snatch up his other wingtip, and this one catches him in the back. "We couldn't afford it, but you wouldn't take no for an answer. You said it would last a lifetime." I rip at the all-cotton sheets, yanking them off the mattress. "I just bought these at Macy's. I changed the bed yesterday. You told me polyester blends make you sweat. So does she!" I yell, jerking my arm towards the cowering blonde and fighting the fury twisting inside my gut.

Jerome approaches the closet. His hairy bare rear with its Orphan Annie blank orbs shines in the morning light. I tug on the curtains, and as the metal rod falls we both reach for it. He twists hard, and I let go causing him to lose his balance and send the pole clattering against the oak flooring. I swoop up the rod in a death grip and connect with the back of his knees. He falls to the rug and writhes in agony.

"Stop," he shouts.

"Sure," I say, launching myself on top of him and boxing his ears. "How's this?"

He rolls to the side throwing me off, and my face plants onto the carpet. I scramble to my feet and collect the scattered clothing, stumbling down the hallway to the spare bedroom.

Think, Sofia. Think.

I throw the lock and hit my palm against my forehead wincing as my brain sends out shooting stars. I inhale, and an ache accompanies the air and settles into my stomach with an unpleasant heaviness that signals I won't dislodge the pain anytime in the near future.

The dark place crowds the edges of my vision, and I move my eyes in a circle to keep it at bay. The dark place is number two on my list of worst things ever to happen to me. Finding Jerome in bed with Mandy follows close behind, displacing losing my childhood dog to a freak motorcycle-chasing accident, which now drops to fourth on my nasty-memory hit parade.

Jerome raps on the door. "Sofia, Sofia."

Rap, rap.

He calls louder. "Sofia, open up. I want to talk to you."

Rap, rap, rap.

"Go away."

He rattles the knob and bangs harder.

I spy my cell on the floor and collect it. If I hadn't forgotten my phone I never would've returned home. My schedule usually goes off like clockwork. Nyack Meals on Wheels by eight o'clock followed by the office an hour and a half later.

My hands tremble, and I clutch the side of the desk. "Do you do this often? Do you have it planned to the minute I go out?" My question comes out eerily calm.

No answer.

An urge to leave becomes unbearable. I seize my purse and two plastic Wal-Mart sacks intended for donations to Goodwill. Shaking out the bags I fill them methodically with a few of the clothes I store in the spare closet, the ones that don't fit in the overstuffed master bedroom closet, the master bedroom closet opposite the mahogany king I shared with Jerome for the past twenty-six years, the bed where Jerome and Mandy were doing the nasty. The edges around my eyes flood with black ink. I stuff Jerome's and Mandy's things into another bag and blink hard.

Jerome bangs so hard the hinges shake. I force myself to finish packing, unlock the door, and push past still-naked Jerome. At the sight of his pasty body, my stomach lurches and sends sour liquid into my throat. My eyes burn.

"Do you know what day today is?" I will my tears not to flow. Why give him that satisfaction?

Three paperbacks stand ready for donation at the top of the stairs. Though he dodges, the second one hits him on the side of the head and he yelps in pain. Too bad it's a softcover. Too bad there's nothing else to loft his way.

As I hurry down the stairs, my bags bump against my legs and my mind screams a million things at once. Jerome limps along naked behind me. Miss leggy-blondeness stays out of sight.

I open the front door, and my husband steps back, hiding from the eyes of the neighbors.

"Sof, where are you going? Wait."

I call over my shoulder, "You're an asshole, Jerome. You always were."

I haul the barbecue from the garage and dump Jerome's and Mandy's clothes onto the grill, dousing them with lighter fluid and striking a match. Flames shoot into the air. The fire smells good.

Scrutinizing the neat houses of the neighborhood, I'm irritated by how no one stirs behind the well-maintained structures. Without a doubt they watch and listen. I barely recognize the neighbors. They stay away and rebuff all attempts at socialization. Maybe they know something I don't. Maybe one of the things they know is that Jerome brings women home in my absence.

I fling the door of my Camry wide and retrieve the keys in my purse. I toss the bag that holds my things into the back seat.

Jerome calls out from behind the half-open door. "If I'm so bad, why the hell did you marry me?"

"Because I was an even bigger asshole than you." I pause. "It's taken me years to figure this out. You've been a dog for as long as I can remember. It's good to finally admit it."

"Sof, don't go. I can explain."

"You always have a reason. I'm sick of it, Jerome. I really used to care about you. No more. Go explain whatever it is you want to explain to her." I jerk my head in the direction of the house.

I climb into the car and back up out of the driveway. Out of habit I hit the brake and avoid Jerome's red Porsche parked on the curb. Jerome awarded himself the fancy vehicle when he won his latest anti-trust case. I hesitate. Why not smack into his trophy and ruin it the way he ruined my life? But then my Camry would be wrecked.

An idea dawns. I grab my house keys from my bag, pull alongside the Porsche, and jump from my sedan. Standing in front of the coupe, I carefully carve the letter "P" then "R" on the hood. Flakes of red paint coat the key.

"Sof. Stop! Not the car." Jerome's voice trembles with anguish. He scans frantically for something to cover himself and disappears. His unwillingness to be seen naked in public amuses me in an ironic way. The man is capable of shame, but not about shame for things that really matter like our relationship. I want to tell Doc Phelps about this insight. But I've sworn not to see him again. I'm better. I can do this on my own.

I dig with new resolve at the finish. The "I" forms easily, and so does the "C." The "K" comes out badly, but it's still readable. I underscore the word twice. The key scrapes against the paint, and the whine sends an enjoyable chill up my spine.

Jerome stands on the front walk wearing only the boxers he's apparently gone upstairs for and donned in haste. He stubs his toe on the concrete and hops on one foot in distress.

I climb into the car and send him a one-fingered salute. Gunning the engine I tear down the block, glancing in the rearview mirror at the man who for many years centered my existence. His arms flail wildly, and he limps towards his Porsche.

As I turn the corner, the house and Jerome recede. But Jerome fails to vanish. He and Mandy materialize right there with me in the front seat, making love with abandon, Jerome's head bobbing, and Mandy's hands gripping his megaphone-like ears.

Oh, oh, mmmm, mmmm.

The sounds repeat in my head, making me want to clap my hands over my ears, but I'm not so messed up to let go of the steering wheel. What a sad and infuriating situation. The darkness creeps around the back of my eyeballs.

I dial on my car phone and grind my teeth as the electronic version of Amy's voice fills the space. The recording tells me to leave a message for A&S Decorators. A for Amy, S for Sofia. My brain says time to add another S. A-S-S. Only an ass possesses the ability to stay with someone like Jerome.

I blurt, "Call me. Quick. The bastard. I'm through with him this time. You were right. Oh, crap, I won't be in today. I'll check with you later." I punch the end key on the screen keyboard, cross with myself for being so upset. But it hurts to have found Jerome with Mandy. It hurts so badly. All his promises and declarations of love made since the last time I accused him of straying ring hollowly in my ears. I so want to believe in him, and in love. Amy warned me not to trust him. But I chose to remember the good times in the beginning of our relationship and to rely on the little deposits of faith left in our relationship bank.

A sign for the Garden State Parkway catches my attention. I turn onto the parkway and press down on the accelerator.

No matter how fast I go, Jerome and Mandy keep up with me. Jerome's backside glares and stares in the sunlight. A ball of anxiety grows in my stomach and bounces up and down, up and down, the way Jerome's head bopped between Mandy's legs.

Details of the scene come into focus. Mandy's head lolls off to the side, her eyes closed. She wears a bored expression, like she's thinking about how many loads of laundry she needs to wash before the end of the day. Not that I ever grew bored during sex with Jerome. Well, not at first. I slam the steering wheel with my fist. The dark place descends and enshrouds my brain. I need to go through the exercise Doc Phelps has given me, but the steps become jumbled. Do I breathe and then count or count and then breathe?

Ideas race and the lump in my throat aches.

Why had I pretended we had a marriage for so long? Why had I needed to stay with a man who grew increasingly distant?

The solution eludes me. I concentrate on driving, calling out the mile markers and exit signs to keep from thinking, to keep the darkness away.

I leave the parkway at Bradley Beach, a town I summered in several times with my parents and grandparents. Back then the beach, sun, and sand occupied the days and family dinners capped off each evening. We played board games and charades to amuse ourselves. I learned to fish and to swim long distances. We all donned silly costumes for the Fourth of July parade. We laughed more than we cried.

The comforting memories swaddle me. Life used to make sense. No other place beckons. Why not land here?

I follow signs to Main Street and pull into the lot for the first real estate agency on the block: Paradise Realty. A passing car blares Springsteen, and I close my eyes and listen.

Jerome despises my passion for Springsteen. I love how Bruce understands things like anguish and the uncertainty of life. He knows bad times lurk around every corner ready to lay anyone low. Jerome calls me a dolt when I say things like that.

Unlike me, Jerome hurdles through his days with sure footing and single-minded purpose. He sneers at everyone who fails to keep up, me included. As the years went by, I found myself further and further back. In spite of Jerome, I know where I am is okay. Bruce gives me hope. He understands the darkness and illuminates the way.

The familiar chords of "Badlands" pour over me, and I lose myself in the driving beat and mournful sax. I like how "Badlands" ties up what I'm feeling in a neat package. The angry, driving call to push on no matter what nightmares I encounter shields me against the darkness, and I cling to the tune mentally and physically, folding my arms around my chest and bursting into song. Recognizing the bad taste of fear, I sing loud and rock until the dark place recedes from the small confines of the car and calm takes over. I repeat over and over the line about being caught in crossfire that makes no sense at all.

I let out my breath and turn off the car's engine, wishing The Boss's songs possessed the power to permanently erase the image of Mandy and Jerome from my memory.

I straighten from a slump and, lifting my chin, call out into the distance. "You can do this, Sofia. You know you can."

If only I can believe my inner cheerleader.

CHAPTER TWO

Born in the USA

A FTER A FEW MOMENTS, I step inside the air-cooled Paradise Realty office. I discover a woman in black, cotton pants and a white blazer trimmed with black piping checking house listings on her computer. Her desk plate reads "Terri Randall, Bradley Beach Broker of the Year." Her hair shouts too blonde, but her smile radiates genuineness and, when she says hello, her eyes emanate kindness.

I learned long ago that someone's eyes tell me far more than their words or appearance. Terri Randall's pale blue orbs gleam mischievously and leave me with the impression she embodies more than hard-driving real estate saleswoman. Terri's eyes linger on mine in a caring gaze.

I unclench my fists as she introduces herself and points to a seat opposite her old, mahogany desk. The interior designer in me notices faded brown curtains hanging on the front window and an orange area rug, that's seen better days, covering the floor in the front hall. The lack of modern furnishings surprises me, given Terri's smart appearance.

Terri sends a welcoming smile as I sink into the chair. "Are you new to the area?"

I wipe at my brow and offer a terse, "Yes."

"It's a bear out there today, isn't it, hon?"

She's trying to put me at ease, but I can't bring myself to chit chat. I nod and rub my thighs.

"What can I do for you? Are you looking to rent or buy?"

"Rent."

I know she's studying me and probably trying to figure out the meaning behind my monosyllabic answers.

Terri rises. She's doll-like and perfectly proportioned, unlike tall-and-big-all-over me. "How about a cool drink?"

"Thanks."

She pauses and winks. "I can offer you a soda or water. I also might have a little brandy back there if you'd rather."

My back goes straight. Is my tension so obvious?

"Water would be fine."

"I didn't offend you, did I? I'm sorry." Terri idly fingers a blue-green pendant that I recognize as Larimar, a stone Jerome once said reminded him of my eyes. I avert my gaze.

"Water sounds perfect." I'm not averse to liquor. I developed a taste for Jameson long ago from my Irish granny. But better to stay sober in strange surroundings with someone I know nothing about.

Terri hands over a Poland Spring, and I uncap the bottle. I drink slowly and count the sips. Once. Twice. Three times quickly. The fog of fury and distress abates with the cool liquid, and soon Terri's patter about Bradley's real estate market blocks out all other thoughts. Within fifteen minutes she finishes assembling the paperwork for viewing properties to rent.

"My car's out back," Terri says, and I follow her outside, glad to leave the dank office.

Terri looks to be about fifty, a birthday creeping up on me in a few months. She appears comfortable in her body and clothes; something I find soothing and admirable. Plus, Terri hasn't probed about why I showed up in Bradley Beach with the demeanor of a crazed, displaced animal. She understands or at least she respects privacy. All these factors make her likable. And her offer of a shot of brandy, which in retrospect might have done me good, tips the scales even further in her favor. I decide I like her.

Terri beeps open her Mercedes. "You'll be amazed at how easy it is to get to know this town and how close by everything is."

It's good to be with a stranger, good to pretend life is normal. I tell myself the best part is I'm going to be able to escape from Jerome and move forward without him.

Freedom beckons. I'm my own woman again.

The flutter in my gut leaves me nauseated, and my armpits dampen with apprehension.

"I have six places to show you." Terri hands over a stack of listings. She flashes a grin. "Your dream place on the water may be one of these. End of summer season is the perfect time to be rental shopping."

Inside the car the cream-colored leather clings to the back of my thighs with annoying persistence, the result of a strong summer sun and high humidity. I push my baggy capris down past my knees and try hard to concentrate on Terri's words, but instead of the realtor's voice, Grandpa Pinto's mantra about healing echoes in my ears. *The saltwater heals everything, Cara.* He always called me Cara, the Italian word for dear. Jerome, on the other hand, abhors pet names.

The image of bobble-headed Jerome between Mandy's legs punches me in the stomach, and the anxiety ball makes a little turn. I try to remember the last time Jerome's head disappeared between my thighs, but come up blank. What makes matters worse is Mandy is half my age, half jerky Jerome's age.

Terri's spiel comes as a welcome intrusion. "Bradley Beach is a tiny town with a huge heart." I center my attention on her chatter and stop my inner dialog.

"We did really well in Superstorm Sandy thanks to our man-made dunes. Not much damage to the town and we're grateful for that. The dunes saved us."

I nod. "So many places were destroyed."

"Our dunes are built from old Christmas trees topped with sand and sea grass. The storm washed the old dunes away but the town gathered new trees after the holiday. It smelled like Christmas around the beach for the longest time till they covered them over with sand."

"That's a great aroma."

"Not what you'd expect when walking on the boardwalk; however, it's become a reassuring fragrance to the town."

I remember that piney scent with fondness. My childhood jobs included watering our Christmas fir and sweeping up the fragrant circle of needles that fell to our handmade, colorful tree skirt.

Terri pulls her Mercedes into a driveway and rolls to a stop. The structure before us appears welcoming, tidy, and a little down and out. The home radiates something special, something that makes me happy instantly. Architectural details add to its allure. While any place decent will do, this goes well beyond decent. I want to fly under the radar and hide, and this quiet neighborhood gives me the impression of being a perfect place to hunker down and be away from prying eyes.

Behind us a car's radio blares "Born in the USA." Curious, I turn and watch a black convertible pull into the driveway next door. The sandy-haired man in the driver's seat sings at the top of his lungs and bangs his hands on the steering wheel. He alternates his drumming with a little air guitar. He does neither well.

Mr. Air Guitar gives off an aura of happiness and an appearance that says "I'm carefree" that annoys me. I dislike him, even if he's a fellow Springsteen fan. He makes me think about the huge pack of trouble I'm trying to unload, the one named Jerome, the one who routinely porks his trainer. Still, nothing requires me to be friends with the neighbors.

Terri opens her door and climbs out. She waves at Mr. Air Guitar, but the man remains engrossed in his playing and fails to notice. He strums a muscled arm again to the blast of the radio, and my ears grow hot. The guy probably knows nothing about the meaning of the song he sings. The mantra "Born in the USA" isn't a rallying cry for overzealous patriots no matter how many times they try to claim it. The howl embodies the pain of fighting and the despair of returning after war while having no job or place in the world, wrapped up in the flag and the confusion of life. The sadness and futility of the lyrics make me uncomfortable. Something deep in my head laughs at me. I hate that sound. Doc Phelps wants me to keep track of when I hear it.

"This is a good block," Terri says, "and the house is charming." I make an effort to concentrate on the structure in front of me, to take my mind from the music and the laughter in my head. The place appears to be a 1920s Colonial, a vintage I have some experience with. The front porch sags, and the cracked wood siding bears one too many coats of paint. I brush at my khaki, collared shirt and brown capris. The faded beige siding of the house and its accompanying taupe trim remind me of my own attire. How pathetic. Even my hair exhibits an eminently unnoticeable mousey brown. Gads, I need to take control and change my dreadful appearance.

The music stops, and the neighbor springs from his car pressing a cell phone to his ear. His shoulders taper to a narrow waist, and he exhibits a grating cheerful walk of youth, further cementing my displeasure.

Terri says, "You can hear the water from here. And you can see it really well from the top floor. We should go inside."

To the right, a block away, the ocean rolls to the shore, only a short walk from the house. The soft whoosh of the waves filters towards me, and I unclench my fists. My nails have cut lines into my palms. Off in the distance, church bells toll. Closing my eyes I draw in the scent of salt and allow the humid air to coat my nostrils. Maybe Grandpa is right about the healing properties of the ocean.

Terri calls from the front porch, "Come on. We have a lot of places to visit." She glances at her watch and flashes the grin again. Her teeth gleam too white, but I fail to find the glow irritating. Terri harbors realness and solidity beneath the fluorescent smile and out-of-place-in-a-beach-community sky blue stilettos. I bet Terri doesn't have a man who cheats on her with his trainer. She possesses too many smarts to allow such a thing to happen.

I smooth my hair in the passenger mirror. Stepping from the car, I gaze at the cottage and turn to the beach. I stop the rational side of my brain from protesting and go with my gut.

"I'll take it."

Terri's mouth drops open. "Don't you think you should see the inside?"

"This place is great. I want to rent it." I send her a smile and know from the expression on her face she thinks I'm loony. Terri's nailed it. But this type of impulsive crazy makes sense at the moment. Nothing else in my life does. The straight and narrow, good-wife path has led to a sea of chaos.

I did so much right for so long. I volunteered at the local church soup kitchen. I drove for Meals on Wheels. I worked hard to establish my interior design business. I enjoyed all those things and loved the people I cared for, worked with, and met. I still do. Most of all, I took care of Jerome. I nursed him through illnesses and celebrated his victories. I listened to his complaints and kept him company when he was down. I even made sure to keep the house stocked with the foods he liked, though I never ate them.

I kept the dark place at bay for ages and never burdened him when it threatened. I hate how I encased myself in a false bubble of belief that those motions protected me from arriving where I am today.

"Sign me up," I call. The image of Jerome and Mandy flashes again. The anxiety ball does a dipsy-do, and a shooting star rounds the bend and lights up the back of my eyelids.

How could he?

Terri removes the key from the lockbox. She beckons. "You have to come inside and see more than you can from out here. Hear me?"

Terri is definitely a good egg.

"Fine. I'm coming."

CHAPTER THREE

Dancing in the Dark

I CLIMB THE STEPS AND JOIN Terri in the front entryway. The constant maintenance and demands of an old home hold no appeal, but I note with relief that in spite of the advanced years of the cottage, the interior shines with new renovations. Jerome and I lived in a 1926 Colonial at one point, and the decrepit structure sucked money the way a vampire sucks blood.

Terri sweeps a hand through the air. "It's furnished completely. Cassandra, the owner, used to be a furniture buyer, before she became a yoga instructor. I love the way she contrasts modern stuff with old. And it's pet friendly too. Cassie loves animals."

"Where is she now?"

Terri grins. "She took off with one of her students, a widower. Last I heard they were opening a yoga studio in the Bahamas."

"She doesn't want to sell?"

Terri shakes her head. "Cassie's practical about keeping options open. She always comes back. At least she has in the past."

The words settle over me. "How long is the lease for?"

"A year."

"And if she comes back?"

"Not to worry. Cassie has a lot of friends in town. She'd stay with them. If you have a lease, it's yours for the duration."

I follow Terri into the tiny but well-thought-out kitchen. Stainless steel appliances shine, and a tan, speckled granite counter gleams in the strong light that filters through the windows. The space makes me feel at home.

"When can I move in?"

Terri cocks her head. "We have five other houses to visit."

"I don't want to see any others."

Terri meets my gaze.

"I'm serious. I want this place."

"You have to see the back." She pushes me towards the rear door of the house where a tidy yard with a well-kept garden greets us.

My heart jumps at the site of the roses, hydrangeas, and hostas that line the fence along the property boundary. Grandpa used to tend a garden with the same plants. Jerome hates gardens; he tells me they take too much time. He hires gardeners and landscapers to keep up with the neighborhood standards but refuses to grow flowers in the yard. Too frilly and frou-frou. Only evergreens and grasses pass his test of appropriateness.

I volunteer at a community garden to be around plants, vegetables, and colorful foliage. Digging in the dirt allows me to escape the tragedy that haunts me. I hum when I bring the cut flowers and the veggies to the local soup kitchen. Jerome calls my immersion in activities of this sort my "projects." I ignore the scorn in his voice when he says the word.

Terri points to the right then the left. "I don't want you to move in without seeing what's next to you." The yard on the right, the one owned by the air-guitarist, appears pristine. The neighbor to the left possesses other ideas. The clutter makes me dizzy.

"Is that an airline seat? And a sink?" My brain struggles with wrapping order around the mess. "Is he a junk dealer?" Dozens of objects, small and large, cover almost the entire yard.

Terri laughs. "A logical guess." She sighs. "The Cornells are, let's say, not your usual family."

"Where do they get all that stuff?"

Terri shrugs. "I'm not sure. All I know is that it comes and it goes. Whenever I show this house there are new things back there." She whispers, "Ellie and Walt Cornell are eccentric but harmless."

I pass my gaze back to the well-tended yard. The landscape segues right into Cassie's. In fact, the same plants spill across the rear fence. They must've shared gardeners or lives in the past. Where the property meets the Cornells', landscaping hell breaks loose. A jungle of weeds in varying states of death clings to the Cornells' back border. Mr. Air Guitar's yard is like a well-groomed show dog, the Cornells' a mangy mutt. At least a low fence defines the boundary to the Cornells' and contains some of the jungle.

"So, do you want to go see the other places?" Terri fumbles in her white hobo bag and comes up with her keys.

"Nope."

The realtor cocks her head.

"When can I move in?" I ask again.

"When do you want to move in?"

"Right now."

Terri purses her lips in thought. "I'm the exclusive agent on this one. And I know Cassie." She studies me.

"I can give you references. I run an interior design firm. I'll be able to provide whatever funds you need for security." Amy would vouch for me. Luckily my checking gives me access to the small inheritance my dad left me. My father's cheery "What a woman needs is money of her own to get that room of her own" pops into my head. Like Springsteen, Dad, and Virginia Woolf, can always be counted on to steer me in the right direction.

Terri smiles. "You're an interior designer? We'll talk. I recently took over that office and it could use freshening." She checks her watch. "We can sign the lease today if you want. I'll need a security deposit and first month's rent." She opens her palms. "I don't want to rush you. You can take a little time if you need it. Think it over a couple of days."

"That's not necessary. Let's get the papers signed. I can write you a check." I locate my checkbook in my purse in the compartment next to my cellphone. The sight of the phone sends me back to the house in Nyack and Jerome and Mandy. Her splayed legs. His white butt. Her hands on his ears. *Ohmigod.*

"Are you feeling all right?"

"It was the long drive. I'm a little tired."

Back at Terri's office, we formalize the lease and legal papers. While I'm waiting for my copies I take in more of the dated décor. Dark wood paneling and molding accompany olive paint on the walls. Two dingy overhead lights provide a somber glow. Without Terri's happy jabbering I fight to cast off the vibe of the depressing room.

An hour and a half later I sit on the porch of my new home by the ocean. I turn on my phone and crank up the music. "Dancing in the Dark" blasts through my earbuds. Like the lyrics, I too want to change my clothes, hair, and face. But I don't want to dance in the dark or daylight. Panic rises in my chest. What on earth am I going to do in this strange place? The anxiety ball bounces rapidly. The darkness hovers on the edge of my eyes, and the laughter in my head grows louder.

Sitting still becomes impossible. I jump up and stride rapidly towards the water. On the boardwalk I sit on one of the benches that line the ocean front and work hard to catch my breath, hoping the sounds of the sea might calm me. Instead apprehension takes root. The waves crash and gulls caw overhead. I grip the wooden slats beneath my thighs until my fingers grow numb.

My thoughts spin wildly. What folly it was to stay with Jerome and his cheating ass for so many years. The signs of his dalliance pass through my brain. At the gym Christmas party, Jerome left to get me an Irish whiskey and when he failed to return I searched and found him at the bar chatting with Mandy. I ordered my own glass of Jameson and joined them. Agonizing awareness gripped me as Jerome's eyes strayed and lingered on the swell that rose from Mandy's holiday red T-shirt. *Ho, ho, ho.*

The gulls laugh, and I turn up the music. Running from Jerome isn't the best of ideas. But staying with him is worse.

The strains of "Dancing in the Dark" fill my head again. The lyrics offer no solace. I lean back, allowing sadness to grow. A dark curtain lowers, and chilling grief covers me.

Jerome's affair with Mandy doesn't cause my distress. Sure his betrayal is awful, made worse by his use of our bed. His having sex with another woman makes me livid. The unease caused by being uprooted to a new place and being all alone also unsettles me. But this time the darkness stems from Ben, for all I'll never have.

I still miss him, our son, my only child.

Today marks Ben's birthday.

He would've been thirteen.

The anxiety ball falls into the hole in my stomach that opened with his death and never closed. The ache grows particularly bad, so bad it threatens to swallow me. I breathe the way Doc Phelps told me. In my nose, out my mouth. Slowly.

Ben's death is my number one worst thing ever to happen. I can't imagine anything being more terrible. Doc Phelps says it's okay to have a hierarchy and for this to be my worst ever experience. I started seeing Doc Phelps right after I lost Ben and stopped three months ago.

Though Ben passed away five years ago, my gut wrenches as if it were yesterday. Jerome chose to honor the occasion of Ben's birth by taking another woman into our bed. Something tightens in my chest.

I study my playlist to redirect my thinking. Amy says Springsteen is my armor. Maybe she's right. I don't have to talk to anyone or answer questions when I listen to The Boss. I prefer the worlds that exist in his songs and the stories that unfold in the tunes to most conversations. Plus, Bruce usually leads to a direction, if not an answer for whatever dilemma I encounter. He orders the chaos if only for a short while. Bring on the lyrics and let them echo in my mind instead of my racing chaotic thoughts.

My brain refuses to distinguish which of the tunes might help. Maybe I'm not up to the task of living on my own. No matter how smart I am, maybe in this situation my wisdom is outmatched. Maybe I'm not born to run or to dance in the dark. I miss the routine of my life already and am irked at what a creature of habit I've become.

I hit shuffle and lose track of the number of songs that play. I keep breathing slowly. Eventually the soulful "Dancing in the Dark" cycles forward once again. The part of the tune that talks about the uselessness of worrying rings true and soothes me. So what if tiredness and apprehension threaten to overwhelm me. I mustn't sit around waiting.

The notes fade, and after inhaling once more, I switch off the music and rub my cheeks. I rise and take a few steps, aware of the looseness in my sternum. Salty air coats my nostrils, and my mind grows clearer than it's been since leaving Nyack. I head back to my new home with newfound composure.

My feet follow my own internal beat. Black concepts nip at my heels, but I keep ahead of them, grinding my teeth and resolving to give my new attempt at life my all.

A glance at my phone; three missed calls from Jerome and one from Amy. This must be a dead zone. Amy will be worried. A small stab of guilt hits me, and I vow to call her as soon as I arrive at the cottage. The heck with Jerome.

I hit play and crank up the music, warbling along. The singing drowns out all thought, and my insides fly, chasing a small flicker of hope. Note by note I move deeper into the feeling. *Thank you, Bruce.* The sorrow strips away, leaving stillness in its place. I'm lost somewhere good, and though no light shines overhead, I don't need one.

CHAPTER FOUR

Better Days

THE NEXT MORNING, SUNSHINE WAKES me. I stretch and grab for my cellphone. 9AM already? I expected to be up all night, disgusted with Jerome, worried about the future. Instead, my lids closed shortly after turning off the ten o'clock news. I awoke once when I dreamed about the first time I brought Ben to Robert Moses Beach on Long Island.

Ben ran to the waves, his short, sturdy legs hopping over them, and his laughter filling the air with glee. He chased seagulls till he collapsed onto a blanket where he fell asleep moments after. He must have been about three.

After I shower and dress, I decide to itemize the creature comforts I long for in my new home. My stomach growls, reminding me no sustenance has passed my lips since breakfast yesterday. *Shop for food* goes down on the first line of my pad, followed by a number of items to purchase.

A lemon cake.

A bag of lemons.

Jerome hates anything lemon.

Tea bags to brew fresh iced tea.

Lettuce and veggies.
Sliced turkey and reduced-fat mayonnaise.

I pause. I no longer need to buy any of the crap Jerome consumes. Sugar-laden cocoa cereal, salt ridden cheesy puffs. For God's sake. He possesses terrible eating habits. I never allowed Ben to eat empty cereal or snacks, even though boxes stayed stashed in the back of the pantry at Jerome's insistence. Plus, there's Jerome's dried beef stick habit. I shudder. He goes everywhere with one of those rods of desiccated meat that smell like excrement. I intend to implement a healthy diet and lifestyle plan. What better time to start than now?

Except for lemon cake. I absolutely need a slice.

And a bottle of Jameson.

And some chocolate. Dark chocolate is medicinal after all.

Toilet paper and paper towels, soap, and dishwashing liquid are added to the inventory. Lastly I write, *Make reservation for dinner on Saturday,* and put two question marks after it. Maybe after a few days, Amy might be able to visit. Last night's hour-long phone venting session about Jerome helped, though nothing compares to having Amy cheer me up in person. Before we hung up, she took time to set my mind at ease with regard to our business, promising to run interference for me for the next few days and reminding me that with the wonders of video and the internet we can operate remotely from anywhere. Amy smooths out my life with the ease of someone smoothing out bed sheets.

My list finished, I don sneakers, a pair of shorts, and a baggy T-shirt. I ignore my rumbling stomach. Stuffing in my earbuds, I set out for a jog. It's time to begin a running program. Being healthy means taking care of me from first thing in the morning.

The song "Better Days" comes on. Bruce croons about sitting around idly and thinking about when life might start, and about feeling sorry for yourself and leaving that type of negativity behind. I listen carefully to the perfect summation of where I am and what I need to do. I fight to keep pace with the beat. After a block my chest constricts and breathing becomes difficult. I slow to a fast walk, accepting the decrease in velocity with disappointment. I need to work up to running speed.

Several people out power-walking move by quickly. A bicycle zooms past. Pairs of women chat and jog ahead. Most of the people approaching wave hello or say good morning. I smile and return the greeting. I wonder how many of the happy faces are hiding problems like mine. The ocean keeps peaceful watch over all. Maybe the sea hides things too.

My breathing returns to normal so I increase my walking tempo. Within minutes, my legs grow heavy. I draw deep drafts of air into my nose and blow them out my mouth, vowing to keep going till I hear at least an album's worth of songs. Eventually the boardwalk crosses into Asbury Park where I stop to recover. Irritation at my bad shape makes me grind my teeth.

A sign with a silhouette of a black horse and the words The Stone Pony emblazoned in black draws my attention. The sight of the most famous rock-and-roll club in history lifts my mood. I remember reading how Springsteen and Bon Jovi often showed up to play at the Pony and how Patti Scialfa met Springsteen there and later married him. Scialfa was also a member of the bar house band. She and Soozie Tyrell made a perfect guitar and violin duo and played together as Trickster.

I hear Amy's voice in my head calling me a rock-facts junky, a rock geek, and I laugh. Jerome prefers classical. He hates all rock music, leaving us polar opposites in musical taste. In spite of his disdain, I never gave up on rock and roll. This part of the shore with its wonderful bands and rock history promises to be a great place to indulge in my passion and also forget about jerky Jerome.

Jerome.

The vision of his naked body standing in the doorway of our home pops into my head. I stomp my feet on the boardwalk and press my lids closed for a second to dispel the sight. I pick up my walking pace and trot into a jog. The pounding of my legs on the boards causes Jerome to vanish. I gasp for air but continue on the path.

To the left lies another landmark: Madam Marie's fortune-telling booth. I search on my phone for the song that mentions Madam Marie to distract myself from the exhaustion that threatens. The name comes to me. "Sandy. Fourth of July."

Even though the famed fortuneteller passed away a few years ago, the family keeps the business alive. The lights glow inside the booth, and a slender brunette in a flowing gown wipes down the counter.

A woman standing on the boardwalk waves. It's an insistent back and forth clearly meant to get my attention. Who could I possibly know in this area after less than twenty-four hours?

I place the figure.

Terri Randall.

Dressed in a peach tank, orange shorts, and matching sneakers, she must be out for a morning walk. I lift my hand and make the effort to move my fingers in a return greeting.

"Hello, hello," Terri shouts.

I pull in air hard through my mouth and slow down. Running any further definitely isn't wise. I shut off my music. The heat and humidity crowd out my air supply, and I suck at the small breeze. My head grows fuzzy and woozy. Everything becomes too bright. The shafts of lightning behind my eyelids join together into one big ball, and I fall into a dark and colorful place.

For a few wonderful moments I become untethered to the earth. I soar through a dazzling, colored canvas where nothing matters, nothing at all. I want to go on like this forever.

I wake up on a stretcher in unfamiliar, ill-lit surroundings. Someone says, "You're back. That's good. Don't worry." A hand pats my arm.

Adrenaline surges through me, and I struggle to get up. I slap at the hand. An arm attempts to hold me down.

Something pricks my forearm, and I fade out once more.

I come to lying on scratchy sheets. A sign on the wall reads Jersey Shore emergency room bed 301. The smell of antiseptic leaves me in a panic. The last time I went to the hospital was with Ben. *Oh God.* He was eight. I block out images of him on the stretcher with blood everywhere.

Terri rises from a chair across the room and moves to the foot of the bed. "Are you feeling better, hon? You took a nasty fall." Her brow knits in worry. "They gave you a shot to calm you down. You were a little out of it. Do you remember much?"

I shake my head and press my hand to my forehead. A large lump protrudes from the left side and a dull throbbing tattoos my skull.

Terri pats my foot. "The doctor will be here soon." Her small, gold, hoop earrings gleam in the overhead lights.

"I'm at the hospital? How long have I been here?" I swivel my neck to find a clock, and pain stabs down my back. The time reads 11:30.

"Lucky for you the volunteer ambulance squad was doing a training session on the boardwalk. They said all your vitals were fine. They loaded you up and brought you here. It's been a couple of hours."

"I was on the boardwalk. I remember seeing you waving at me."

Terri nods. "You collapsed. Went down like a little puppet whose strings had been cut."

"How embarrassing." I attempt to sit up but dizziness overwhelms me. The IV in my arm tortures me each time I move.

Terri clears her throat. "Listen, your phone was ringing when we were checking you in. The emergency room tech gave it to me."

I groan. Not Jerome calling again. The vision of old megaphone ears and miss big-and-bouncy shoots into my brain.

"It was a woman named Amy. I told her what happened."

"Was she upset?" Foolish question. How could Amy not be upset?

Terri grins. "She talked so fast it took me a while to get a word in edgewise. I hope it's okay I told her where you are and what happened. She sounds like a dear friend."

"She is."

"She's on her way, hon."

"What?"

"When I said we'd taken you to the hospital, she said to let you know she was going home to collect a few things and would be here as soon as possible." Terri contemplates her sport watch. "That was more than an hour ago."

I roll into my pillow and bite the cover. "Oh, no."

"You don't want to see her?"

"I'm mortified. I hate to be trouble. Amy has work to do." One of us has to keep up with the orders, and I'm certainly not pulling my weight. While I want to see her, I don't want to be a burden or be seen as unable to cope.

Terri sits. "Do you want to talk about it? Or would you rather I left? Your friend should be here in a few minutes." She peers over her shoulder, looking to see who might be in earshot. Satisfied no one stands nearby, she leans in. "I'm sorry, hon. I know this is none of my business. I'm a little worried about you. Amy said I should stay till she arrived. I'm not sure what's going on, but Amy mentioned you were having family problems."

I exhale slowly. "I might as well learn how to say this." I clear my throat. "I left my husband. I caught him cheating on me and I took off. I'm not going back."

Terri laughs. "Is that all? I thought you were running from far worse."

"There's worse?"

"Oh, honey, this isn't the end of the world. Odds are you're way better off without him. It's about time you got to live your life the way you deserve."

Spoken like someone who's been through the mill.

A rap on the door causes both of us to glance up. "Mrs. Catherwood?" His crisp white coat matches his manner. He's young and handsome, and, if I stand beside him, I'll barely come up to his chin.

Terri rises. "Let me give you a little privacy." She slides past the doctor to the hallway.

The chiseled one smiles at me. "You have a nasty bump on your head but no concussion. I'd recommend you get a physical soon if you haven't had one lately. Have you?"

Not again. Last time the tests indicated my cholesterol was

too high. Same for my blood pressure. I make a mental search and decide my most recent physical occurred several years ago; no, more than several years ago. I went to the doctor before Ben's accident and that means over five years ago.

"It's been a few years." I brace for the reproach.

"Do you have a physician in the area?"

"I only moved here yesterday. To Bradley Beach."

He writes on a pad and hands me the top sheet. "Dr. Salter isn't far from you. Here's his address. Go see him. What do you remember about this morning?" He studies my chart.

"Running hard on the boardwalk and falling. I got dizzy."

"And after that?"

"Waking up here."

"It appears that you've gone through a TGA."

"What's that?"

"Transient Global Amnesia. TGA for short. It's a temporary loss of memory that can happen after strenuous physical activity like intense running. You were confused when you came in and had trouble answering questions. You also made a few statements about the darkness and kept repeating the same questions and comments over and over."

"I did?" I remember nothing of my questions or statements. My armpits pool with sweat.

"It's rare, but not something to worry about, unless it happens again."

"It can happen again?"

He hands me two pamphlets. "You should have some tests done. The sooner the better to rule out anything else. They'll have more information at the front desk."

I take the brightly colored leaflets. His instructions annoy me, and I forget about being distressed.

The doctor continues, "When did you last eat or drink?"

"Some time yesterday."

"You're going to have to pay attention to your food intake. Blood sugar can drop dramatically, dehydration can occur. Without the right food and drink at regular intervals you're at risk for something happening medically." He makes a note in the chart and continues his flat patter. "I'm going to have the nurse send in a meal, and once you've eaten you can leave. I'll have them take out the IV too."

He stops scribbling and studies me with clinical dispassion without ever meeting my eyes. "Eat and drink, Mrs. Catherwood, on a regular basis. Do you understand?"

He's speaking to me as though I'm a child. I suppose I deserve a lecture. But what does he know about stress so severe it makes you lose the desire to eat? He, in his white coat, who in all likelihood is never rejected by anyone. The nurses are no doubt falling all over his ass. Eventually he'll marry one and wind up screwing another. I fume.

"Are you all right, Mrs. Catherwood?"

"Fine. I'm fine."

He surveys me, clearly on a mission. "I'm going to ask you a few routine questions."

"Sure."

"Have you been feeling sad or empty lately?"

I shake my head and fight back tears.

"Do you find yourself crying a lot?"

"Some. I've gone through a recent separation from my husband."

"How's your sleep?"

"You're worried I'm depressed, aren't you?"

"Sometimes these types of incidents are brought on by depression. And acute emotional distress can also cause a TGA."

"I suppose I'm depressed some, but who wouldn't be in this situation?"

"Your answer then?"

"I'm sleeping fine."

"Any problems concentrating, or with energy? Any thoughts of death or suicide?"

"No. Not at all."

"Problems getting out of bed? Getting things done."

"No."

He taps his pen on his pad. "I can recommend someone to prescribe you a course of anti-depressants if they're needed. Sometimes that's helpful."

"I'm fine. I need a little time to get my head adjusted."

"I see. One more thing. What does controlling the darkness mean to you? You mentioned that a couple of times."

"I have an active imagination and a lot of odd dreams. I guess that was one of them." I refuse to discuss the dark place with this stranger. I know how to keep things manageable without his intrusion.

"You have my number on those pamphlets. If you change your mind give me a call."

He exits the room, and Terri moves back inside. "What's the news?"

"I have to remember to eat and drink."

"Sounds serious." She sends me a small smile.

"He's worried I'm depressed."

Terri shoots me a look of concern.

"I'm not. Maybe a little, but I don't need medication. I can work through this."

She smiles some more. "Been there done that. You seem pretty good to me. You should've seen me after my Wally passed away."

"I'm sorry about your loss."

She waves me off. "I'm good now, hon."

"And I'm sorry to have put you through all this trouble. I can't believe I don't remember what happened. That's more than a little scary."

Terri pats my hand. "You'll be okay, dear. The nurses told me they see a fair number of people like this." She probes her white, cross-body purse. "Here. I didn't want this to disappear." She hands me my phone. "Springsteen fan, huh? I saw your playlist."

I take the phone and place it on the bed beside me. "I've been a fan forever."

"Me too. Of course, in this part of the shore you'd have a tough time not being a fan of his. It might be dangerous." She laughs and shakes a finger.

"No worries there."

Terri continues, "He used to live not far from where you do, right in Bradley Beach. And E Street, as in The E Street Band, is a little to the south of us, in Belmar."

"No kidding?"

"Scout's honor."

"Maybe I'll make the entire Bruce repertoire my anti-depressant playlist. I bet I'd have a lot better result than going on drugs—though some of the meds can be pretty amazing."

Terri laughs. "An excellent idea. No matter how bad things are Bruce usually takes me someplace better. I love seeing him live. How about you?"

"At concerts it's almost like there's praying going on. His songs, they're the gospel and the hymnal."

Terri nods in agreement. "He's a preacher in the church of rock and roll. I've been a disciple for ages."

I'm thrilled we've bonded over Bruce.

A nurse appears with a tray. I push up on the pillows and eye the unappetizing array in the gray, plastic compartments. Cupping my hands around the carton of orange juice, I down the sugary liquid in a few gulps. Hunger rears in my stomach. I eat the eggs, the toast, and the small container of Jell-O. I wipe my mouth with the napkin.

The door opens, and Amy moves quickly into the room accompanied by her signature grassy scent. My spirits immediately lift.

"Oh God, Fi. I came as fast as I could." Amy's called me Fi since we were kids, though she makes an effort to use my full name with our clients. Her use of the pet name makes my insides warm.

I peer over Amy's shoulder. "You're alone, right?"

Amy nods. "Jerome's been calling me every fifteen minutes but I don't answer."

I grin at her. Perfect. Let him stew. Let him rot forever. I turn to Terri and introduce her.

"Thanks for updating me, Terri." Amy crosses the room and hugs Terri. Like me, Amy towers over the petite blond. Amy holds Terri for an extra beat. A stranger would've assumed they'd known each other for years.

Amy's cheerfulness and confidence attract nearly everyone, and Terri immediately falls under her spell. For the millionth time, I notice how Amy's dark curls shine and cascade in soft waves past her shoulders. My hand goes to my own barely tamable brown locks that I fight to blow-out straight every morning. My hair bristles beneath my fingers, reminding me that this morning the blow-out never happened. I want to shower and wash away the events of the day.

"Please," I say, "can we go home?"

Amy cocks an eyebrow. Her golden eyes sparkle with amusement at the urgency in my voice. "What, this resort isn't to your liking?"

I let out a deep sigh. "I'm exhausted. It's a little frightening not remembering how the heck I got here."

"No worries. We'll be on our way as soon as we can." Her pressed, white shirt sets off the light tan of her arms. I wonder if someday I might be able to borrow what I assess to be a new pair of jeans with a cute floral detail on the cuff. They're far nicer than anything I own.

I lean back on the pillows. "I'm so glad I rented a place by the water that has a couple of spare rooms." I smile at Terri. "And if you don't love it, Terri will never forgive you. Me either."

CHAPTER FIVE

Atlantic City

BACK AT HOME, AMY GRABS the shopping list from my hand.

"I'm on this. You do whatever you want. Take a nap. Read a book."

"Don't be silly."

"See you later." Amy charges out the door in full throttle woman-on-a-food-foraging-mission mode and never looks back.

I shower and change into a pair of faded jeans and a beige tank top. The freshening up revives me and leaves me energized. I turn up my music and tour each room in the house while Bruce wails in my ears. I tour them all again. I'm fond of the house, but nervousness at having so much free time plagues me. Without Jerome's constant lists of tasks to be done, I'm unmoored. That upsets me. Sure, the interior design business beckons and no doubt will continue to occupy some of my time, but my job only filled part of my days. In Nyack, I volunteered and enjoyed helping out wherever needed.

I realize I need to call in to Meals on Wheels and let them know what's going on, and I dial the number from memory. The receptionist tells me not to worry about not being able to show up. Several subs are on a list waiting to work on my scheduling tasks. Though the kind woman who takes my message means to be helpful, being so easily replaced bothers me. I put Bruce on again.

I push open the door to the backyard and spy a cluster of purple flowers growing along the fence. The type and name escape me. The blossoms stir in the breeze and beckon in the strong sun.

In a few paces I reach the border of the property where I verify the purple flowers are indeed unfamiliar ones. I bend and cup one between my fingers. The downbeat, murky message of Springsteen's "Atlantic City" blasts through my skull with its harrowing tale of poverty, crime, and most of all fear; fear of losing your home, your job, your loved ones, coupled with the desperation that drives you to do things you would never think of doing. I hear the enthusiastic promise about everything coming back, but it rings hollow today. The song's refrain of how everything must die brings me to the verge of tears. The voice in my head cackles and competes with the tune. My fingers switch off the music.

An uncontrollable urge grips me, and I tug at the flower and detach the bloom from the stem. I pull the petals apart and scatter them on the ground. I tear away another flower, and another, and dismember them one by one, grinding the petals beneath my sandals.

A cough startles me. My air-guitar-playing neighbor stands at the border of our yards. A strange creature, that wriggles non-stop, dances at his feet. A pink, cotton cord that could hardly be called a leash tethers the animal to its owner.

Is it really a dog?

I study the pooch. Other than tufts of white around delicate ankles, no hair grows anywhere on the body of the canine. A shock of platinum hair on its head hangs in a chandelier-like manner, reminding me of a style I wore ages ago. The dog looks particularly incongruous next to the large man who holds the cord in thick hands.

The fellow points to the purple pile on the ground. "Those aren't daisies."

He must see the puzzlement on my face because he continues, "He loves me, he loves me not. People don't use clematis for that. Or for stomping on usually."

I focus on the plant and the remaining clutch of purple blossoms that raise their heads to the sun.

"Clematis is the name of this flower?"

He nods.

A guy who knows flowers and controls a dog with a pink leash poses no romantic threat and is not someone to worry about. However, his witnessing my destruction of the blooms causes embarrassment and anguish to wash through me. I don't want him to think ill of me but figure I've lost that battle. What kind of person draws satisfaction from crushing poor defenseless flowers? Maybe all things of beauty aren't safe around me.

I recall how now and then, Jerome pushed me too far and I went into what he called my "el destructo" mode. Once I flung a chicken cutlet across the table. Another time I tossed the salad too high. My temper flared and erupted but usually remorse caught hold before I did anything too terrible.

My neighbor shoots me a mischievous grin that makes me want to smile back. Instead I hold off and gaze at him. I assess him to be no more than forty. The green of his eyes reminds me of an emerald my grandmother used to wear. The playfulness in them masks something I recognize. Heartache.

"My sisters told me the names of all the flowers in the yard." He nods towards the house. "They're the ones who stopped me from ripping out the entire garden." He bends and picks up the dog who licks at his cheeks. "I think they were right to make me keep them. Please don't tell them or I'll never hear the end of it."

My phone rings, and I fish it from my pocket. Jerome's name flashes on the screen. I grit my teeth, turn away from my neighbor, and shout into the phone. "Don't call me. Ever. You're an asshole." I punch the "end call" button and shove the phone back into my pocket. Oh man, my new neighbor must think I'm a real nutcase. I rally behind my newfound self, brought to life courtesy of jerky Jerome. What do I care what this guy assumes? The better to keep him on his side of the property line.

I turn back and face him, surprised he still stands tranquilly in the same spot. He has to be a little crazy to continue hanging around after witnessing my nasty behavior. First the flower destruction and then the phone call.

The dog whimpers, and he strokes its ridiculous hairdo. His hand practically swallows the dog's head, though it's a gentle swallowing. The dog emits a cheery air that makes me want to rub its funny noggin too. Handsome man and silly-looking dog amount to a tonic. A laugh bubbles up, and I immediately choke off the sound. My eyes water with the effort.

"It's all right," he says. "Killer's used to people laughing when they meet him. It's the standard reaction. Right, Killer?" At the mention of his name, the dog's ears perk up, and he lets out a small yip. Killer's owner continues, "We have a rather volatile household ourselves. You should see what goes on in my kitchen."

"What breed is Killer?"

"Chinese Crested." He leans towards me and whispers, "They're famous for winning the funniest-looking dog contest for several years. But we don't let Killer know that." He winks.

I reach over and pat Killer. Such soft and warm skin. Blotches that look like gigantic freckles cover his hide. Killer licks my hand. He possesses intense eyes and an adorable nose that twitches like a rabbit's.

"He theoretically belongs to Greta. She's my older sister. She's inside making June's life miserable. But Killer is most at home in my man cave."

"And June is?"

"The middle child. Then came me."

Great. The baby of the family. *Needy, needy, needy.*

I stick out my hand. "I'm Sofia. Sofia Catherwood." I spit out the last part. Jerome's name on my tongue makes my organs snarl.

"Sam Flaherty." He shakes firmly and holds the grip a moment too long. "Most people call me Sammy."

"Do you live with your sisters?"

"Heck, no. I have enough trouble keeping them out of my business with them being close enough to drive here whenever they want." He rubs the dog beneath its neck. "But it's not all bad. They're both great cooks. They're in there fighting about what to make for lunch now. June's a fan of chef salads. Greta wants soup and sandwiches."

"You're lucky to have them."

"Yeah, I am. Even if June and Greta are always trying to find the perfect woman for me."

I cross my arms. "It's always amazed me how much easier it is for men to be taken care of than women. Not that women need taking care of."

In spite of the snark I put into my voice, he gapes at me in a fashion that makes me believe he hangs on each word. Great. If he doesn't pick up on the fact that I'm pushing him away with a ten-foot pole he should be awarded a certificate for denseness. Another reason to keep my distance.

Sammy speaks softly. "Listen, I don't want to pry but if you need any help with moving in, I'm happy to oblige."

The unexpected offer of assistance takes me by surprise. "I'll keep it in mind."

A tall woman appears on the back deck of Sammy's house. She shades her eyes. Moments later she lowers her hand and climbs down the steps to the yard.

Sammy purses his lips. "June's on her way. You have about three seconds before she..."

"Hello there, new neighbor." Red-headed June takes a few long strides and arrives at the edge of Sammy's property. Angular cheekbones, a lot like Sammy's, dominate her face. A dimple appears in her left cheek, and her smile, though fleeting, is stellar, apparently a family trait.

"This is my sister, June. June, meet Sofia." Sammy glares at June. "Am I late for lunch? Sofia was about to go inside."

June extends her hand. "Welcome to the neighborhood. To Sammy's neighborhood, I should say." She lets out a pleasant laugh. I shake her hand.

Sammy says, "June's living in Avon."

"Is that nearby?"

"It's the next town to the south."

June sends him a sideways glance. Then she faces me. "What brings you to Bradley Beach?"

Sammy clears his throat. "Is that Greta calling us?"

"I don't think so. Gret's decided she wanted to make grilled veggies to go with the soup and salad. She's busy cutting up zucchini and eggplant." She turns her gaze back towards me. June assesses me and gives me the once over with a scrutiny so intense and judgmental that a chill passes down my spine. I'm clearly under a microscope. Sammy's face shows discomfort. He thrusts Killer at his sister.

"He needs to be walked. You might want to go out on the street by his favorite bushes."

I watch Amy's car turn into the driveway and take the opportunity to back away from Sammy and his sister. "Excuse me. My friend's going to need help unloading. It was a pleasure meeting you."

Sammy catches my eye. "Don't forget. If you need any help over there, I'm around most evenings after six."

I nod slightly and try my best to appear impassive and noncommittal. I don't want him thinking I'll be calling him up to visit. No way. He should stay in his own house with his overbearing sister June who clearly pigeonholes me as a person her brother needs protection from. Oh God, it must be the age difference. Being suddenly almost single and almost fifty certainly causes new complications in life. A divorcee on the prowl for younger or even older men? No way. The quicker Sammy and his sister learn that the better. I smile at the now stone-faced June, wave goodbye, and hurry towards Amy's car.

CHAPTER SIX

Hearts of Stone

"WHAT?" I ASK AS I join Amy at the rear of her Volkswagen.

Amy eyes me with a silly smile. I recognize that grin. She watched what went on in the backyard and now stands poised to comment on Sammy. She reaches in the trunk and hands me two Shop-Rite bags.

"He doesn't come off as married." Amy's smirk broadens, and her eyebrows move up and down.

"Who?" I wheel around and climb the porch steps with Amy following right behind. I open the screen door, and Amy grabs the frame.

"You know who. Mr. Smiley next door."

I turn the handle of the interior, oak entrance door and shove it with my hip. "I didn't notice him smiling."

"If you paid attention to him you would have. He was grinning. At you." She pushes her dark curls behind her ear.

"The last thing I need is a fool of a man smiling at me. I'm over the relationship disease. Jerome cured me."

I rush down the hall with Amy in hot pursuit. "If I thought

I could get him to smile at me I'd tell you to forget about him. Then I'd go over there and chat him up. The guy is hot. How old do you think he is?"

I ignore the question. We unload the bags of groceries onto the kitchen counter.

Amy stares at me. "Are you going to tell me what went on back there? Is that his girlfriend who was glaring at you?"

"You're lucky I like you and don't mind your incessant prodding."

Amy chuckles.

"I mean it. You're the nosiest person I know." I store a box of crackers and close the door of the pantry.

Amy lets out a small sigh. "She's not his girlfriend. She can't be."

"What makes you say such a thing?"

"She didn't touch him. If I were his girlfriend I'd have slipped an arm around his waist while greeting the attractive new neighbor."

I laugh. "Not everyone is so possessive or shows it that way."

"Maybe they should."

"She's his older sister. And she's clearly not happy to have a cougar like me living next door to her precious little brother."

Amy crows with delight. "I knew it. I knew she wasn't his girlfriend."

"He also has a dog with a pink leash. And he knows the names of the flowers in the back yard. I'm not so sure you'd get too far with attracting him."

Amy shrugs. "We'll see."

"How about helping me put the rest of the stuff away, Sherlock? Regardless, he's got two sisters. They're a modern, two-headed Cerberus guarding the gates of hell."

"They're sisters. Not in the picture at all."

"I've barely left Jerome. It's a little early to be drawing pictures." I fold the paper bags, stuff them beneath the sink and face my friend. I need to set her straight. I don't require a social director and don't want meddling in my life. "I'm content to live here on my own without knowing any of the neighbors. In fact, it's my goal. To not meet anyone. Ever." I add extra emphasis to the last word.

The added force makes no impression.

"Never say ever." Amy shrugs, and her eyes dance. "Besides, meeting a man and doing things would be good for you. It'll take your mind off Jerome."

"That might be a good plan for you, Amy. I've never been one to switch gears so quickly."

"And how has that worked for you?"

I know this side of my pal. She gets an idea in her head and clings to it tighter than a bulldog with a new bone. I turn away and ignore her, hoping to end the discussion.

"You need to eat. It'll make you feel better and think more clearly."

My back burns with the heat of Amy's glare.

Amy continues, "Come on. I'll throw a couple of omelets together for us." She taps me on the shoulder, unwilling to let go of the conversation. "I'm betting you'll feel differently in a couple of days. I think he's fortyish. That's a nice gap. You're almost fifty, he's forty or so."

I sigh.

Amy withdraws a pie from a paper bag and beams. "You said get lemon things. How's this?"

"Perfect." Lemon meringue. "Definitely Jerome's most hated dessert of all time. One of my favorites."

Amy puts a shiny skillet on the stove, places a tablespoon of olive oil in it and turns the gas on medium high. She prepares vegetable omelets while I dig in the closets and find tableware. I flip the old countertop radio on to a classic rock station and the soulful "Hearts of Stone" permeates the space. The song's wistful ache of love gone wrong sets me back for a moment, and I listen hard. The lamentation that things are not the way they were before and there's no way to go back is sad, but for me, today, the message is also freeing.

I offer plates to Amy.

"This place is so well-equipped," Amy says. "It doesn't have a rental feel."

"That's because the owner lives here when it's not a rental."

Amy strokes the woven placemats. "She has excellent taste."

She points a manicured finger. "Your taste. I can see why you chose this spot."

"I didn't see any other places, didn't need to."

"No kidding?" She chuckles. "And it comes with a cute neighbor."

I shoot daggers at her.

Once the omelets are ready, we dig in. I can't believe how hungry I am and how much I enjoy the meal. Amy's presence and her light-hearted way work the usual magic.

"Thanks," I say, mopping up the last of the stray veggies with my toast.

"It's an omelet, not a gourmet meal. I'm not a wiz in the kitchen."

"It's the best omelet I've ever had. And the thanks are for more than the eggs. I'm glad you're here."

The doorbell rings, and we exchange glances. "Maybe it's Sammy." Amy raises her eyebrows.

I grouse. "He's eating lunch with his sisters and would never pop up like that. If he does, he's too desperate for words." I rise and beeline for the front of the house. "It's probably Terri. She said she might come by."

I open the door and immediately try to close it again, but the man on the other side possesses too much strength.

Jerome and his stinky beef jerky breath leave me gasping for air.

CHAPTER SEVEN

Wrecking Ball

JEROME SHOVES HIS SHOULDER IN the gap and prevents the door from shutting. "Sofia, stop. We need to talk."

"Go away." I lean into the wood and breathe through my mouth to avoid the stench that wafts from his jaw. I shout in the direction of the kitchen. "Did you call him? Did you, Amy?"

Amy's heels click towards me. "Heck, no. How could you think that?"

"It's called a family locator app, Sofia. We installed it ages ago." Jerome pushes against the door.

"Why are you here?"

"I was worried, goddammit."

Amy says, "Want me to do anything?"

"Call 911. Tell them we've got an intruder."

Jerome yells, "Don't do it, Amy."

"Sof?" Amy asks. "What do you want me to do?"

"Call them. Quick."

Amy hurries to the back of the house.

"Hurry."

"My cell's in the kitchen somewhere."

"Don't call them," Jerome shouts and shoves at the door again.

Hot venom sweeps into my veins and fans through my chest. If I were a dragon, flames would erupt from my nostrils. I wish I could breathe fire. Jerome deserves to be blasted, and I deserve to be able to annihilate him.

"You had no right to do what you did and then come here."

"Sofi, please, I need to talk."

"We're beyond talking, Jerome. We haven't talked for years. Why start now?"

Jerome presses hard on the door, and my feet slide along the polished, oak floor. My attempt to hold him back fails. He steps quickly into the house. Why is he so strong?

"The police are coming. Leave now."

"Sof, I screwed up. I know that."

"Are you trying to make me feel better? It's not working." He's a child trapped in a six-foot-four body, someone I never should've married. It's taken me almost half my life to admit the mistake. Time still remains to be Jerome-less. "Don't you have a meeting at work to be at? Or a personal trainer to screw?"

"I took vacation for the next month. And I broke it off with Mandy."

"That's rich. You never had time for vacation before. Maybe you should take it with her?"

"I'm trying to apologize. Don't you get it?" The muscles in his forehead constrict, and I know that means full-blown rage isn't far off. Fury pours off him—his usual reaction in difficult situations. Jerome fine-tunes rage. His anger frequently sends a wrecking ball through our relationship. I dig deep and channel Bruce's railing and resilience in the song "Wrecking Ball." Well, bring on that wrecking ball, Jerome.

I shout, "I get it fine. They're empty words, Jerome. I want you out of here."

"Sof, stop—"

"We've been over for a long time. It took me till now to understand where we are. There's nothing left to save." I mean it. If our relationship is a plant, it's now a dried-out stick ready for the garbage. I eye him, and the anger that pumps through my middle turns to an ache so bad I want to double over. Emptiness fills me. I force myself to stay erect and ignore the horrid laughter in my head.

Jerome's face pales. Have I wounded him? Now he understands what it's like to hurt.

He rests against the wall and shuts his eyes. His hand moves to his chest. I catch my breath. A few seconds later he slumps into the hallway and anxiety rises up in a sickening wave.

Oh, no. This isn't happening.

Yes, it is.

I yell, "Amy, get out here. Now." My heart moves wildly. I squat beside him and tap his hand. He fails to respond.

"Come on, Jerome, come on," I say, drumming on his forearm.

Amy pokes her head out of the kitchen. "I found my phone. Give me a sec." She spots Jerome and me on the floor and moves quickly towards us. "What's going on?"

"Can you hear me, Jerome?" I ask.

He presses his lips together. "Pain." His chin dips to his chest.

"Call an ambulance," I say. "I think he's having a heart attack."

My anger fades, and worry and guilt move in. I might hate him, but I don't want him to die or fall ill. I've been after him for months to see a cardiologist. He's complained of intermittent stabbing pain in his chest more than once. After the second time, I glowered at him and told him to grow up and take care of himself. After the third, I shouted, "Get to a doctor."

Now, here he is, slumped in the hallway. God, what a child. And here I am, once again, in the role of his caretaker. I slam my fist against the wall. I want to be free of him, free to be angry at him. But he's coiled around my neck, strangling me. He doesn't deserve my help.

Amy presses numbers on her cellphone and hurries to the front porch. While she's rapid firing our information to the dispatcher, I crouch beside my husband. "We're going to bring you to a hospital, Jerome. They'll be able to help you."

Jerome's eyes open wide with terror and discomfort. "Please," he says, his voice a scratchy whisper. "Stay with me, Sof."

I reach over and take his hand. "I'm here. Don't worry."

Then you can get your cheating ass out of my sight forever.

CHAPTER EIGHT

Loose Ends

A MY AND I SIT IN the visitor's lounge and sip cups of weak green tea while we wait for news of Jerome. I draw deep, measured breaths and study my phone apps. Within seconds of our arrival at Jersey Shore Medical, the emergency team took over and hastened Jerome away. I glance at my watch. Three hours have passed.

"Amy, why don't you leave? I can call you when I hear anything." I press the delete button and banish the family locator app.

Amy sniffs. "I'd rather be here with you."

I muster a reassuring tone. "I appreciate your willingness to stay. But I feel awful keeping you here."

"Are you kidding? I wouldn't miss this for the world. Besides, it's going to make a great story for my future grandkids. How I kept my best friend company while she waited for her cheating husband to have a heart procedure." She pauses. "That was really insensitive of me, Fi. I think I'll blame the five cups of green tea I've swilled."

I lean back and rest my head against the wall. I want to leave, don't want to be here helping Jerome, but I can't possibly go. I wouldn't ignore a stray cat outside in the cold. How can I possibly desert asshole Jerome?

I pat Amy's knee. "Speaking of grandkids, how's your daughter?"

"I spoke to her a couple of days ago."

"Her pregnancy is going good?"

"Emma's fine. California agrees with her. Me, I can't believe I'm going to be a grandma."

"You'll be a fun, youthful granny."

"I'm more likely to be an exhausted, grumpy Nana. It's good she's having her first now." Amy's forehead wrinkles. "How long have we been friends, Fi? Was it third grade at St. Ann's?"

"Fourth. I moved to Nyack that year."

"Your parents and mine hit it off, remember? And so did we. Two only kids."

I feel a smile forming. "You were the sister I dreamed about having."

Amy fixes her gaze in the distance. "I miss those days. I miss my folks."

"It's hard to believe they're all gone."

"I still hear my parents' voices in my head. I was hoping my mom would last to see her great-grandkid. That didn't happen."

I rub Amy's hand. "I bet you'll have a passel of grandkids. Your son is bound to find someone eventually. And Emma will probably have another baby."

Amy massages her cheek. "Remember how we always said we'd do everything together?"

"You're on your own with the granny situation."

She sends me a kindly gaze. "Life might surprise you. There are lots of new types of blended families. Who knows what's out there."

A door opens, and a middle-aged doctor in scrubs enters the lounge. Amy's warm hand closes around my shoulder. I steel myself.

"Mrs. Catherwood?"

"Over here."

"Your husband's resting."

"Can I see him?"

He shakes his head. "Not right now."

I exhale slowly. "But soon?"

Amy wrings her hands, and I knead my temples, suddenly aware of my exhaustion. "Is he okay? I mean, will he be okay?"

The doctor pushes his glasses up onto the bridge of his nose. "He's doing well but there were some complications, so we'd like to keep him for a day or maybe two."

My breath hitches. "What kind of complications?"

"He had an allergic reaction. We're resolving that."

"What about his heart?"

"You brought him here with moments to spare. We placed a stent and opened the artery successfully. He had a significant blockage."

An involuntary moan escapes my lips.

"He'll be up and around quickly. I'd recommend he take part in a cardio rehab program after release."

"Do you have any idea when we can see him?"

"Really, it's a good idea for you to go home and get some rest." He hesitates. "He's asked not to have visitors. No exceptions."

I stiffen. He's already close to being back to controlling, nasty Jerome.

The doctor continues, "When he's released, he'll need to take it easy for a couple of weeks." He smiles. "He's lucky to have you."

Amy grips my shoulder, and I see her eyes roll to the ceiling.

The doctor clearly wants to leave. He looks over his shoulder and motions to a nurse waiting nearby. After a perfunctory nod, he retreats from the room.

"What on earth am I going to do, Amy? Could my life get any more screwed up?"

"Let's not go there. In all likelihood I can come up with a dozen scenarios far worse than this."

She speaks the truth. But that fails to make the current state of affairs any easier. This situation truly sucks.

"Do you think you should call Mandy?"

"I'm not doing that." The hair on the back of my neck stands at attention. Attack mode flashes through my gut. "She can figure out on her own what's going on. He said it was over."

"He wouldn't lie about her, would he?"

"Of course he would. I don't give a rat's ass if he did. I'm not calling her."

Amy taps her finger on her cheek. "What about Jerome's sister? Doesn't he have one?"

I nod. "Bernadette's been M.I.A. for years. The last time we saw her was at our wedding."

"That's a long time ago."

"She's a free spirit. A couple of years ago we got a postcard that said she'd become a scuba instructor in Phuket. I have no idea how to find her. And even if I did, what's the likelihood a scuba-diving-crunchy-granola-free-spirit would come home to care for a brother she barely acknowledges?" I worry my lip with my tongue. "There's no one to call. I'm afraid I'm all he has."

"You'd think he'd have taken better care of his relationship with you. What's to stop you from walking out and leaving him here?"

I smile weakly. "You tell me."

"He chose wisely, the dirt bag."

My gut rails at the thought of abandoning him and next wrenches at the option of caring for him till he returns to health. Neither choice offers me relief. The anxiety ball bounces rapidly.

Amy squares her shoulders. "He was a bastard after Ben died. I'll never forgive him for how he treated you then. He's such an angry creep."

"You got me through that."

"You got yourself through. I sat around and jabbered while you baked incessantly."

"I was a regular Betty Crocker."

Amy sends me a wink. "My waist still hasn't recovered."

"Listen, would you mind calling Jerome's office for me? He says he was on vacation for a month so they won't be missing him. There might be health forms he'll need to fill out." I rub the bridge of my nose and massage my forehead. The cackle starts up, and I shake it away.

"I'm on that. I have the office number in my contacts from

the time we were going to meet him for lunch and I called for directions."

I smile. Last winter Jerome had taken on an important client and decided to treat us both to lunch at The Commons, his private club. Amy and I dressed for the occasion and showed up on time. Jerome never appeared. An important meeting took him away at the last minute. He didn't bother to call me. Instead he instructed the club's head waiter to inform us of the situation and take care of us. The waiter explained to "Missus" that we should order anything we wanted. What I wanted was Jerome there with me and my best friend.

The afternoon had not turned out badly. Amy met an old friend, Marcus Voight, and he joined us. He dated Amy on and off since then—mostly off. He was a charming fellow, though I still remain unsure of what he does for a living. His answers to my questions were less than forthcoming. He mumbled about sailboats in the Caribbean, and whenever I pressed for details, he lifted his hand and said, "Let's have another bottle of wine, shall we?"

At the end of the day I went home alone and sat in the empty kitchen. I baked four trays of scones that night and delivered them the next morning to my local food pantry along with a twenty-three pound frozen turkey. Because the center's lot was full, I parked at the top of their long icy driveway. The first trip down with the scones passed uneventfully. But when I stepped out of the car with the unwieldy turkey, I lost my balance and fell face down on the bird. I clung to the fowl whose weight catapulted me along the icy hill, depositing me at the rear door, legs spread wide behind me and face covered in snow. Someone inside clapped and yelled, "Nice turkey sled. No good deed goes unpunished." I can't imagine the punishment that now awaits me when I help Jerome.

I rise, and Amy follows me to the parking lot. We drive home in silence. Once there I retreat to my bedroom and slap on my oldest and most comfortable jeans. So many holes poke through the fabric that I worry each time I wash them they might become unwearable. An old baggy T-shirt with a Madonna theme tops the pants. I find my phone and descend the stairs.

"I'm going out for a while," I say to Amy. "I need air."

"No running, okay? Not till you get checked out at the doctor's. One Catherwood in the hospital at a time, if you please."

I wave my fingers and stride to the door. Outside I crank up The Boss. The harrowing, questioning of "Loose Ends" fractures my heart. Bruce asks how did things get so bad when they used to be so good? How, indeed. The air smells salty and sweet, and I want to revel in it and enjoy its invitation to life. Instead, Jerome's idiocy and neediness strangle me. Talk about being at loose ends.

A niggling feeling makes itself known. Perhaps Jerome's not the only one to blame.

I grow unable to draw enough air into my lungs no matter how hard I try. Rubbing my neck does nothing to stop the noose from growing tighter. My new life shatters around me.

CHAPTER NINE

Light of Day

AFTER BREAKFAST THE NEXT MORNING, I pass by Sammy's cottage. Pushing my earbuds in tight, I keep my head down and fix my eyes on the path at my feet. This is a keep-to-myself-because-I-am-stressed-to-the-limit type of day. The last thing I want is to talk to Sammy, or worse, one of his sisters. Meddlesome neighbors amount to a complication worthy of avoidance at all costs. Pausing at the corner, I turn the volume on high and wait for a large truck to rumble through the cross walk.

Springsteen wails "Light of Day." A good night's sleep allows the lyrics to fan the spark of optimism flickering in my soul. The incessant mantra of hope, of that light of day being at the next corner, saturates my brain, and I find myself smiling in spite of the circumstances.

A tap on my arm startles me, and I rip out my earbuds.

"Taking a walk?" Sammy gazes down with a friendly and disarming look.

I nod and trip over my feet. My clumsiness makes me groan inwardly but I regroup and collect myself.

"I saw the ambulance at your house yesterday."

I'm aware I'm clenching my jaw. Small-town living and its lack of privacy might not be for me after all.

"Was it your friend?"

"No, no. Amy's fine."

His eyebrows arch. He wants information.

"She left early this morning to handle some business for our design firm and to go shopping at the Jersey Shore Outlets." It's a half-truth lacking the details about the hospital and Jerome. I know he expects more but I offer nothing. Too many complications muddle my life. I fiddle with my phone.

Sammy steps into the crosswalk. Without hesitation he walks away from me and to my astonishment his leaving bothers me. He apparently harbors no interest in what I have to say. Why should he ask another question? Why should I care? We barely know one another, so he merely makes pleasant superficial conversation in passing. Or perhaps my evasiveness has succeeded in shutting him out completely.

He reaches the other side of the street, turns to me and grins. Sammy wears jeans, sandals and a white, V-neck shirt that stretches across his broad chest. I'm mesmerized by the way the fabric clings to his pecs. Something stirs within me. *Oh, no.* I stop myself from staring.

He calls, "You picked a good day to walk by the ocean." He positions himself on the curb with his legs splayed slightly and waits for me to catch up.

As I join him, he falls into step beside me. He stands almost half a foot taller and possesses a longer stride than mine, but matches my gait seamlessly. We amble side by side to the ocean and the boardwalk. The easy companionship strikes me as odd and confuses me, especially in contrast to the volatile encounter and turmoil with Jerome yesterday.

The thoughts of Jerome and the hospital make me cringe. I called earlier and the nursing station said he was still groggy but doing well. Amy and I plan to visit this afternoon to check on him in spite of his no-visitors-allowed mandate.

Sammy points a finger to the north. "Today's the Ocean Grove flea market. It's twice a year."

"I'm usually a neatnik, but I love the clutter of a flea market."

"I know what you mean. You mentioned you have a design firm. What kind?"

"Interior. Amy, my partner, she's got a really good eye. I'm good, but she's on a whole 'nother level."

"There'll be a ton of vintage stuff today. It might appeal to both of you."

"I love old things. Not only for decorating. I can't help wondering about the past lives of the items. Old bottles, plates, bowls, and knickknacks remind me of my mother's and grandmother's kitchens. Lots of good times and memories." I'm babbling like an idiot.

He points at my phone. "What are you listening to?"

"Springsteen."

"He's the perfect accompaniment for a walk. I sense I'm in the presence of a believer in rock and roll. I didn't mean to interrupt you."

I shove the phone into my pocket. Sammy smells fresh out the shower, and the fragrance of soap and aftershave infatuate me. I don't mind shelving the music.

"I do love Springsteen. Jazz, folk, rock, country, gospel. He's done it all. I've been a fan for years."

"Me too. His words are inspiring and the music, what can I say? Nothing better."

"A lot of people say music isn't about the lyrics. But with Springsteen you get both."

"How cool is that?"

The wind picks up, sending a refreshing breeze our way. A strong tang of salt meets my nostrils, and I draw it in, letting it settle into my lungs. Tension drains from my muscles.

I ask, "So is there anything in particular you like at flea markets?"

He holds up his hand and points to the ocean. "Whoa. Do you see what's out there?"

I follow his finger but spot nothing other than an endless blue sky that meets a sea green horizon. What a gorgeous day.

He repeats in an eager voice. "Do you see them?"

"Who?"

"Dolphins. Keep looking and you'll see two of them jumping." He points again and places his arm over mine, holding my hand to the horizon. I try to ignore the heat that rises at the spot our bare skin meets. Unlike me, he appears completely comfortable.

"Got them now?"

Two creatures leap from the water and follow one another along the coastline. My heart soars at their magnificence, even this far off shore. "Yes, now I do."

"They're special, don't you think?" he asks.

The two dolphins rise from the ocean again, their sides gleaming in the strong sunlight. He's right. They affect me on a level I don't understand. My eyes well, and I drop my arm from his. I dig in my pocket for a tissue but come up empty-handed.

Sammy clears his throat. "Are you okay?"

I nod, unable to get the words out. I expect him to disappear now, to run screaming from an overly emotional and obviously unstable woman. Instead, he withdraws an old-fashioned handkerchief from his pocket.

I recover my voice. "I haven't seen a handkerchief since grade school."

He winks and offers it to me. "That's one of the things I buy at flea markets."

The white cloth feels soft against my eyes. "Thank you. I'm not usually this emotional, honest. I'll return the handkerchief when I do laundry." I examine it. The letters SF are on the corner.

"I was lucky to find a few with my initials."

"It's pretty. Nice embroidery." I stroke the fabric. "Almost too nice to use." I smile at him.

"I'd be upset if you didn't."

I blow my nose and pocket the hankie, embarrassed by his steady gaze.

Sammy carries a handkerchief, a square pressed and folded neatly. I envision him gathering his things in the morning and taking the time to place the cloth in his pocket. Only a thoughtful person carries a handkerchief. The quirky habit gives him an appealing dimension. Perhaps there's more to this fellow than lousy air-guitar playing. He's taken my mind off what awaits me back at the cottage and that elevates him to almost savior status.

We continue walking and soon cross over from the stone pavers of Bradley Beach to the wooden boardwalk of Ocean Grove. The boards are dry and splintered but they give resiliently and pleasingly underfoot, unlike the pavers. They provide an automatic spring to my step. Many people, alone, in couples, or in small groups, stroll in our direction.

Sammy points. "The market's on the Great Lawn, in front of the town auditorium."

White tents and tables dot a large expanse of lawn. Brightly painted Victorian homes line the perimeter of the gathering place and crowds throng the green landscape. Some visit the vendors, others eat at food stalls, and many sun themselves on benches.

We cross the street and enter the flea market. "Are you shopping for anything in particular other than handkerchiefs?" I ask.

"Lots of things. None in particular." He scans several booths in our vicinity and approaches one laden with glass and kitchen ware. Sammy slides a set of three mixing bowls towards him and turns them over to find a price.

A pleasant memory warms me. "My mom had a set similar to those. She's gone now, but I still have those bowls. Hers have polka dots. They remind me of her every time I use them."

"It's vintage Pyrex. A reasonable collectible now."

I pick up a cream-colored vase and hold it to the light.

"That's milk glass, like the bowls," he says. "We don't make it anymore in the States. The process turned out to be too dangerous, and they didn't want the fluoride leaching into the rivers. Too bad because the stuff is gorgeous, especially in sunshine like this."

He motions that he wants to pay, pulls out his wallet, and hands bills to the vendor who never ends his cellphone conversation. Still gabbing, the vendor pockets the money and holds out a plastic bag. Sammy places the bowls carefully inside.

"You didn't bargain?" I ask as we walk away.

"It was a fair price. I don't like to squeeze these guys for the last penny."

A voice from a nearby table calls out in greeting. "Sammy. Hey. I figured you'd pop up today."

Sammy smiles and approaches the seller. Postcards and picture frames line his battered card table.

"How're you doing, Pete?" Sammy shakes his hand heartily.

"Can't complain. It's a sunny day. This weather should make them come out. I've been selling decent." He displays a playful smirk. His waggling coal-black unibrow and dark-rimmed glasses remind me of Groucho Marx.

"Since Sammy's being rude let me introduce myself. Pete Lambert." He extends his hand and we shake.

"Leave her alone, Pete. She's not interested in the crap you sell."

"Hey, it's not crap. Besides, what you're selling is no better." He grins at Sammy and studies me. Pete strikes me as being about my age, though his ill-fitting Hawaiian shirt and baggy shorts make him appear older. His high forehead meets up neatly with an India-ink hairline. He possesses enviably straight hair.

Sammy taps the card table. "Listen, I could use a selection of vintage postcards for the holidays. Think you could come by with some?"

Pete grins wider. "You bet. I'll stop over next week."

"Wednesday would be best."

"Say hi to June for me. Let me know if you want anything else." An elderly woman asks for a price on an ornate cane, and Pete turns to her. He helps remove the shopping bags from her arms and presents her with the cane with a slight bow. "You've picked a really interesting item. Let me tell you about it."

Sammy takes the opportunity to steer me away from Pete, out to a section of less-crowded stalls that line the interior of the grass mall. He runs his gaze up and down the aisle. "This is going to take me a while. Are you okay with moseying along slowly through all this junk?"

"It's a great flea market." I hesitate. "Would you prefer if I went off on my own?"

"Frankly, no." He smiles. "It's good to have the company."

I'm not sure if I should leave him. But he's so upbeat, his mood is irresistible, and I want to prolong the walk.

Sammy resumes his patter. "Up by the auditorium there're usually a few dealers I like to visit. Come on. We can see what they have today."

"Lead the way."

We progress through the crowd to the middle of the mall, and I take in the surroundings.

"The Victorian homes are beautiful here. Such colorful gingerbread on their façades."

"There're more of them here than almost anywhere in America." He shoots me an impish smile. "Aren't you going to ask about why Pete's bringing me things like postcards?"

"Nope."

"Why not?"

I laugh. "You haven't told me about it and I figure there's a reason."

"I wanted to surprise you. Now I'm afraid it's ruined." He stops and studies me.

"Not necessarily. I bet you'll still surprise me. It was all kind of cryptic." I beam. "I love surprises. So surprise away."

"You're on." He takes me by the elbow and leads me back in the direction of the boardwalk.

"No more flea market?"

"It's here all day. We can always come back after."

"After what?" This sounds intriguing, and I'm grateful my schedule for the day is uncluttered. Amy claims the business is on auto-pilot and still refuses to let me worry about it until the situation with Jerome clears up.

Sammy fixes me with a serious gaze. "You'll have to be patient."

We walk north on the boardwalk and leave the Victorian splendor behind for Asbury Park. The boards turn older here, and a number of them stick up treacherously. Off to the right the ocean rolls gently to the shore. Where is Sammy headed?

For the first time in a long time my organs fire with something I don't think I should ever experience again. I struggle to stop them, but the incipient flames prove resistant to being dashed. I concentrate hard and attempt to figure out what's searing my ribcage so I can smother it. I recognize the feeling of desire with its tagalong-buddy longing. They're long gone, and I want them to stay far away. Besides, he's so young, and so not interested in me. And I'm still tied to Jerome.

What a foolish older woman. He's being kind, neighborly. But, oh, how that white shirt and those arms call to me.

I finally extinguish the last of the flickering ashes and chalk the sparks up to being a reaction to jerky Jerome. Dealing with a new fellow holds much more appeal than coping with Jerome and all his crap, Jerome who lies sick in the hospital. Discomfort seizes me. Even though Jerome's blameworthy, the fact that we're barely separated dogs me.

I take out my phone and discover a text from Amy. *All is well. Saw Jerome. He's fine, still drugged. Don't come. C u later.*

CHAPTER TEN

4th of July, Asbury Park, (Sandy)

W E STROLL ALONG THE BOARDWALK in Asbury Park and Sammy says, "It's so uplifting to see this place coming alive again. I remember when it was a great spot to visit and then it fell on hard times. It got better and bam, Super Storm Sandy hit. But it's really turned around again. Talk about resilience."

I study the vacant lot to the left. A gritty charm permeates the area. Decaying pillars mix with newly laid foundations and buildings. Signs of renovation speak of promise and a difficult rebirth. A longing to explore the stores we pass takes hold, and I make a vow to return another day.

A few yards later Sammy stops in front of a small shop. "We're here."

I lean in and shade my eyes against the glass. The display window holds an array of vintage items arranged artfully.

"This is my place. The Emporium." He bows slightly. "At your service, madam."

"You own an antiques store?" I'm thrown off balance. Sammy's large physique seems more suited to an outdoorsy type of venture.

"It's not really antiques. It's more 'previously loved items.'" He digs in his pocket and locates a key. "I don't open till noon on Saturdays usually. We have time for you to poke around before the customers arrive."

The door swings open, and Sammy ushers me inside. A familiar scent sends me back in time. Bowls of lavender rest on a pair of gleaming, mahogany, antique dressers. My grandmother loved all things lavender. I used to primp at her dressing table, spritzing myself with her purple atomizer. I helped gather countless armloads of the plant's blooms from her garden to be dried and turned into beautiful sachets.

"I'm officially surprised." I lean down and take a big whiff of the dried buds. "Oh, that smells good."

"I rearrange the place periodically and put out different things depending on the season. I've been working on my fall display." Sammy throws his keys on the counter.

I stroke a burgundy, velvet club chair and sink onto a green couch covered in vintage fringed pillows.

He smiles. "What do you think?"

"I could move in here and be extremely happy with never changing a thing."

He laughs. "Perfect. Your reaction is what I'm trying to induce. I want people to want to buy a complete lifestyle."

"I'm sold. It's like being in a Victorian parlor. It's perfect for all those old houses in Ocean Grove."

"Lots of them exist here in Asbury too. The area has a rich architectural history."

"Amy and I can definitely use some items for our clients."

"Come back anytime. We get new things every day."

I finger a beaded and tasseled lampshade. "This is so precious. It makes me want to curl up and read a good book with a cup of tea."

He grins. "Would madam care for a cup of tea?"

I laugh and go along with the script. "Why of course. And a crumpet, please."

He saunters to the back of the room. A cupboard slams shut and another squeaks open. I peer through the doorway as he arranges things on a counter.

"You're serious about the tea?"

"Dead serious. I have a microwave back here. No crumpets, but I have something else that should do fine. Is Jasmine good?"

"Now I'm doubly surprised. I thought you were kidding. Jasmine is perfect."

Sammy takes a silver tray from a shelf. He fills a glass Pyrex measuring cup with water and places it in the microwave. A few minutes later he carries the laden tray across the room and sets it down on the table in front of me. He shoots me a quick look and turns his head downward and away, clearly self-conscious.

I offer a cheery, "What a gorgeous spread," hoping to relieve his anxiety. The tray holds an antique, floral teapot and matching cups, two scones, and a small pot of jam. "The tea cups are so pretty."

A small smile appears. "I haven't been able to part with this set. All the objects in the store are for sale, but I do tend to hang onto some of them longer." He motions to the scones. "Courtesy of the Scone Pony in Spring Lake." The smile grows. "I had to think twice about sharing them with you."

I bend forward and pour two cups of tea. The heady, floral aroma drifts upward and spreads out into the rooms. "Can I speak frankly?"

"Of course." He picks up the cup and has trouble holding the slim handle. He wraps his hands around the body of the thin china instead.

"I didn't think you were the kind of guy who'd treasure a tea set."

"So there's another surprise for you."

I raise my eyebrows. "For sure."

Still it doesn't match up, doesn't mesh with the rugged hands and thick arms.

"You forget those sisters of mine. I went to more tea parties than I should admit. But I did manage to escape and play ball. Basketball, baseball, skeeball." He grips the china so tightly I'm afraid it may shatter. "This pattern's the same as one our grandmother had. I keep a couple of tea sets for my sisters. When they come in they like using them. June enjoys having tea more than Greta, but Gret's a good sport."

"You're lucky to have June and Greta. I always wanted a sister. I bugged my folks to have a baby girl. I'd even have settled for a brother."

"Hey, what's wrong with brothers?" He shoots me a look of mock-injury.

"I'll leave that for your sisters to answer." The bantering feels good.

Sammy sips his tea. "Are your parents nearby?"

"They passed away a few years ago. But I do have Amy."

The door to the shop opens, and we both swivel towards the entranceway.

Sammy calls out, "June bug. You're early. I wasn't expecting you till after one."

I sink back into the couch. The dreaded June eyeballs me, up and down. Maybe I need to put a price tag on my head, a really expensive one—or a lampshade. She drops Killer to the floor, and the dog races to me. Killer clambers onto my lap and licks at my face wildly.

"I missed you too, buddy," I say, holding him aloft. His chandelier of hair shakes happily.

"I figured I'd come in and catch up on the bookkeeping." June holds my gaze. "If he bothers you, put him on the floor. He doesn't realize not everyone likes being drooled over."

Sammy positions himself between us. "Sofia was at the flea market. I thought she might enjoy seeing what we do when we're not being beach bums."

June drops her large, black purse behind the counter. She could fit a week's worth of clothes in its many compartments and still have room to spare. She marches purposefully to the back of the store, her long, floral dress flapping behind her. A tortoise clip at the nape of her neck restrains her auburn hair. Not one strand escapes.

"Want a cup of tea?" Sammy asks.

"Not right now." She slips behind a curtain and disappears. After a few seconds, she pokes her nose out and announces, "Greta's on her way."

June's definitely a frosty one. And I don't need to encounter another of Sammy's sisters. I stand and smooth my pants.

"I'd better get going before Amy sends out a search party."

"You haven't finished your tea or your scone. You should stay and meet Greta. She's the one with taste, not me. Greta's got a real sense of color. June handles the books. I'm not sure why they keep me around."

I take a final sip and place the cup back on its saucer. "Thanks for this. And for the tour. I enjoyed it." Being with Sammy made me forget completely about the long list of things that bother me—no Jerome, no sadness, no worry about getting to a doctor to have tests done. This little excursion leaves my innards merry. I scratch Killer behind the ears, and he pants in appreciation. What a funny face. I cup his cheeks between my hands and lean in to his expressive eyes. Killer's tongue covers my cheeks and tickles like mad. He jumps to the floor and races to the back room.

Sammy rises and follows me to the door. "Come by anytime. I'm here most days."

I send him a smile and pull my phone from my pocket. "Take care, Sammy. It's a really fascinating store." The place begs me to spend more time delving into the memorabilia.

June calls, "Hey. Are you leaving already?"

Sammy catches my eye. "She'll put you to work if you hang around too long. June's the practical one. Greta, she's the dreamer. She forgets to show up, especially when she's got a gig playing guitar."

"Your sister plays guitar?"

"Blues guitar. She's good, right, June?"

June floats across the room and faces me. Other things than Greta's blues guitar playing clearly occupy her mind.

"Would you like to come to dinner at our place? We need to welcome you to the neighborhood."

How interesting. Is the she-wolf inviting me into her lair? The unexpected request throws me. I clear my throat. "Thanks. That'd be nice someday."

June stares. Her eyes shine the bright green of a gemstone. Their eerie similarity to Sammy's makes me blink to ensure which Flaherty owns them.

"We close early on Wednesdays and have a family gathering at Sammy's. Want to join us?"

Whoa. An invite with a definite time and place?

Sammy studies his sister with an odd smile I decide says *I'm old enough to find my own women, sis.*

"I'm not sure I can make it then. I think I already have something that night." The lame excuse hangs in the air. I need to avoid making any social commitments, what with Jerome in the hospital and with the events of the past few days swirling like mad in my mind.

"Bring your friend." June presses on, not wanting to take no for an answer. She eyes Sammy. "And Helene might come too. I've mentioned her to you."

Sammy groans. "I told you I didn't want you to invite Helene to dinner."

"Too late. She's going to let me know later today."

Sammy turns to me. "I'm sorry you can't make it. We'll do dinner another day."

"I appreciate the offer." I'm not sure if Sammy wants to get me off the hook, or if he wants to avoid having me to dinner along with the dreaded Helene. In spite of the fact that June continues to size me up, my interaction with the Flaherty clan makes me want to spend more time with them. They have an easygoing relationship and are comfortable enough to disagree amiably without it becoming an all-out war.

The door opens, and a stocky woman in a black motorcycle jacket and straight-legged jeans enters. I estimate she stands barely five-foot-three. She wipes her tan work boots on the welcome mat and shoves her hands in her pockets.

Sammy sends her a wave. "Hey, Greta. Come say hi to Sofia."

Greta runs her fingers through her dark, spiky hair. She clomps over and extends a hand. Her high cheekbones and perfect nose with a diamond stud captivate me. She raises her friendly brown eyes to meet mine and chocolate kisses come to mind.

Sammy adds, "Sofia's our new next door neighbor."

Greta circles me, boots scuffing. "You're not from around here, are you? I haven't seen jeans like those in ages. And your Madonna top, it's so eighties. If you have more like them at home and want to sell we'd like to buy them."

Sammy places his hands on his sister's shoulders. "Don't mind Greta. She's wild about women's clothes. Has been since high school, though she's more of a collector than a wearer herself."

"And men's," Greta says, moving out of Sammy's grasp. "I like them too, but there's so much more drama in women's clothing." Greta's sincere gaze secures her place as the less severe and judgmental of the two sisters.

"I'll keep your store in mind when I do my annual closet purge." In spite of what Greta said, I wish I'd worn something a little more fashionable than my ripped jeans and old T-shirt, which definitely needs a wash.

Sammy walks me to the door. Once outside in the sunshine I wave at the three siblings through the window of The Emporium. Killer paws at the glass, and I tap a farewell. Sammy speaks to June who exhibits a stern look, but I can't make out the words.

I take a few steps towards home and plug in my earbuds. The cry of "4th of July, Asbury Park, (Sandy)" grips my soul and I soar with the music, marveling at how Springsteen captures so many of my memories of the shore: the smell of salty air, the taste of love on the beach, and the raucous sound of carnival music. Nothing like summer at the seaside to order the chaos and allow you to live large for a short while. I laugh at the line that mentions Madam Marie. I know the exact location of the parlor on the boardwalk in Asbury Park, and I remember how I collapsed there. My pace quickens. Wait till Amy hears about my adventure.

A small boy runs up ahead, and I stop and inhale deeply. His kite trails behind him. The ache in my being comes alive, but this time I let the soreness wash over me. Today the anguish strikes me as comforting and familiar, as much a part of me as my inability to pass a homeless person or musician on the street without making a small offering. The boy races by, oblivious to my presence. His strawberry blonde hair gleams in the sun the way Ben's used to. If only Ben could be here.

He isn't and never will be.

I walk briskly and concentrate on the air in my lungs and the sweet smell of the last of the roses that line the dunes. I turn into the flea market. I want to look around some, and a mission comes to mind. Amy collects peace paraphernalia. She mentioned once that she longed for a decent pin.

A joyful crow escapes my lips when I discover a shiny round brooch with rhinestones that form a peace symbol. A perfect gift.

Amy texts to let me know she's back from shopping, and head home. How fine to have Amy waiting. Years ago I waited for Jerome. Even while I shopped or spent days behind a desk, I knew he was coming back at night and a part of me waited for the reunion to happen each evening. Jerome occupied my center and grounded me. He was background music of which I wasn't always aware but was conscious of. He was there any time I wanted to listen. Yes. I always waited for him back then.

Along the way I stopped waiting.

I switch on my music and find the Fourth of July song again. "Sandy," I croon, my voice growing louder. This time, the swell of Danny Federici's accordion sends icy waves down my spine. I can see The Boss's aurora rising behind me as he spews his poignant paean to the bittersweet end of a summer romance and the changes that are coming. It's far more than a boardwalk serenade. He's singing of loving someone forever, but he's also singing about the impossibility of loving anyone for that long. The on point dichotomy cuts deeply. I ignore the amused stares of the joggers and people on benches. Bruce flows through my veins and out my mouth. I imagine telling Amy about the meeting with Sammy, and I break into a fast jog. My lungs expand and carry me a little further than the last time I ran this route.

CHAPTER ELEVEN

Crush on You

AT HOME, I COME ACROSS Amy stretched-out on the front porch loveseat with her chin tilting to the sky. The sight of her with her long curls up in a clip and her eyes closed throws me back to our teen years when we drove to beaches all over the area in search of the perfect tan. Our sun equipment included baby oil and iodine in a spray bottle and a sun catcher made of aluminum foil to reflect the rays.

Amy and I still worship the sun, though in a much more conservative fashion. I spray on SPF 45 and sport a wide-brimmed hat. Amy protects herself with sunscreen too, on a sporadic basis. She hates the idea of blocking out what she calls "the therapeutic rays." She frequently regales anyone who listens with tales of how she becomes a better person when she spends time in the sun. Today her fair skin appears reddened and blotchy in places. She lowers her head and opens her eyes in response to the sound of my feet on the wooden stairs.

"You're more than a little fried, Amy. How long have you been out?"

She strokes her cheeks and winces. "Uh oh. I forgot to put sun cream on this morning and I walked a lot at the mall. How can something like the sun make you feel so good and be bad for you?"

"Three shots of raspberry vodka will make you feel great. That doesn't mean it's good for you."

"Wise ass," Amy says. "Hey, did you have a fun walk?"

"I did." I make an effort to tamp down my grin.

Amy leans forward. "Hmm. That's an intriguing half-smile you're giving me."

"One of these days we may be going to dinner with the neighbors. They invited us." I pause. "I'm not sure it's smart to go."

"Anyone cooking for me is a fine idea. Sammy asked you? I knew it. He likes you."

"Actually, it was his sister, not him. I'm too old for him. What would he see in me?"

"A sexy, intelligent woman."

"He's an infant."

"Back up a little. How did this invite occur?"

"Don't make more of this than it is."

"Tell me what happened, Fi."

I decide to give her a short version. "I went for a walk and bumped into Sammy. It turns out he has an antiques store. You'd love it. It's filled with cool stuff. We went there after the flea market, and his sister asked me to come to dinner."

"You went to a flea market with him?"

I hold out the peace pin. "Here. I got this for you." I don't want to think about the possibility that Amy's right about Sammy.

She launches into a warped version of "He's Got a Crush on You." "Oooh, oooh. Someone's definitely crushin' on you." The words are wrong but heartfelt. She breaks out laughing. "Your Springsteen obsession is rubbing off on me." She snaps up the brooch and places it on her shirt. "It's adorable. I'm going to wear it every day. You know me so well."

"How was Jerome?"

Amy studies her lap. "He's fine. Making progress."

"Did he talk to you?" Guilt punches me in the stomach. "I have to visit him but I dread going."

"Don't bother. I spent an hour with him. He's kind of sleepy from all the meds."

"What did you talk about?"

Amy lets out a long sigh. "He's such a prick."

The hair on the back of my neck revolts. "That's a given. What did he say?"

"You should stay right here. He's good."

"What happened, Amy?"

Amy twists the peace pin on her shirt. "He thought I was Mandy a couple of times. He kept saying her name over and over. And mentioning various body parts. And geez…lots of stocks to buy. I'm sorry, Fi."

My gut wrenches. "At least he's consistent. I think he loves stocks more than anything."

A loud noise from the Cornells' house startles us.

Amy says, "Whoa, sounds like big doings over at the neighbors." We peer in the direction of the low hedges between the properties.

Two voices shout loudly. The first belongs to a man, the second a woman.

"Those are not happy people sounds." Amy stands and tries to get a glimpse.

"Stop being nosy. They'll see you."

"So? Maybe they'll go back to their corners if they know we're watching."

I tug on her shorts. "I don't want to meet them."

"You never want to talk to anyone." Amy wags a finger. "Aren't you glad you met sexy Sammy next door? Who knows what waits over on the other side of us?"

"Whatever it is, I have a feeling we're better off without it."

"You're far too pessimistic for your age." Amy bends so far over the front porch railing, I fear she might fall.

The voices become clearer. The man and woman stand in their side yard now. "Walt, if you don't replace that pile of wood, I'm leaving you." Her hands rest on her hips.

"Wouldn't be the first time, Ellie."

I join Amy at the side railing. The woman wears her gray hair pulled back into a neat ponytail. Her faded jeans and work shirt jive with her no-nonsense directives.

"This is serious, Walt. I want the wood in the kitchen where I stuck it, not outside." She shouts, "Leave it in there and don't move it!"

She advances and stares up at him. She only comes up to his armpits, but that doesn't affect her ability to challenge the big fellow. "Do you hear me?"

"Ellie, the kitchen is no place for this much wood. You're losing it, woman." He leans toward her, clearly angered. I hold my breath. He unclenches his fists, and his body relaxes. So does mine.

Walt says, "Stop it. You stop telling me what to do and what you're going to do."

I muse about the object of the fight. A wood pile. Couples quarrel over anything and everything. I know all about disputes like that from Jerome. He makes a habit of being right about things. He argues about the best type of garbage can liner; whether it's the hottest August on record; which state possesses the most apple orchards. Argumentativeness and the ability to split hairs come naturally to him and nourish him. His hostile confrontations about trivial matters far outnumber any caring words or actions. We never talk about things that really bother either of us; instead we hide behind a wall of disagreements.

I cough forcefully. I want the two of them to cease their bickering. I'm used to people who talk at top volume. My Italian grandparents filled conversations with loud and volatile speeches that erupted violently and passed quickly. I never took their arguing seriously. However, I'm not sure of the level of the Cornells' anger. My exposure to Jerome's brand of fury leaves me confused about the dangers of rage that might be present in their home.

My coughing works. The Cornells both turn their gaze to the porch, then back at one another.

"Hello," shouts Amy. "Beautiful day, isn't it?"

I kick her in the shin, not too hard, but with enough force to get her attention. Amy whispers, "Hey, what did you want me to say? You're the one who hacked and got them looking over here."

"I was trying to embarrass them into stopping."

"Brilliant. But now they're both training their headlights on us."

The Cornells exchange glances again. Ellie wipes her palms on her jeans and nods towards the porch. Her husband digs his hands into his pockets and glares across the low hedge. His gray hair curls around the edges of the collar of a worn, plaid shirt.

"Hi. I'm your new neighbor. I'm Sofia. This is my friend, Amy."

The couple stands mute.

I continue, "I'm enjoying the area so much. It's a fun place to live."

Walt pulls on the gristle on his chin. Ellie says nothing. She stomps towards the back of the house, her ponytail flapping behind her.

"Friendly, aren't they," Amy whispers.

Walt's brow lines with concern. "The lady who lived here before, she's okay, isn't she?"

Clearly he doesn't have much of a relationship with his neighbors.

"She's teaching yoga in the Bahamas. I rented the place from her."

He glances at his back yard. A door slams, and a crash comes from inside the house.

"It's nice to meet you." Walt turns and follows his wife's path. He picks up his pace and calls, "Ellie, stay away from that wood. You hear me? You'll hurt yourself. I'll make room for the rest of it."

He disappears inside, and the back door shuts. Their discussion carries outside, but now it's muffled by walls and the intensity diminishes. Laughter erupts, and my gut unwinds. In spite of their previous argument, the present tone suggests they care about one another.

"I hope they confine their fighting to during the day," Amy says.

My cellphone rings. The caller ID glows the name and number, and my temples immediately throb.

"It's the hospital. It must be about Jerome." I thrust the handset at my friend. "You answer it."

"Me?"

I nod vigorously.

Amy presses the phone to her ear. She mouths, "It's the nursing department."

I mouth back, "Pretend you're me."

Amy shakes her head. I cross my arms, and dramatically mouth, "Please. Please. Do it."

She rolls her eyes. "Yes, this is Mrs. Catherwood." She pays attention intently for a few seconds. Her face pales.

I grip the railing for support. A wild flutter in my chest sends my pulse into overdrive. I want Jerome to exit the hospital and return to Nyack and leave me to my new life.

Amy hands back my phone.

I say softly, "Is he okay?"

"He's good. No worries."

I know Amy too well to accept the blank statement without an explanation. "Your nose is twitching. What's going on?"

"Don't get upset." She hesitates. "They expect to release him tomorrow. He told them he's ready to come home." She clears her throat. "That means to you."

CHAPTER TWELVE

I'm on Fire

"HE'S SO OUT OF IT, Amy." I glance in the rearview mirror at Jerome dozing in the backseat of my Camry.

"Do you think we'll be able to get him inside?" Amy twists in the passenger seat for a better look.

"We managed to load him into the car. It can't be much more difficult to move him to the house."

"I saw him pop a couple of pills as soon as we showed up. They said he was good to go but he's incoherent."

"Damn. He's always believed in what he loves to call 'Better Living Through Chemistry.'"

I remember after Ben died Jerome appeared to be in a fog. He sought comfort in a vial he carried in his pocket. When I asked about it he told me to mind my own business.

"You'll have to wake him, Fi. We can't drag him up the stairs while he's sleeping. He weighs too much, and we might hurt him."

Jerome snores. Other than a couple of muttered phrases, he hasn't spoken since we collected him at the hospital. His always wavy, dark hair, shot through with gray, stands straight up in a fashion that reminds me of our youth when he often forgot to brush it down. Today his locks look particularly unkempt. In spite of the bad hair day, and his odd ears, he still possesses a certain allure—the creep.

I grip the steering wheel and think about the attraction he has for the opposite sex. The nature of his job as a skilled trial attorney and adjunct law professor presents many chances to mingle with women—most of them far younger than I. Women like Mandy always circle around him. Besides cutting a trim figure, he often displays a befuddled countenance that draws women to him like toddlers to electric sockets. Unfortunately, his readiness to make the most of those opportunities grew exponentially with the passage of time. I realize now that I often looked the other way rather than attempt to confront him.

Amy taps me. "Are you doing okay?"

"Fine."

"Then why do you look like you're sucking lemons?"

I shoot her a don't-be-a-pain-in-the-butt gaze.

She grins at me. "What's bugging you?"

Once again, Amy keeps me from spiraling off into the insane depths of my brain.

"You mean other than the fool in the back seat?" His snores intensify.

Amy studies Jerome. "He's pathetic right now, isn't he? And noisy. It's hard to believe he's the same dashing man who belongs to The Commons. Take a gander at his hair." She laughs.

"He's always been a challenge to clean up. I don't get it. For someone whose job requires him to have an impeccable appearance he's never been able to avoid looking rumpled. If I didn't throw away his old clothes and replace them he'd wear them till they were in shreds."

Jerome chokes mid-snore and sputters. His eyes shoot open, and he closes them again. He mumbles something twice.

Amy leans towards him as he babbles again. "What's he saying?"

"Darned if I know."

"It sounds like 'grilled cheese.'"

I nod. "That's his comfort food. Grilled cheese. And

cheeseburgers. And let's not forget beef jerky. Boy, is he in for a shock when he wakes up. No more artery-clogging stuff. Not while he's in my house. I want him healthy and gone."

"You can do it," Amy says.

My tongue probes the sore spot that has opened in my cheek. "I can deal with a few days. But it's going to be difficult not to antagonize him. I don't want to make him worse. I feel bad, Amy."

"It's not your fault he had a heart attack. He's been hard driving for as long as I've known you."

I do my best to ignore my throbbing temples. "It's really amazing that he managed to find a way to keep me taking care of him."

"Can't you dispatch him back to Nyack?"

"I'll gut it out for a day or two. The discharge papers say he only needs a little time to recuperate."

"Maybe he's having second thoughts about living with you too and will leave fast."

"I doubt it."

Not much later we pull into the driveway, and I turn to address him. "Jerome," I say. I repeat his name loudly.

"He's definitely not hearing you."

"He's immune to my voice. He hasn't heard me in years." I extend a hand and jiggle his knee. "Wake up, you lying piece of garbage." His eyelids flutter. "Back to earth and your horrible existence."

He peers at me through half-lidded eyes and smiles sweetly. "Sof? It's you? I'm not dreaming?" He sounds thrilled to see me. My blood boils in spite of the fact that his voice carries a tone I haven't heard since our first years of marriage. Usually he barks instructions at me without meeting my gaze. He also prefers studying his phone to looking at me.

Amy chuckles. "I want whatever he's taking."

I tap his thigh. "Let's go inside. You can take a long nap."

He blinks and stares out the window, confusion crossing his face. "Where are we?"

"My home. You showed up here the other day and promptly had a coronary."

"Oh, yeah." Embarrassment cascades through his features.

Amy takes one arm, and I the other. We lead Jerome up the front stairs and into the guest room on the first floor where he falls prostrate onto the bed and mutters. "So tired. Sell Sentius. Buy Magnolia."

"What's he babbling?"

I shrug. "Who knows."

I put the bag of things the hospital gave me into the drawers of an empty dresser. Amy takes off his shoes and pulls a comforter over him.

She leans down to his ear. "We're right outside if you need anything."

By the time we exit the bedroom, Jerome snores loudly again. Amy shuts the door and smiles. "That wasn't too bad."

"He's practically lovable when he's drugged."

"Come on. Go sit outside. I want you to avoid having your own heart attack."

I press my eyes closed and open them. "Is it wrong to be so pissed off at him?"

"Nope. Not at all. This is a challenge. I'd say it's one of the bigger ones you've ever faced." She cocks her head. "I'm sure you're up to it. Like you said, the bum doesn't have anywhere to go. You're stuck."

"I don't like the sound of that." I scrutinize Amy. "Are you leaving me alone with him?"

"Not a chance. I'll hang around. Luckily I can do most of what we were hired to do right from here." She bows. "So, if you'll excuse me, while you sit on the porch and contemplate your navel, or dream up ways to rid yourself of Jerome, I'll take this opportunity to go earn us a living. I must have 150 emails to answer from anxious customers."

"I want to help. I can help."

"I know you can, Fi. I did send you a few questions about some of the accounts. When you're up to it, you can take a look and let me know what you think."

I blow her a kiss and drag myself to the front porch where I collapse into a large, white rocker. The song "Dollhouse" appears on my playlist, and I ball my hands into fists. Gee, that one says it all. For so long I was just another doll of Jerome's, one rarely taken out to play. Now the whole structure is falling down.

Leaning into the hard back, I set the chair in motion. I used to rock Ben. We'd purchased a chair similar to this one after I gave birth. I smile, remembering how the only thing guaranteed to quiet baby Ben was movement. If it wasn't the rocker, we relied on a bouncy seat I kept at my feet while we ate, or a swing Jerome wound up and let him ride. The swing gave us about half an hour, enough of an interval to down our dinner and a glass of wine. Occasionally, when nothing worked and Ben still wailed, Jerome bundled him up, strapped him into the car seat, and rode him up and down the neighborhood hills.

Life held fullness then. But before I knew it that richness grew overwhelming and our relationship suffered. Taking care of Ben and working left little time for Jerome. Our intimacy dwindled.

I shift in my seat uncomfortable with the memories of my increasing refusals of Jerome. Not only time for intimacy, but time for doing little things together fell by the wayside.

Though the bedroom door is closed, Jerome's snores carry through the thin wood, the racket piercing my ears. He roars on the breath in and on the breath out. How does he do that? He moves on to shouting names of companies and what I surmise to be stocks. The eruptions grate on my nerves. Standing, I push the rocker towards the other end of the porch and listen hard. At first I still hear the ruckus. It comes at me like an annoying song that plays over and over in my head, an earworm of noise that burrows so deep I fear I'll hear it for hours after he stops.

There. The sound finally is out of reach and not in my skull. I push the chair a little more to ensure occupancy of a snore-free zone. Silence at last.

"Rearranging furniture?"

I jump in fright and turn to find Sammy standing in front of me.

"A little."

Sammy points to the ocean. "The view is better from the other side of your porch so you might want to put your chair over there."

"You're right, but I like it over here." I sit down on the rocker. The side he refers to is near Jerome and his bone-shattering commotion.

Sammy proffers a basket. "This is from my sisters. Welcome to the neighborhood."

"That's so thoughtful." Perhaps I need to reassess the sisters from hell.

An array of goodies resides on a fluffy kitchen towel lining the wicker. Jars of olives and tomato bruschetta, crackers, and packages of candies catch my eye. Butter cookies peek through cellophane wrapped around an attractive tray.

"All of these things? Amy will be thrilled too."

"Those cookies from Del Ponte's bakery barely made it here." He grins.

"Thanks so much. It looks terrific."

Sammy places the straw container on the porch and points in the direction of the ocean. He clears his throat. "Listen, there's going to be a board-in tomorrow. I thought you might want to see it."

"A board-in?"

Sammy nods. "It's a thing surfers do to remember their buddies. One of the old-timers passed away a while back and a bunch of us are going to gather on the beach for a ceremony with our surfboards."

I shift in my seat. "I wouldn't want to intrude."

"You're not intruding. I can stop by and we can walk down together." He pauses. "It's just a thought. You don't have to come if you're worried it might be upsetting. I can understand that but, honest, this should be pretty uplifting." Discomfiture spreads over his face, as though he thinks he may have gone too far. Or maybe he fears my rejecting him, though I figure that's my own wishful thinking.

"Where exactly is this ceremony?"

"Right at the end of the block. On the beach."

I send him a smile. "Sounds like a plan."

He slaps his thighs and turns to go. The corners of his lips turn up slightly. "I'll be by around six."

Sammy bounds down the steps, whistling. He whistles

marginally better than he sings. I recognize the tune.

"'I'm on Fire,'" I call.

He turns. "Excuse me."

A blush creeps up my neck and warms my cheeks. "'I'm on Fire.' That's the song you were whistling."

He winks and resumes his trek to his house. His whistling fades, and behind me Jerome's snoring intensifies. He shouts sell and buy every now and then. He must be involved in a big deal.

I find my phone and go through my playlist. "I'm on fire," I whisper and press play, drowning out the snoring. The memory of Sammy's whistling fills the middle of my skull and heats my insides. I call out the lyrics loudly in union with Bruce's intense warbling about excitement, desire, and the glorious soaking sweaty aftermath of sex until I'm drenched and happily exhausted.

CHAPTER THIRTEEN

Missing

THE NEXT MORNING I DECIDE to explore the main thoroughfare of the town. After a short walk I arrive on the festive street. I look in on a gift shop displaying coasters, scarves and everything imaginable in a beach theme. Mugs with pink and green flip flops and white trays emblazoned with the words Bradley Beach in navy blue catch my eye for future presents. All along Main Street I spy flowers hanging from lamp posts and planters filled with gorgeous blooms. A couple of vacant storefronts catch my eye, and for an instant I consider setting up our business here.

I reach Terri's Paradise Realty and when I hold my hand to the front glass and peer inside, Terri frantically waves. She can't be that happy to see me.

She dashes to the door and throws it open.

"I need a favor, hon." She motions me inside. Smartly dressed as ever, she wears a yellow blazer over a navy blue and yellow shift.

"I have to pick up my grandkids." Her bright lemon platforms with Minnie Mouse bows shuffle across the linoleum floor to her chair where she hefts a mammoth navy purse.

I lift a gold frame from her desk. "Is this picture of them? They're adorable."

Terri leans over and taps the photo. "This is Birkin. He's six. And his sister, Prada. She's five. They're my most precious gifts."

"Your grandkids have designer names?" I'm unable to keep a laugh from escaping.

"My daughter-in-law has a thing for pocketbooks."

"Is there a pet?"

Terri doesn't miss a beat. "Coach. Their ferret."

I can't resist. "Poor ferret. That's a little downmarket."

Terri guffaws. "I'm the mother-in-law. No say in the names. I've gotten used to them now though."

"What do you need me to do?"

"Can you mind the store till I get back, hon? I won't be long. Fifteen or twenty minutes. The receptionist is out sick, and my daughter's stuck in traffic on the Parkway, so I need to shuttle them home. The grands are out of camp early."

"I hope I don't have to do anything other than sit here. Are you sure you don't want to lock up and put a sign on the door."

"I'm expecting a delivery and I bet it comes when I leave. You'll be fine. It's a slow time of the day for people looking at houses."

Terri blows me a kiss. The door slams behind her before I can ask any questions.

The sun shines outside but you'd never know it inside dank Paradise Realty. I sit behind Terri's old, mahogany desk and watch the sparse foot traffic of the town. The large, picture window sheds coffee-colored light on the dated and depressing atmosphere.

I locate a piece of paper and start listing all the things that need to be changed to make the office a more welcoming place.

I manage to decode the complex coffee pot sitting on her desk, treating myself to one of her cookies and sipping my cup of coffee while I sketch ideas. The phone rings twice. I enjoy pretending to be the receptionist. The UPS man delivers a package which I sign for.

Terri's twenty minutes turn into thirty, and I keep drawing. She finally reappears and plops down in the chair opposite me. "I love those kids, but goodness, they're impossible to keep track of. Thank heavens my daughter was home by the time I got to her house." She sends me a sincere gaze. "I can't thank you enough, hon."

I stand to leave. Terri appears crushed. "You can stay. I like the company."

"I need to get back."

"To an empty house? Pish, hon."

"It's not empty." I pause. "My ex is there. "

"The one you told me about leaving when we were at the hospital? Oh, dear."

"He's recuperating from a heart problem. Lucky me." I fill her in on the details of Jerome's appearance and collapse.

Terri shudders. "That's a lot of stress."

"Nothing that a good jog and music can't help with though."

"Run over here anytime you like, okay?"

"You might regret that offer."

Terri smiles and accompanies me to the door. A young couple passes me on the way in, and Terri launches into her spiel about the wonders of the beach area. I chuckle in spite of what I know is waiting for me back home.

Courtesy of the stash of his drugs, Jerome sleeps for most of the day. I hear him stirring and venture into his room. He shoots me a sullen glare. Good. His eyes are clear, and he's looking like himself.

"You're supposed to move around."

"I'm aware of what I have to do."

"You're in bed. Maybe get up and walk some?"

"I'm busy, Sofia."

"You have to do things differently now. Eat better."

"Says who? Those doctors? Why should I believe any of that medical bull?"

I bite my tongue and depart. His argumentativeness signals

he's better, but I don't want to face him down. Not yet. I arrange for Amy to bring him whatever he requests.

Later in the day Amy reports that he showered and reluctantly ate a bowl of soup and asked her to call for a cheeseburger. Though he remains in bed, we hear him yelling on his cellphone. That evening, Sammy rings the bell at a little before six. I perform a quick check of my annoying mate's snoring; he's emitting the familiar strident sound that he's always insisted exists only in my imagination. The uproar increased over time, generally proportionate with the amount of stress endured during his work day. I took to sleeping in the guest room on particularly loud nights.

Amy shoos me from Jerome's door. "Get out of here. I'll keep tabs on him while you're gone. He's got good color in his face already. "

"He's always been strong."

"Go on, get to that board thing with Ole Green Eyes."

"What if he doesn't go?"

"Maybe he'll be bored with us."

I uncurl my fingers. I want to stay calm and prevent a nasty interaction when we do converse, but my irritation chafes badly, leaving me with little emotional reserve. I doubt I can control all the horrible things I want to say to him. Last night, the nasty cackle grew louder after dark, and I resorted to turning on a night light. I remember Doc Phelps telling me to do whatever it takes to get myself back to the present moment, and the light helped.

I shake my head and try to send thoughts about Jerome away before greeting Sammy. As I open the door my lips instantly curl upward. Sammy wears board shorts, and his broad chest is bare. I drop my gaze to Killer, not wanting to stare at Sammy and wanting to at the same time. The dog sports a floral bandana and licks at Sammy's bare feet.

"Hey." Sammy picks up Killer and shifts him from one arm to the other. The dog squirms against his torso and leans towards me. Killer laps at the air.

"Hey," I answer, disturbed by the lifelessness in my voice. I wish I'd been able to put a little more oomph into the word. If my voice rings out that way to me I can only imagine how much worse it sounds in reality. I scratch Killer on the head and let his tongue run over my hand. His body shakes with glee.

Sammy eyes me. "You okay?"

"It's been a long day."

"There still might be time to snag a cuppa at the food truck if that appeals?"

"No thanks. I'll be great as soon as I get a hit of ocean air." I force myself to smile warmly and notice with relief that the action makes me feel better. Apparently the putting-on-a-happy-face studies to improve mood that Doc Phelps told me about are true. I stretch my lips a little wider. The grin lingers, this time due to muscled Sammy dancing in front of me with goofy Killer in his arms. The pooch alone amounts to a grumpiness annihilator of the first degree. With Sammy waving a paw at me, the effect is better than having downed a couple of Red Bulls.

Sammy stops moving, and Killer cocks his head. His focused gaze makes him seem like he knows my thoughts. The steady stare amps up his cuteness. I laugh easily. In return, Killer wags his oddly fluffy tail. Tonight it resembles a quill pen with sections missing.

Sammy scratches Killer behind the ears. "Are you going to let me in on the joke?"

I shake my head. "Not till I know you a lot better."

"I like the sound of that."

Sammy and I amble along to the oceanfront, letting Killer take the lead. "He has a routine," Sammy says. "Watch what he does when we reach the picket fence at the next house."

We arrive at the white fencing, and Killer plants his rear at the front gate facing the home's porch. He barks three times. Then again three more times.

A black lab appears behind the glass storm door. His tail wags furiously, and he yips. He and Killer exchange yips and barks.

"That's Corky. The two of them have some sort of thing going on. I can't go past here without having this conversation."

The lab retreats into the house, and Killer tugs on his leash. "Ready to go, boy?" Sammy says. "We're outta here."

"They're a lot smarter than we give them credit for, aren't they?"

"Definitely." Sammy pulls a plastic bag from his pocket and shakes it. "Look at this. I have to carry a bag around with me to clean up after him. Think about that. I'd say dogs have *us* trained and not the other way around. Heck, if we did half of what they do in public we'd be in prison."

"Or an insane asylum."

"Exactly."

We both laugh.

Once we reach the boardwalk Sammy points to the sand. "My board's down there with my buddy. Looks like they're waving me over now. I'll leave you under the protection of my fierce companion."

I take a seat on a bench, and Sammy hands over Killer's leash. The dog jumps into my lap, licking furiously at my arm.

"Geez, Killer. Take it easy." He pushes away his snout but Killer returns to my skin with ferocity.

"His tongue tickles. He's such a cute dog."

Sammy sends me a crooked grin. "He makes a great wing man."

Sammy bounds down the stairs and joins the knot of men gathered near the water. One of them hands each surfer a rose. Before Sammy walks into the ocean with his board, he turns and finds me. He waves, and I return the gesture. The man next to him nudges Sammy in the side. The group wades in and paddles out through the breakers to where the ocean lies peaceful beneath the growing dusk.

I hug Killer, not sure what to expect. The surfers bob in the water. Without saying a word, in unison they form their boards into a long row and drop the flowers into the sea. They watch the tide carry the blooms out. Cheering and raising arms overhead, they burst into "For He's a Jolly Good Fellow."

I'm relieved this is a happy ceremony. Killer barks and wags his tail. He barks again staring away from the beach.

"What's up, boy?" I twist and see a figure standing behind us. At first I fail to recognize the man but then his face registers. "Hello, Walt."

He starts, apparently not expecting me to address him. He scuffs a shoe on the ground. "It's turned out nicely, hasn't it?" He runs his fingers through his hair.

"You knew Phil?"

He grins. "No one ever really knew Phil. He was the most infuriating and lovable character."

"I wish I'd have met him."

"You'd have liked him. Everyone did."

Walt joins me on the bench, and we watch the rest of the ceremony together. The surfers return to shore and dry off. They plant their boards in the sand upright and join hands for a few seconds, and then they erupt into an immediately recognizable old Journey song—"Don't Stop Believing." They sway and belt the lyrics, thoroughly enjoying themselves. A couple of young fellows link elbows and twirl on the sand.

The singing stops, and the surfers clap one another on the back and gather their things. Walt stands and says, "I'm glad I came. They did a fine job. Phil would approve." He bows slightly and says, "Good night."

Killer wags his tail and yips at Walt's departing back.

Sammy takes a seat beside me. "Was that Walter?"

"He was a friend of Phil."

"Amazing. I had no idea. But I'm not surprised. Phil charmed everyone." He towels his legs dry. "Thanks for coming. I'm glad we were able to do this for old Phil. That was his favorite song, and we all wanted to sing it for him."

"What a lovely tribute. He must have been a special guy."

"He was." Sammy studies the horizon. "He was always up for keeping me company on the waves. He had such a great sense of humor. I miss him. We all do."

Killer licks at my cheeks. The lyrics of "Missing" fill my head and bring my demons to life. Some mornings I still hear Ben's feet clomping down the stairs in his soccer cleats. I wake in the middle of the night, my arms outstretched towards the vision in my dreams. I smell him in the hallway like Bruce says. God, I miss him.

Sammy slaps his thigh. "The night's young. Let me drop off my board and change and then I think it's time I introduced you to one of the finer establishments the shore has to offer."

I pat Killer. "A walk with this fine canine is all I need."

"You'll have your walk and more. Plus, Killer will be extremely happy when we get where we're going." Sammy's eyes are sparkling.

Nothing but the present moment matters, and my heart soars in the comforting space.

CHAPTER FOURTEEN

The Last Carnival

"WELCOME TO YAPPY HOUR AT the Wonder Bar," Sammy says.

A white fence surrounds a patio and yard teeming with a casually dressed crowd. Sammy opens the latch to the Wonder Bar's large outdoor deck, and we follow Killer into the enclosure. Killer strains at the leash, and his tail wags wildly. Thirty or so dogs and twice that many people roam the space.

"Yappy Hour? I love it."

"I bet no one else has ever taken you to a cocktail hour for dogs. It's an Asbury Park specialty and not-to-be missed event." He scoops up Killer into his arms.

An attractive woman in a pink T-shirt and blue jeans approaches, and Sammy waves hello. Her cropped, blonde hair frames her smiling face. Though she dresses in casual attire like all the other patrons, her attitude signals the role of being in charge.

After she greets Sammy, she says, "There're some new puppies Killer might like to meet." She runs her palm over Killer's head. He wiggles and shakes so hard Sammy can barely hold onto him. She strokes Killer along his spine. "You're one happy Chinese Crested, aren't you, boy?"

Sammy introduces the woman as Kate, head of the volunteers at the Wonder Bar. "You came on a good night. Lots going on," Kate says. "Part of the proceeds of tonight's sales will benefit the boardwalk stray cats." She hands me a flyer. "And we have a group of doggies waiting for adoption tonight too. They're the ones wearing blue bandanas."

I scan the open area and spy a few puppies with tiny, blue kerchiefs around their necks. A cluster of people gather around them, and the little ones display their puppy best in order to attract an owner. Off to the side, a cute beagle with a bandana sits on a young woman's lap.

At the end of an outdoor bar, I notice another dog wearing a blue bandana. This one's older, quite pudgy, and looks like the saddest dog in the world.

Kate rubs her palms together. "We've already had four adoptions this evening. I'm so relieved."

"What's the story with that one?" I point at the sorry-looking creature.

Kate follows my finger. "You mean poor Phoebe?"

"She's not a breed I recognize."

"She's a mix of a Sharpei and Dachshund. She's the biggest darn Dachshund mix I've ever seen. She must weigh forty pounds."

Phoebe's muzzle is salt and pepper, and her skin sags all the way to her ankles in unattractive wrinkles. Her ears droop, and her rolls of flesh wriggle like Jell-O when she scratches herself. The color of her coat reminds me of damp sand.

"She's a little old for adoption, isn't she?" My eyes stay riveted on Phoebe.

"Her owner got tired of taking care of her." A frown wrinkles Kate's brow. "Phoebe's been here three times and no one's taken her. It's distressing. This could be the last time she comes."

I blink. "You're not saying anything bad will happen to her if she isn't adopted, are you?"

"We've had a great track record till now." Kate bites her lip.

"That's terrible."

Kate blinks rapidly. "We don't have any control over what happens to them. The animal rescue people bring them here and usually they're adopted by the end of the evening." Her voice chokes.

"Will they kill her?"

Kate looks away and leaves the question unanswered. "The puppies are always taken." She points to three little dogs surrounded by doting patrons. "The young ones are lucky. Everyone wants a pup. But an older, overweight dog like Phoebe…" Her voice trails off.

Another customer enters, and Kate hurries to greet him.

Sammy leans down and unleashes Killer with a "Go get 'em, boy." Killer immediately dashes to the far side of the penned area. He joins a pack of canines that race into a fenced lot where they run at top speed. Round and round they go. They charge in a broad circle and miraculously avoid collisions with each other or the fences.

"Let's get something to drink." Sammy gestures to the outdoor bar, clasps my hand, and leads me through the crowd. The warmth and strength of his grip calm something deep inside me. Along the way I sidestep a couple of Jack Russells and a Westie who lunge playfully at one another. I take a seat on a high stool next to Sammy. We both order the special beer of the day. I lean back and smile, charmed by the beautiful evening and demonstrative camaraderie of the dogs and their masters. My eyes periodically return to sad-sack Phoebe sitting at the end of the bar.

I tear myself away from watching her. "So who enjoys this more, the dogs or their owners?"

"It's a tossup." Sammy takes a swig of his beer. He's wearing khaki shorts tonight. A pale green, V-neck shirt intensifies the color of his eyes.

Killer finds a friend to race and charges to the outdoor pen again. Poor Phoebe wedges herself into a quiet spot beneath the bar and scratches at her ear.

I study Kate's flyer with its display of all types of cats. Sammy taps the front cover. "The boardwalk's home to a lot of strays, and they make sure to place them with good owners. They set traps out and house them in one of the empty buildings. Otherwise they'd either freeze over winter or animal control would get them and put them to death. The cats used to roam free but with all the redevelopment they've become outcasts."

"It's terrific someone does that."

"It's a noble cause. They run another benefit called Woofstock too." He winks. "I'll have to have more than one beer, you know, to support these admirable causes."

"Heck, I'll have to join you."

I glance at Phoebe, still beneath the bar, protected from the rush of activity. Her middle bulges out several inches from her sides, and her fur needs brushing. Phoebe closes her eyes, seemingly resigned to her fate. My pulse flutters.

Sammy interrupts my musing. He inclines towards me and says, "So, can you tell which of the dogs belongs to which owner?"

I look at the sea of pets and owners. "That's a challenge I doubt I'm up to." The patrons are as colorful and varied a group as the dogs, and many times their pets are nowhere to be seen. At the far end of the bar, a man in African garb and a woman in a sari converse with a pair of Asian men whose arms drape around each other. A white-bearded man in a Harley Davidson jacket pets a Schnauzer held by a woman wearing a head scarf.

"How about I go first," Sammy says. "You pick a dog that's not clearly with anyone, and I'll see if I can guess the owner."

"You're on."

A well-groomed poodle wearing a rhinestone collar catches my attention. The dog stands off to the side of the deck aloof from the rest of the pack. I point, and Sammy follows the direction of my finger.

"The dapper poodle. Hmm..." He pans the enclosure, turns, and angles his head towards the fence that runs along the back of the area. He snaps his fingers. "The owner is the lady back there with the black and white hat."

The black and white hat is an Easter bonnet strikingly out of place in the casual surroundings. Then again, so is the elegant poodle. The rest of the middle-aged woman's outfit consists of a full, black skirt with a wide, patent leather belt, matching shiny pumps, and a pressed, white blouse as pale as her face. The woman's getup is appropriate for a night on the town circa 1948. She completes the picture with bright, red lipstick and a glass of white wine. She sips slowly and could've been at a cocktail party instead of on an outdoor deck.

I laugh. "They do make a logical pair. Both a little overdressed." The poodle advances and lies down at her feet.

"Score," Sammy says. "Your turn. This time you pick out a dog and find its owner."

I run my gaze over the deck and hone in on a pair of small Chihuahuas with pink collars. The duo hang out under a table and beg for French fries.

"I'm working on those Chihuahuas."

No likely owner comes into view. I continue searching unsure what to look for, panning back and forth in slow motion.

"Tick, tock, tick, tock," Sammy says, wagging his finger like a metronome.

Finally my brain seizes on a clue. Two tall, thin men in matching baby-blue T-shirts stand on the far side of the yard next to a white, bone-shaped doggie swimming pool. They gesture at each other in animated fashion. I nudge Sammy.

"Straight ahead." I nod in the direction of the two men who appear to be in their mid-twenties. "Baby-blue shirts over there own pink-collared Chihuahuas over that way."

"Way too easy. Their shirts have Chihuahuas on them."

"Hah. Let's see what you come up with."

Sammy points at a gigantic, black mastiff approaching a table nearby. The dog sits down and drools on a young woman's leg.

Sammy says, "He doesn't belong to her. She's too uneasy." The woman tries her best to act comfortable with the strings of drool that fall to her pressed jeans. She strokes the dog's head and shoves him away gently. The dog refuses to be deterred. His dripping saliva lands on her pedicured, sandaled feet, and frustration passes over the woman's face. The dog rests against her leg and plops his massive, wet snout onto her lap. Her brave front collapses and segues into wide-eyed repulsion. The dog stares at her as though she were the only person in the world. My laugh causes the young woman to turn towards me. She clearly hopes for salvation.

"Is he yours?" Her brown eyes are wide and anxious.

I shake my head. "Sorry."

Sammy whispers, "Wanna bet that's his owner over there?" Sammy points. "Biker jacket. Black leather pants. The tall one."

I judge Sammy's candidate to be in his early forties. He stands beside a similarly attired man. Both of them sip sullenly from beer bottles.

"What on earth is telling you to make a connection between that guy and the drool factory?"

Sammy grins. "Amazing, huh? Are you impressed?"

"Only if you're right."

"I'm right."

"We'll see."

The girl lets out a groan and heaves the dog's head from her lap. "Nice doggie, good doggie," she says. In desperation she stands and wipes at her pants with a napkin.

"I don't think she's a dog owner at all," I say.

"Not a drooling dog's owner, that's for sure."

The tall, biker-jacketed fellow notices the woman's dilemma with the mastiff. He slaps his hand on his thigh and calls, "Andy, come here. Now."

The dog yawns and stands his ground. He leans against the girl's leg and raises an enormous paw to her thigh. She holds onto the table, steadying herself against the weight.

The owner whistles. "Come on, Andy. Get over here."

After a mighty shake of his head that sprays strands in all directions, the mastiff backs away. The woman's shoulders relax, and she sits down in her chair. Andy's owner comes over to her with a towel and offers to help her dry off.

"Damn. You were right. I can't believe it. It's not at all obvious."

A twinkle appears in Sammy's eyes. "Pretty good, huh?"

"What's the smug look about? No one loves a gloater."

"Says who? I bet you're cute when you gloat."

I glare at him.

"Hey...what's that look for? I wasn't gloating. This is my usual smirk."

"I'm not buying it. Something's going on. Spill."

He clears his throat. "I was here last week and so were Andy the drooling mastiff and his beer-guzzling master. Andy likes the young ladies. So does his owner." He points at Andy's owner who now sits beside the young woman.

I frown. "You knew."

"You're not pissed, are you?"

"You mean because obviously this shows you're a deceptive, smooth-talking con artist capable of God knows what else?"

"Hey. It's a dog and its owner. I'm not Bernie Madoff trying to make off with millions."

I avoid his gaze and feign anger. When I glance towards him, he displays a look of worry but, seeing my smirk, he smiles and nudges me tentatively in the side. I laugh.

He sends me a crooked grin. Sexy. So youthful.

"Nicely done, Sofia. You had me going."

"We're even, then."

Killer appears and rubs against Sammy's leg. Sammy reaches down and scratches him behind the ears. "Having fun, buddy?"

Killer licks at Sammy's hand. Sammy pours a few drops of beer onto his palm. "Here you go." Killer laps at the beer, and his entire body wags. His head snaps left, and he runs off at top speed to join a pair of Labradors taking turns bathing in the white, bone-shaped pool. The pool's size makes it impossible for more than one of them to enter at a time. Each Lab noses the other out after a few moments.

Sammy wipes his hands on his jeans. "Is this a hoot or what?"

"It's special. Really special," I say. "The people are so happy, and the dogs are in canine heaven. It's made me remember my own dogs from when I was a kid."

"More than one?"

"Flapper and then Rex. They were my best friends. Flapper lived with us till my teen years, and Rex till I graduated from college."

"I still miss my childhood pets. I think we owned almost every animal you can think of. A rabbit, two dogs, a couple of cats. I wasn't fond of Gret's gerbil, but I did love those dogs and cats."

"Have you noticed how so much of life is about what you lost, not what you had?" Ben's face flashes before me. The ache in my chest grows more noticeable. "I'm sorry. That's what beer does to me. I'm not usually so maudlin."

I catch the sound of lyrics and listen hard to bring myself back to the present. Inside the bar, "The Last Carnival" plays with its insistent yearning for lost love.

"Do you hear that song?" I ask.

Sammy cocks his head in the direction of the music. "That's the one about the trapeze daredevils who defy death every show every day. Great song."

"You do know your Springsteen."

"I like how it captures how emptiness and loss cut everyone the same. Even daredevils who are willing to take a leap don't have any more protection than the average couple."

"But at least they experienced that leap."

Our eyes meet and something passes between us.

A scuffle arises by the pool. A large dog corners a smaller one and snarls at the yapping and terrified pooch. The smaller dog yelps in fear and pain.

I jolt upright. Killer's neck lies beneath the large paws of a huge pit bull.

CHAPTER FIFTEEN

How Can I Keep From Singing?

SAMMY BOLTS FROM HIS STOOL. He makes it to the dog pool in a matter of seconds and scoops Killer away from the snarling dog and his menacing behavior. The pit bull loops around them, periodically jumping up. Killer cowers against Sammy's chest.

I scan the deck in a desperate search for the owner of the dog. Sammy crosses to the far side of the enclosure and confronts a tall, sandy-haired fellow in a navy blue bandana.

"Your dog's at it again, Ernie."

Ernie hooks a thumb through the loop on his jeans. "Maybe you and your rat dog should leave."

Sammy's jaw sets. His fingers curl, and he hugs Killer to him tightly.

"You know the rules as well as I do."

Ernie takes a long swig of his beer and burps. "He's not bothering anyone except your weird-looking dog. It's your dog's hair that's setting him off."

Sammy pulls himself up to his full height and glares at Ernie. I want to grab Sammy and tell him it's time to go. The hairs on the back of my neck rise in anticipation of what might happen next.

Kate appears and steps between the two men. She disrupts what threatens to deteriorate into a dog owner version of the O.K. Corral gunfight. Ernie grips the pit bull by the collar and attempts to soothe him but the dog continues snarling. The dog finally whines and heels.

Kate leans into Ernie and whispers in his ear. Sammy spins around and strides back to his barstool.

"There's always one," Sammy mutters in a voice that rings out more than a tad too loud. Sammy signals the bartender and orders another round. He kicks at the sand beneath his barstool.

Across the yard, Kate discusses matters with Ernie. Her hands rest firmly on her hips, and she holds her back ramrod straight. A few seconds later, Ernie throws his bandana to the ground. He and his growling dog leave the enclosure.

I relax. Maybe the study I read about men and confrontation was right. According to the researchers, once men directly face each other a primal urge to dominate takes over and that prevents them from getting along. To achieve cooperation guys need to sit side by side the way they do when watching TV and sports. Throw in a threatening situation such as the one between Killer and the pit bull, and all hell breaking loose between two men who are facing off becomes highly likely.

Sammy lets out a sigh of relief and places Killer on the ground. Killer races back to the pool with the labs.

"I shouldn't let Ernie get to me." Sammy takes a gulp of beer. "I vow I'm not going to get angry and promise myself no matter what happens I'll keep cool." He shakes his head. "Doesn't work. I was ready to smash his obnoxious face in." He hesitates. "I'm not violent. Really."

"Uh huh."

Sammy shifts in his chair and turns to me. "His dog attacked Killer a few months ago."

"Here?"

Sammy stiffens. "I was out walking Killer late at night over by the Convention Center, near the jetty. I didn't hear them coming up behind us on the sand. The guy's a regular stealth bomber."

He takes another swallow. "He thinks it's funny when his dog scares or attacks the other ones. He's one of those people that give the whole pit bull breed a bad name. Such a shame to train a dog to do stuff like that. They're really protective wonderful animals."

"Did Killer get hurt?"

Sammy nods. "I had to bring him to the vet. He took a few stitches."

"Poor Killer. That's horrible."

"Ernie doesn't show up too often. Kate's thrown him out a few times."

"Good for her."

Sammy drains the last of his bottle. "Ready to go? I think we've had enough Yappy Hour excitement for one night."

I hop off my stool. Sammy whistles for Killer who continues bouncing in and out of the water. The pool and the labs hold far too much interest for a whistle from his master to distract him.

"He'll sleep well tonight." He smiles.

"Me too." I sigh then hold up my hand. "Be back in a minute."

I locate Kate and speak to her. After a few moments we exchange texts, shake hands, and I return to Sammy. He snaps Killer's leash to his collar as Kate leads Phoebe over to us.

"Give me a call if you have any questions. She's been here so many times that I know a lot about her. I'll send along her papers." She hands me the leash.

Sammy chuckles. "You're adopting Phoebe?"

"It's her lucky day," I say. "Mine too."

I have an inkling I might regret this, but my apprehension quickly dissipates when Phoebe turns her large, brown eyes on me. My insides melt under the soulful gaze. Taking Phoebe home makes perfect sense.

We wave goodbye to Kate, and on the boardwalk Sammy stops to study the ocean. A pair of surfers rides the small swells. Killer and Phoebe sniff at one another.

I push Killer away from Phoebe's rear. "You just met her, Killer, behave."

Sammy points to the surfers. "The white dude is Leon, the black one is Mack."

"How do you know? They're so far away."

"Ain't nobody else out there. Mack and Leon are always out boarding in this spot or close by. The surf may be shitty but they'll drag their butts out even in February."

"What dedication."

"They live for music and the surf. You'll see them playing backup in the local bars. They're really happy guys."

"I'll be on the lookout for them. It's nice they like what they do. A lot of people I know are caught up in work but aren't enjoying it much."

Sammy shifts his gaze from the horizon, and his laser green eyes lock onto mine.

God. I want to fall into them and I want to kiss him.

I bite my lip. That comes out of nowhere.

I try to stop the thought from intensifying and tell myself he's too young. Also, I'm so not-yet-divorced. What a fantasy to think a sexy guy like Sammy harbors any interest in me. A lovely fantasy.

"You don't know the right people," he says, waving a hand in the air. "You hang around here long enough, the water and sand will do their magic and you'll only know people who like what they do."

"Oh really?"

I take in his broad shoulders. I wish I possessed the strength he gives off. Once, long ago, I was strong and unbreakable—a woman with plans.

He turns, and I follow him along the boardwalk back through the decaying structure that leads out of Asbury Park, into Ocean Grove, and on to Bradley Beach. The dogs move ahead of us. Killer runs, and Phoebe ambles. Phoebe definitely ought to lose more than a few pounds. Maybe we can get back to fighting weight together.

"If you need any dog supplies let me know. I have more than enough to get you through a couple of days till you can buy what you want for Phoebe."

"Thanks. I think we'll be fine. I should be okay getting what she needs at the grocery store."

Phoebe tugs hard on her leash and takes a sharp left. I tumble behind her down a few stairs to the beach. She's sniffing the sand and struggling to move under the boardwalk.

"Whoa," I say, choking up on the leash.

Sammy and Killer reach us, and Sammy laughs. "She's a strong one. Wants us to go under the boardwalk."

I peer into the dark space beneath the wooden planks, remembering the Drifters song. "That doesn't look inviting right now. I don't care what that old tune says."

"You mean 'Under the Boardwalk?' All that's under this one is cats and the rats they're chasing. And sometimes a homeless person or two."

On cue, a black and white feline darts out of the darkness and takes off in front of us. The cat races back under the wooden structure. It takes all my strength to control Phoebe. The noise coming from her is deafening, somewhere between baying and ear-shattering howl.

Sammy reaches in his pocket and removes a treat. "Hang on," he says, breaking the biscuit in half and feeding one piece to Killer. He waves the other in Phoebe's direction. She stops making noise and dollops towards him. He hands her the treat.

Sammy whistles, and Phoebe follows him up the stairs, sniffing at his shorts.

"Thanks for the distraction," I say.

We fall into a comfortable silence with the two dogs padding beside us. I want the walk home to last longer. Regardless of whatever baggage Sammy carries around, the world grows brighter with him beside me. Phoebe's presence makes the experience even better. Sammy interrupts my reverie. "Hey, where are you?"

I shrug. "I'm right here."

"Uh huh."

I'm surprised he's so aware of my being lost in thought. Jerome barely knows if I'm in the same room. Sammy's paying attention to me, to my moods, is so unusual I forget to watch where I'm walking on the old, uneven boardwalk. I lose my footing, and Sammy reaches out to steady me, his touch searing my flesh. A torrent of ardor cascades up my arm.

"Careful," he says.

His attentive behavior and his kindly tone impress me. He's a protective soul,

comfortable with jumping immediately into action to save Killer, steady me, or divert Phoebe's focus. And our banter at the bar revealed his sharp sense of humor. I'm aware of throbbing in my nether region.

When we come to his house, he and Killer proceed down the walk without hesitation.

Sammy never looks back. I guide Phoebe up my porch steps and glance over as Sammy pauses beneath his front door light. A grin spreads over his face. He waves one of Killer's paws at me, nods, and slips inside.

A curious mix of joy and sadness floods me. I close my eyes to savor the moment. The expressive richness and promise of fulfillment of "How Can I Keep from Singing" bubbles up soundlessly, radiating through my core. How wonderful, that, in all the darkness, something bright flickers and makes my entire being want to sing.

"Have a good night?"

I jump at the voice and catch myself before I slip off the top step.

Jerome sits in the shadows of the porch.

CHAPTER SIXTEEN

Fade Away

"I SEE YOU'RE FINALLY UP." I make my voice steady and pull Phoebe's leash close.

"I'm tired of being in bed."

"Where's Amy?"

"She went out to pick up a new prescription and some snacks." My hand reaches for the door knob. Jerome stands and approaches me.

"Who is he, Sof?"

"A neighbor."

"A friendly neighbor. Young, too." His voice drips sarcasm.

"It's none of your business."

"You're still my wife. Coming home with a strange man is a cause for concern."

I shake my head. "You've got to be kidding."

He glares at me, radiating anger. Isn't that rich. Then he wrinkles his nose. "Where'd you find the dog? God, it stinks."

"Good night, Jerome."

"No, Sof. We're going to talk it out."

"There isn't anything to say." I hasten inside and into the living room with Jerome following close behind. He moves quickly for a man who recently suffered a coronary episode. Phoebe, bless her soul, lowers her head and growls. I pet her matted coat and soothe her.

"You must be feeling better." I remind myself to measure my words. I don't want him to land in the hospital again.

"Geez, what a miserable-looking mutt. Who's the poor person who owns her?"

"She's mine. I adopted her." The warmth of the house grows oppressive, and I cross to the air conditioner. I hit the on button. The unit immediately streams a steady coolness into the space.

"We don't need that thing."

Jerome hates air conditioning as much as he hates animals. He likes to sweat and he accomplishes perspiring with proud success. The beads on his forehead glisten in the light of the living room lamp.

Phoebe flops down in the path of the cool air, watching Jerome closely. Her dog scent fans into the room, and Jerome covers his nostrils with his hand. I turn the knob to high and face him.

"My house, my rules. Speaking of rules, you're supposed to take it easy. And enroll in cardio rehab."

He lets go of his nose and breathes through his mouth. "Forget it. I'm not interested in lining their pockets. I'm feeling great." He thumps his chest.

He's definitely better.

He clears his throat. "What I did was wrong. But it's over. I made a mistake, Sof, a big mistake."

The cool air hits me in the back; however, I need more than a chilly blast to stop the growing wetness beneath my arms.

"It's not about mistakes, Jerome."

"I know that. It's about Mandy."

I cut him off. "It's more than your young bimbo."

I sink onto the couch. The air conditioner hums loudly, the only sound in the room. He stares at me intently, as though he really cares about the conversation. He exhibits a look that I remember from long ago. In spite of what has passed, my interior melts. The hollow behind my knees surges with heat.

I force myself back to the present, and the fond memory

dissolves rapidly.

"We've had this discussion before," I say. "Lots of apologies, lots of broken promises."

"Name one."

"I'm not going to do this again."

"If you don't tell me what's bothering you, how can I fix it?"

"Besides Mandy? Do you remember last summer? When you didn't come home for a couple of days? It was around our anniversary."

He blanches slightly.

"That's one. You told me there would never be anyone but me. That I mattered more to you than anything else."

"It's true, Sof."

I press the bridge of my nose tightly. "I think you mean that when you say it. But then you take off with someone else."

"I'll never stop loving you."

"You have a strange way of showing your love."

Mandy represents one in a continuous long line of women.

"That fellow you came home with is awfully young."

"Stop it. There's no comparison. He's fully grown for starters, unlike Mandy." I cross my arms. "Do you realize we haven't spoken about anything of significance in months, and now you're acting like we talk to one another on a daily basis?"

"We talk."

"No we don't. We talk about the weather and about what time you'll be home for dinner the one or two days you make it home a month. That's it."

He scowls at me.

"I don't trust you, Jerome. I haven't for a long time. Why on earth would I—or should I?" I rise to leave. When I reach the stairs the heat of his stare bores into my back.

"Let's give it another go, babe."

I mount the first two steps.

"I'll take that as a yes."

"You really have nerve. You might believe your bullshit, but I don't."

He glowers at me full-on now.

"We're done. Over." A huge weight lifts. The words free me,

but the relief that streams through my center takes me aback. "Why do you want to keep up this charade? Let's put this relationship out of its misery."

"Why now?" Jerome clenches and unclenches his fists.

"I don't know. It's the right thing to do."

"You're not making any sense."

But I am. "Phoebe and I are going to get some sleep." I pause. "This is her home, Jerome, not yours."

"You can't be serious about that animal." He snorts, and my fury grows.

"I know you think dogs are messy and inconvenient. Well they're nothing compared to you. For twenty-six years I've cleaned up after you and let you have your way. No more."

Jerome drops onto an easy chair, and for an instant I wonder if my rant has stung him. He appears lost in concentration. Has he retreated? Is he licking his wounds?

No, not at all.

He's not injured by my remarks. The look on his face says he's regrouping and planning his next line of attack. The thrill of the chase. Some things never change. I shake my head. "Don't waste your time figuring out what to say or do to win this."

His eyes shine icy blue. "What?"

I know he hasn't missed my words. "You heard me."

"Don't flatter yourself."

"I want you to leave. You're obviously well enough to be on your own. The sooner you're out the better. I'll call the cops if I have to."

I lift my chin. A part of me fears I'll never be rid of him.

Without warning, he bolts toward me and his fist cocks back. Phoebe lunges at him. In a flash she grabs onto his pant leg, snarling and pulling the fabric. Jerome kicks her in the side, and she lets go, yelping in pain.

"Stop hurting her!" I yell. Jerome wheels and charges from the room. His door slams shut.

My head reels. I don't know why, but the memories rush at me and time compresses backward. I hear Ben's screams and the roar of the receding snow plow. Then there are no more screams. A bright light flashes behind my eyelids. Red blood seeps onto the white snow. Ben's body lays sprawled on the ground. The plow driver never stopped. He rolled over Ben and continued along his morning route only noticing the red tracks that led from our house on his return pass. I cradled Ben and rocked him until Jerome arrived and pried my fingers from his body. I didn't believe he was dead until the doctor at the hospital told us there was nothing they could do.

My tears spill over and cascade down my cheeks. I wipe at my face with numb fingers, unable to staunch the hot stream dripping from my chin. My sobs ring out, and Phoebe whines loudly, stirring me from the horrible remembrance. Rubbing my knuckles into my eyes forces me back to the present.

We climb the stairs to the bedroom where I throw the lock and bend to comfort Phoebe. A large welt rises at the spot Jerome's foot connected with her ribcage.

"I'm so sorry, Pheebs. He's never done that before. I didn't expect it. Thanks for saving me." I find a washcloth in the bathroom and soak it in cold water, wringing out the excess. As I press the cool cloth onto her side she licks my hand and I'm grateful for the soothing contact.

After a few minutes, Phoebe claims a comfortable spot on a throw rug at the foot of the bed. I turn on my music and scroll through the list of tunes. "Come on, come on," I mutter, searching for one that will dispel the mood taking root. I control my breathing drawing in air deeply and exhaling slowly.

The title "Fade Away" catches my attention. I press play and listen hard, choking back tears as the agonizing ballad makes my skin crawl. No love or trust exists between Jerome and me anymore, leaving us in a sad state that cannot be fixed. Things haven't been good for so long. Now they're worse than ever. I hear Doc Phelps voice saying there comes a time to cut losses and not to fear the result.

My melancholy grows. I shut off the music, inhaling deeply and pacing around the room until intense tiredness engulfs me. I change into ash sweatpants and a large, cotton T-shirt. I used to wear normal pajamas to bed—cute silk shorties, long jewel-toned lounge pants, cotton ones with tiny bird prints or seashells. Jerome bought me pajama-grams more than one

Valentine's Day. After Ben's death I started wearing sweatpants and sweatshirts or men's tees for sleepwear. I'm ready to face any emergency in my sweats. Knowing I can flee on a moment's notice usually keeps the panic away and allows me to succumb to sleep.

A light flickers across the way. The brightness coming from the top floor of Sammy's house makes me smile, and I envision him in his own space, close by but not too close. How beneficial right now to have a friend like Sammy. He forces final thoughts of Jerome and the past out of my mind.

Phoebe lets out a yowl and paws at the air in her sleep. She snores loudly. It's a softer and less irritating snore than Jerome's. I flick on the night light, sending its butterscotch glow into the room, and I slide between the sheets and hug my knees to my chest. Eventually I surrender to dreamless darkness.

CHAPTER SEVENTEEN

Jungleland

TWO DAYS LATER, I'M FINISHING up a load of laundry when I hear Amy and Terri laughing out on the front porch. It's no surprise that the pair is hitting it off. Other than Amy towering over the petite Terri and being far more boisterous, they harbor a number of similar personality traits. Both are organized, hard-working professionals and stellar saleswomen. Unlike me, they're always ready to try new things. It also strikes me once again that they are far more attractive and put together than I could ever be.

I join them outside, taking a seat on the bamboo loveseat.

"What are you two talking about?" I'm feeling a little left out of their easy conversation.

Terri swivels toward me in her chair. "Amy's been filling me in on her art projects. She's so creative."

"They're not that funny," Amy says, tapping her black pump on the floorboards. She's chosen a pair of gray, polished, cotton pants with a pale gray, silk top today. I've seen her don this outfit to meet with clients.

"Has she told you about any of the disastrous ones?" I pour a glass of iced tea from the pitcher Amy's brought outside. The cold liquid slips down my throat, leaving the taste of raspberry and mint behind. Amy adds two sugars to her glass and stirs. Her gaze lingers on the swirling pink, blue, and green op art pattern of Terri's palazzo pants.

"I have no idea what you're talking about," she says, throwing shade on my comment.

"How about the one with the donuts in the park?" I take a cherry-centered cookie off Amy's plate and bite into the buttery goodness.

"Everyone loves donuts. You have to admit that." She adopts a perfectly crafted look of false annoyance.

"And therein lies the problem."

"I guess I didn't think that part through."

"The donuts were gone before we set up the camera equipment for the shoot."

"The ravens enjoyed them." Amy moans and explains to Terri, "The glazing took me a really long time. I arranged them in the shape of the flag. Red, white, and blue. It looked so pretty. I didn't get one picture."

"A donut flag? What were you trying to say?" Terri squeezes her lips together, trying hard to hold back her amusement.

"I was trying to make a comment on conformity in America. Instead it became a testament to catastrophe, and a statement on aggression. Raven aggression. I felt like I was in that Hitchcock movie, *The Birds*. They were everywhere."

"And so was bird poop. My hair got hit a few times. Gross." I stroke my curls and untangle a few.

Terri chuckles. "They say it's good luck if a bird craps on your hair."

"Well if that's good luck what the heck is bad?" Amy wipes her mouth on a napkin. "Have you noticed there are a lot of annoying things that are supposed to be good-luck charms? Like rain on your wedding."

"It rained on mine," I say, cupping the icy glass. "Didn't help at all."

Terri says, "Finding a spider on your wedding dress is supposed to be good luck too." She shudders. "I managed to have a good marriage without any crawly critters."

Terri reaches to the floor and hands me a freezer bag. "Before I forget, I stopped by to give this to you. I figured you can use some take-out. It's only soup and some sandwiches." She motions to the house. "How's it going?"

"A car picked him up in the middle of the night. But his stuff is still here. He left after our last conversation." I'm used to these odd hour comings and goings, and given the clutter in the guest room, I figure he'll resurface eventually.

Amy shifts in her seat. "A couple of packages came for him this morning. I took them inside."

Great. More stuff of his in my space.

Terri stands and straightens her palazzo pants. "Time for me to get to the shop. Heavenly Bodies. It's the cutest little lingerie store. You have to come visit."

A store. In addition to being a broker, she runs a shop. The woman's a human version of the Energizer Bunny.

"Hang on," I say. "I have something for you too."

I dash inside, locate a large manila envelope and race back to the porch. I present my find to Terri.

"These are some design mockups I worked on. You mentioned you wanted to remodel, and I figured I'd take a stab at some ideas to update a little. Amy's weighed in too."

Terri takes the envelope. I can tell she's uncomfortable.

"There's no charge. If you want to buy any of the items we can give you a good discount. I really appreciate everything you've done for me."

She beams. "Hon, I'm floored. That's so nice."

Terri's lime green patent shooties gleam in the sun. She minces her way down from the porch and sends us a broad grin. "Good luck. I can't wait to look at your plans."

"Did Sofia tell you where she went with Sammy from next door?" Amy calls.

Terri stops. "Where?"

I throw a balled-up napkin at Amy, but she catches the projectile mid-air. Her face shows a "ha-ha-made you squirm" smirk. She knows how to get to me.

I sigh. "A board-in."

Amy pumps a fist in the air. "And Yappy Hour."

Terri claps her hands. "Really? That's terrific, dear. From what I've heard he usually stays to himself. Kudos to you!"

Not long after Terri leaves, Amy departs for a meeting. Figuring on going for a run, I find Phoebe and clip her leash to her collar. She follows me outside and immediately becomes dead weight on the end of the tether.

"Move it, lard-butt." I tug on Phoebe's leash. She plops her ample rear on the ground, so I pull the tether tight—again to no avail. She lowers her head and yawns.

"We're going jogging. It means we run to the beach from here and keep going." I lift my feet up and down and trot around Phoebe in circles. "Like this. See?"

She stretches out on the pavement and splays her rear legs behind her. "Come on, Phoebe. Humor me."

She rests her head on her paws and licks a spot on the ground. I try pushing at her back end but she becomes limp. My shoving barely budges her. I pull a dog biscuit from my pocket and wave it in front of her face. Her nose twitches. "This was supposed to be your reward after our run." Her eyes track the treat as I brandish it over her head. "You know you want this."

Phoebe's eyes stay locked on the biscuit. She sluggishly finds her feet and trails me, but the moment I pick up the pace, she loses steam. The leash goes taut, and I trip over my sneakers.

I groan. Clearly Phoebe and jogging make a poor match. Defeated, I hand her the treat and she chomps on it, her saliva puddling on the sidewalk.

"You win this time. But I'm not giving up on you. How do you make so much drool?"

After the snack, Phoebe consents to a walk around the block. She finishes her business, and I bring her home following her wide rear as she lumbers up the porch stairs. Once inside she collapses in a pool of light by the front door.

"You might be done for the day, but I'm not." The dog yawns, and I leave her to her laziness, taking a gamble that she is safe from Jerome returning soon.

The sun warms me as I run down the boardwalk, and I crank up my music reveling in the searching violin intro of "Jungleland." The segue into a pulsing rhythm commands me to push harder. The Boss's primal screams tear into me, and I shiver with the understanding that finding love, even if only for small moments, helps with the dark daily struggle and the inevitable dying of dreams. My empty arms ache.

I increase my speed, and my body protests. I encourage myself to stick with my fitness program. *Atta girl, Sofia. Keep going.*

The song's a long one, and I grab for the life preserver of the last line, clinging to the message that though I may be wounded, I'm not dead.

Huffing and puffing, I pass over the Bradley Beach/Ocean Grove border. One town down. A few seconds later, my legs wobble and a dull ache wends through my calves. I gasp for air.

A tap on my shoulder startles me, and I turn to find Sammy.

He grins. "Hey, you."

He sports wrinkled jersey shorts and a once-white T-shirt. His downright cuteness trumps his messy disarray. The thin cotton shows off his lean frame and makes me pull in my gut and stand taller. My legs want to quit but I continue running, hoping to impress him. I pull my earbuds out and smile.

"You headed to your place?"

He nods. "I open later but wanted to check on some inventory. Figured I'd get a run in first."

My lungs threaten to give out. I can't keep up the pace any longer, and I taper to a walk, unable to speak. I stop and wait for the pounding in my chest to decrease refusing to show how much I need to suck air.

I force out words. "How often do you do this?" My ego refuses to give in to the strong urge to bend over and place my hands on my knees. I can't believe how quickly the running became difficult after such a good start. It's going to take time to build up stamina.

"Not often enough."

The thrumming in my chest slows. My breaths come more easily. "Where do you run to?"

He points. "See the tower in Asbury? The one next to the old structure at the end of the boardwalk."

"I haven't made it that far."

"The tall tower is an old heating plant that doesn't work anymore. I run past it, through the old Casino, and over to Convention Hall. And then I head back till I hit the Belmar Bridge, and I finish up either at home or at the store."

I groan. "That's like eight or nine miles. You're a running machine."

"I worked up to it. Those last couple are killers."

Great. Add modesty to the list of his good qualities. "I'm not much of a runner. I only started recently. That distance terrifies me."

He grins. "Don't get down about it. No one can do long distances from the get-go. It helps if you keep at it."

I nod. If only I could believe him. I point in the direction of Asbury Park.

"I better get going again or I'll never finish, and one of the few things I like about this is when I do finish I can collapse. Phoebe and I are in a competition to see who can land first on the sofa with the loudest groan. I'm winning. But only because she has trouble climbing up onto the couch."

He hesitates. "Want company?"

"You could never keep up with my pace." I shoot him a challenging stare.

Sammy emits an easy, deep-throated laugh. "Let's go."

I love his laugh. I want to hear that sound more.

We jog side by side, and I enjoy the companionship and newness of the situation. Jerome doesn't run, though he stays in shape. He sweats his butt off at the gym. He likes an audience for his workouts and the bigger the crowd the better. The treadmill within the view of the most customers claims him every visit. No people that day? A mirror suffices.

"What were you listening to?" Sammy asks.

"Bruce. I need all the distraction I can get."

"Ah. Excellent running music."

"The 'Born to Run' album." I chuckle. "It's not jogging he's talking about. But all that intense need to escape and angst works great for keeping my legs going."

"Lots of energy in that collection."

"He's such a poet. He's been a big part of my life for so long it's like having a buddy along with me."

"He plays around here now and then. In regular concerts, but he also pops up unexpectedly."

"That'd be amazing to see him that way."

"His lyrics capture something special, don't they? They're about life and all its yearnings. And about looking for answers. And they're a reflection of our culture, of where we are as a country." He pauses. "I'm sorry. I don't mean to go off on a Bruce tangent."

"I couldn't have said it better. Bruce is all I listen to lately. Sometimes I don't understand a song, but I still love the way it makes me feel."

"Ah, sounds like you're a candidate for the Spring-Nuts if you're not already one?"

"Spring-Nuts?" He's piqued my curiosity.

"They're fans who love all things Springsteen. I joined up a while ago." A sheepish grin forms, and he sends me a sideways glance. I can tell he's assessing whether his enthusiasm makes me think less of him, but his comments are music to my all-things-Bruce-tuned ears.

"Sounds like my kind of gang." I manage to deliver what I hope is a reassuring smile.

He's no longer hesitant about his ardent fan-dom. "They gather at the Wonder Bar and other spots."

"Another reason to love that bar."

I need to slow down, and Sammy wordlessly accepts the lesser speed. Our easy silence sends me to a welcoming place. Soon, we pass a massive structure with a large crucifix embedded in its cupola.

"What a striking building. I noticed it at the flea market and have been wondering about the history."

Sammy relishes his tour-guide role. "That's the Methodist's Great Auditorium. They worship there though they also use it for other events. The funny thing is Woody Allen donated that big cross on top after making *Stardust Memories* here. They play the film occasionally and everyone in the audience cheers the familiar spots when they appear on screen."

My legs grow tired, but my inner voice tells me to push forward and count on them for a little while longer. I ignore the growing tightness in my chest and stop myself from rubbing it. I fight to wipe the grimace from my face.

Sammy points out a long line of colorful tents. "See those?"

"I was admiring them at the Flea Market."

"The tents go up every year on Memorial Day. The back of each one is attached to a wooden structure that has a kitchen and bathroom. The tent community is governed by the Methodist Camp Meeting Association. They own all the land in the town and grant ninety-nine year leases to buyers of houses and businesses."

"The tents are so close together. They can reach out and shake hands through their windows." Baskets of flowers dangle from the rafters of the small porches. A brightly colored awning marks the approach to each cottage and inviting rocking chairs flank the front doors.

"There are still around a hundred left. The owners come every year for camp meetings. They move in for the summer and take them down on Labor Day. Pretty good accommodations for ten bucks a night."

"You're kidding."

"Can you believe there's a ten-year waiting list? Plus, you have to show you've done good deeds to rent."

As we pass the Auditorium expanse, I see Asbury Park in the distance. I'm barely above a speed walk. I give myself landmarks to keep going. *Make it to the third bench...Now make it past the water fountain.*

When I pass under the rusting steel-frame hulk, with the word Casino overhead, a surge of accomplishment flashes through me. I never expected to run this far. Sammy smiles at me.

"It's a mile and a half from our block to here."

I gulp air. "It felt like five."

"Let's take a break at my store."

That sounds like a terrific idea. I nod, unable to get more words out.

He slows to a walk, and I resist the urge to stop completely.

Big drafts of air fill my lungs, and soon my chest moves in and out normally.

Sammy points to the ocean. "Dolphins again. See them?"

Sure enough, a half dozen fins bob and arc out beyond the waves.

"Do they show up here a lot?"

"You've been lucky. They're actually rare. And even rarer are the whales."

I point to two figures dotting the horizon. "Mack and Leon?"

He laughs. "You were paying attention the other day."

At his storefront, he digs in a pocket for a key. The ocean roars behind us. I need something to drink and to sit. Sweat streams from my brow as I look out to the water and observe three children riding boogie boards. The sight of them stirs up a memory that turns the joy of my accomplishment into sadness.

I was a stronger swimmer than Jerome, so I took on the task of teaching Ben to swim at an early age. He reveled in the sport and all things water-related. At six he expertly rode a boogie board. At seven he graduated to a long board. His laughter echoes in my head.

I bury the memory and enter Sammy's shop.

Sammy waves a hand. "Sit anywhere."

I hesitate, not sure about the appropriate spot to park my sweaty rear. "I'm kind of damp."

"Really, it can take it." Unlike me, Sammy has no trace of wetness on his face.

He brings me a cold bottle of iced tea and opens one for himself. Sammy takes a seat on a couch and puts his feet up on a worn hassock. I join him. A wet, sloppy tongue licks my ankle, and I jump. Killer paws at me from beneath the couch. I wiggle my fingers and locate his head. The dog scrambles out and leaps into my lap. His soft fur and inviting body draw me in.

"He likes you. He usually doesn't come out from under there till his food appears."

I hug Killer and scratch beneath his chin.

"How's Phoebe doing?"

"Fat and lazy as ever. She's not into running. Otherwise she's adjusting nicely."

"She's lucky you took her in." He smiles the little crooked smile that's now familiar. "I'm not being nosy, but I redirected a Peapod delivery to your house a little while ago. The driver was looking for a Jerome Catherwood."

I gasp. "Oh, no. This is awful." I blink a few times. *Peapod.* Jerome's stocking food supplies. This isn't a man who wants to move on and out.

"I've been told I'm an excellent listener. Want to give me a try?"

I let out air through pursed lips. "It's not a pretty story."

"Killer and I both know there's more to life than pretty."

I lower Killer to the floor and try to keep my pulse from racing. "The delivery guy was looking for my husband. He's the same one I was yelling at on the phone when we first met." My fingers clutch the fabric of the seat cushion. "We've separated. It's complicated."

"He's living with you?"

"It's *really* complicated."

Sammy shoves his hands in his pockets. I have trouble beginning, but soon pick up conversational steam and fill him in on why I left Jerome, how he had a heart attack, and now is holing up in my new place. When I relate the part about Jerome kicking poor Phoebe, Sammy's jaw tightens. I swallow hard and blurt my fear that Jerome might not leave, and if he does I might not make ends meet. That part stings. Why would Sammy want to be friends with someone in such dire straits as I am? But I don't care a whit what Sammy thinks about my situation. If he runs, he runs. It's pure and simple me, and I'm not about to lie or cover up the disarray of my life.

Except for one thing.

I never mention Ben. The words about him fail to surface.

Sammy nods at all the right places, and I know he pays attention. When I stop talking, he covers one of my hands with his.

"I'm sorry, Sofia. If you ever feel threatened or need to vent or call me for any reason, please don't hesitate. No one should put up with what you did."

I tell myself, he's kind, nothing more. Nonetheless, his caring gesture causes my intestines to swirl with something fiery. I'm astonished at the intensity.

Uncertainty about how to act takes hold. I want the moment to last. Oh, to stay suspended at this place where things are right between us. My hand burns.

I take him in. "Thanks for listening. I'm glad you're here."

"Me too." His eyes glow with warmth, but underneath I again sense distress.

I pull back my fingers and break away. "Sammy, listen, this is a difficult time for me."

"I understand." A rhythmic rapping on the front door interrupts us. A man's face presses against the glass. His hands shade his eyes. "Anyone there?"

"It's Pete. He must have a delivery." Sammy checks his watch. "He's probably looking for June. Trying to get her to notice him is one of his favorite pastimes. She probably dropped off Killer and went out for something. Guess he's going to be disappointed."

Sammy stands. My unease grows. Sharing so many intimate details of my life confuses me. Maybe it sets me up for sharing other intimacies.

Other intimacies like sex.

I rack my brain for a memory of the last time I had sex with Jerome and come up blank. For years now I figured my desire switch might not ever trip again. The days of lighting up immediately on his touch are long gone.

Young and handsome Sammy listening to me amounts to nothing more than friendship. What coursed through me moments ago is my fantasy, not his.

I'm not doing a great job convincing myself.

I brush off my shorts. "I'd better get back."

"Hang on." Sammy trots to the door, and Pete enters carrying three large bags. He dumps the contents onto the floor. Old shoes cover the area delighting Killer who leaps into the pile. "You're going to love these, Sammy. I can't wait for Greta and June to see them. I bet they'll sell like mad." He sees me and pauses. Waggling his thick, dark unibrow, he shoots Sammy a you-dog expression,

Sammy ignores the look. "You remember Sofia from the flea market. She's my new neighbor." Sammy smiles at me. "She was out for a jog. Would you like something more to drink, Sofia?" The all-business tone sets me back.

I shake my head. "I have a doctor appointment to make."

He arches an eyebrow.

"A checkup. I'm trying to live a healthier lifestyle, and it's time to face the medical music. Cholesterol and all that."

"Been there, done that," Pete says. "Diet and exercise. Don't take the drugs unless they make you."

Outside on the boardwalk, my mind spirals back in time. Before Ben came into our lives, Jerome and I occasionally went to the beach together. Sometimes we sat staring out at the water with his face buried in my hair. Once we made love on the shoreline. The sand made a terrible bed. It wound up in my hair, his mouth, and in other uncomfortable spots. He called it our *From Here to Eternity* moment. We used to laugh about that. The recollection smarts.

I turn on my music and find the "Born to Run" compilation. My slow jog erupts into a punishing run. As my feet pound hard to the music, putting distance between me and my memories, I pray that, like the buildings behind me in Asbury Park, those haunting remembrances will eventually fade into a soft tableau.

I reach my block and taper to a walk aware that I haven't shaken the miasma of dark memories. When I see Terri approaching she has a broad smile on her perfectly made-up face. Her blonde hair shines in the sun.

"Yoohoo," she calls. "I'm so glad I caught you." She tugs a tasseled gold necklace into place.

She leans in to kiss me hello, and I wave her off and wipe my brow. "I'm a sweat ball. Keep that silk away from me."

She chuckles and hands me a card. "All sorts of wonderful new lingerie came in today. We're running a special sale. I want you and Amy to visit soon."

"Me and lingerie." I sigh. "I think this is a waste of everyone's time."

"Nonsense. There's nothing like a pair of pretty undies to make a gal feel good about herself."

I'm not buying what she's selling.

Terri casts a quizzical gaze. "Is everything all right?"

Something about Terri makes me want to come clean and let her know some of what I struggle with on a daily basis.

I bite my tongue. "Have you got a minute?"

"Of course."

"I need some water and to check on Phoebe."

She follows me inside, and I discover Phoebe right where I left her, dozing in the sun. She thumps her tail and yawns in greeting.

In the kitchen I fill two glasses from the tap, and I take a few sips, swallowing hard. Terri sits at the table.

I can't look at her. I fidget with a striped placement on the counter to stop my hands from shaking.

Terri waits quietly with her fingers entwined on her lap.

I blurt, "Terri, I lost a son. I miss him terribly. I feel so alone, so disconnected from everything."

"Oh, hon, I'm so sorry. What a terrible thing to go through. I can't think of anything worse than losing a child."

She stands and wraps her thin arms around me, and we cling to one another. My eyes grow damp. Terri holds me tighter. Her hair smells of gardenias.

After what feels like an hour, I pull away, and everything is lighter and brighter. I swipe at the wetness on my cheeks.

"You okay?" she asks. "You're not alone." She taps me on the shoulder. "Feel that? I'm right here, aren't I?"

I nod. I've never discussed Ben with anyone other than Amy, Jerome, and Doc Phelps.

An impish smirk crosses Terri's lips. She steps back, fans her face with her hand and pinches her nose. "Listen, sweetheart, I'm not minimizing what you've told me, but we do have luscious smelling soaps at Heavenly Bodies. And I think a visit would do you good. What have you got to lose besides that awful stretched-out bra you're wearing?"

"Why do I have the feeling you're as good at selling lingerie as you are at selling real estate?"

"Realtor of the year, three years running."
I slap at her arm, and we laugh.
I can't believe I've made a lingerie date.

CHAPTER EIGHTEEN

Trouble in Paradise

"THE DOCTOR WILL BE WITH you shortly. He's running a little late. There's a gown to change into on the counter." The medical assistant shows me to the examining room and closes the door behind me.

I strip off my shirt and pants, don the blue gown, and climb onto the examination table taking stock of why I'm here. Since Ben's death five years ago, I dodged getting another physical. The only doctor I visited was Doc Phelps, because he gave me the meds to keep the darkness at bay. Doc Phelps said grief immobilized me and made me unable to take the steps necessary to stay fit. Time wore on and then he said survivor guilt replaced the grief and mired me into inaction. That rang true. With Ben dead, I didn't deserve to care about my health.

I swing my legs back and forth off the table. Jerome's antics with Mandy have made me reorganize my priorities. Though I fear the possible results of the tests, I now have the resolve to take control of my health.

"You're the captain of your own ship," my grandfather used to tell me. *"Don't forget to steer."*

Jerome pointed me in whatever direction he wanted. That left me washing up on dire shores. I have myself to blame and now it's time to take the wheel.

I insert my earbuds and turn on my music. The unsettling message of "Trouble in Paradise" makes me think of losing Ben, of my wrecked relationship with Jerome, and of my medical situation. I'm good at ignoring all sorts of red flags, at pretending that nothing is amiss. The music burns deeply, and my adrenaline rises.

Maybe my denial and refusal to take care of myself is coming home to roost. What type of health problems loom in my future? The inner cackle rises up above the music. I calm my forehead with my thumbs to stop the black mood from descending further.

Unnerved, I shut down the device and yank out the earbuds.

A voice interrupts my reverie.

"Hello, Mrs. Catherwood."

I look up. The doctor's the same one who examined me in the hospital. The cute but unlikable young one.

He studies my chart while he washes at the sink.

"I'm Dr. Bartlett. We met at the hospital."

"Where's Dr. Salter?"

"He had an emergency and I'm covering for him."

"It would've been nice if someone told me."

He eyes me and wipes his hands on a paper towel. "How have you been?"

Great. He's ignoring my complaint and not apologizing. An asshole with a God-complex.

I compose myself and say evenly, "I've started jogging a little and walking more. And I'm watching my diet."

"When was your last complete physical?"

"I'm not sure. A while ago."

He picks up his pad. "Any more fainting or periods of forgetfulness?"

"No, thank goodness. That was frightening."

"Still sleeping okay?"

"No problems there."

"Most of your blood tests came back fine. No issues with your thyroid or triglycerides."

I wait for the "but."

He taps his pen on my file. "I'm sending you for a couple of additional screenings. Routine follow-up blood work. There's nothing to worry about." He studies me. "Is anything bothering you?"

You!

Why do I dislike him so much? I control my irrational feelings. A simple no is all it takes to get me out fast. Instead, I answer, "There's one thing…well, maybe two…"

He folds his arms across his sternum and waits for me to finish the thought.

"There's tightness in my chest occasionally."

"Tightness shouldn't be ignored. Where is it?"

I point to my left breast.

"When do you notice the feeling?"

"It comes and goes. Sometimes it's at night, sometimes when I run. It never gets too strong, but I'm aware of something there, something tightening like a rubber band."

"Any family history of heart disease? Diabetes?"

"My father died of a heart attack at eighty-two."

"I want you to get a stress test and a cardio ultrasound." He approaches and places a stethoscope on my back beneath the gown. "Breathe in and out, please."

After a few breaths he moves the instrument to the front.

"Do I need to restrict my activities because of this tightness?"

"Activities?"

"Yes."

"Such as?"

"Jogging."

"I wouldn't go climbing any mountains till we get the stress test results, but if you've been jogging and enjoying it, keep on with it." He taps on an iPad. "Be sure to keep walking and exercising. If you drop a few pounds it'll help, but don't obsess. The most important thing is to get fit and to bring your LDL cholesterol into a normal range. You're more than a little on the high side."

"What's that mean?"

"It means your numbers are well over 200, and your good

cholesterol isn't so hot."

My breath hitches. "What can I do to get into the normal range?"

"Let's try altering your diet, and once we've received the stress test results you can begin increasing your exercise. Sometimes that's all that's needed. Lower your fat intake. Watch the alcohol. We have some literature at reception that spells it out in detail."

The pronouncement of no medications yet is good news. Amy told me several horror stories about friends who developed awful side effects from cholesterol-lowering drugs. This visit gives me the impetus I need to bring my levels into the standard range.

He glances at his watch and hurries out the door without saying goodbye. I dress and stop at the reception area. I charge my co-pay, pick up a few pamphlets, and check the sheet that lists the tests I need to undergo. As I turn to leave, I see a familiar face.

Ellie Cornell frowns at the floor. Her plaid dress hangs on her frail frame, and her skin exhibits a sallowness that makes me shudder. The sign on the door indicates Dr. Salter and his colleagues share office space with an oncologist. A stab of apprehension runs through me.

A woman clad in a pink smock stares at a clipboard and calls out, "Mrs. Cornell." Ellie follows her into the oncologist's office. I wave, but Ellie fails to notice me. A desire to help Ellie with whatever she needs rises, and I exit the office with sorrow in my gut.

I climb into my car and gasp.

My aversion to Dr. Bartlett suddenly makes perfect sense. He looks like the doctor who gave me the news about Ben. The young physician spent only a minute or two with me and Jerome, never meeting my gaze. He told us nothing could be done to save Ben and hightailed it out of the room before I had a chance to ask questions. I grip the steering wheel. The darkness closes in and after a time recedes. The trembling in my hands stops, and I throw the car into gear, desperate to escape all this sadness.

CHAPTER NINETEEN

Your Own Worst Enemy

BACK AT HOME, IN LIVING room, Phoebe gives me a hello thump of her tail on the floor. She closes her eyes after the effort and returns to dozing.

One whiff of the air makes me pinch my nose. "Phoebe, I didn't think you could get any smellier." I approach and rub her behind the ears. "I can't take it anymore. It's bath time, girl."

In the kitchen, I locate a few dog treats and biscuits. Two sticks of beef jerky sit on a shelf in the cabinet. The nasty dried meat goes into my shirt pocket, headed for the garbage.

I wave the mouthwatering treats in the air by Phoebe's nose, and she opens her eyes and yawns. Strings of saliva course onto the floor. She stretches and pushes herself to her feet. I move the snacks in a circle and call, "Come on, girl."

Once I lure Phoebe to the backyard, I toss her a dog-bone shaped biscuit and tie her to the back fence. Phoebe crunches away in happiness, and I turn on the hose.

"Here you go," I say, bending and offering her another dog treat, but Phoebe twists her head away. She whines, and sniffs at the plastic wrapper that peeks out of my shirt pocket.

"Jerky Jerome's jerky, huh? That's what you want?" After peeling away the casing, I break off a small piece. Phoebe drools with pleasure and gulps it down.

In between handing her bites, I struggle to lather her coat. She strains at the leash but eventually she sits and tolerates the washing, head down and tail between her legs. The occasional bit of beef jerky keeps her calm.

I croon Springsteen's "Your Own Worst Enemy" to her over and over. "You are, you know, your own worst enemy, Pheebs. If you'd stop rolling in garbage and eating everything that came your way, you'd really be a lot more pleasant to live with."

Phoebe pants and sends me a knowing doggy stare.

"And then you wouldn't be you, would you?" I sigh. "What have I gotten myself into?"

Phoebe licks her chops. I hug wet dog and choke off the smell. "Forget what I said, honey. You're the best thing ever to come along."

My inner voice tells me maybe Phoebe's not the only one who is her own worst enemy. I don't want to think about being guilty of causing my world to disintegrate.

I pour myself into the task at hand. When I finish hosing her off, my drenched top clings to me, and my hair lies matted on my head. Phoebe shakes mightily and sends a spray of droplets into the air. I shield my eyes with my hands to avoid the soaking. When she stops, I peek through my fingers and laugh at the sight.

Phoebe's stomach bulges in a comical fashion. Her tail resembles a thin stick attached to a huge rear end. It wags back and forth like a pathetic metronome.

"What a pair we make. You're on a diet. Me too. Your cholesterol's probably higher than mine. You've got to lay off the beef jerky." A stench emanates from Phoebe's rear and envelops me, and I cover my nose. "That's worse than ever, Pheebs." I lead her into the house and she promptly rolls on the carpet.

"No, no, no," I call, trying to stop her. "This Oriental isn't for drying dog fur. It's going to smell like damp dog forever if you do that."

I throw a towel over Phoebe and rub at her coat, but she

squirms out from under. I push her down again onto her belly. Phoebe flips over and raises her paws in the air. She grinds her back on the rug in a rhythmic motion. In desperation, I pull her into the bathroom to distract her from the carpet. I glance in the mirror and eye my dripping hair. I turn on the hair dryer and work on my soaked curls.

Phoebe becomes transfixed on the blower. She paws at the tiles and whines with anticipation. I place the setting on medium and aim the nozzle towards her. Phoebe lifts her chin and closes her eyes. Her ears flap in the hot air. She whimpers and wags her tail, thumping it against the floor rapidly.

"You like this? What a girly dog you are."

I use the dryer until all dampness disappears from her fur. My dry dog sits and watches me work on my hair. Done, I stow the hairdryer, bend, and give her a kiss on the head.

"Ah, you smell divine. If you can get those gaseous emissions under control, no one will run from the room when they see you."

Phoebe lets out a little bark of agreement. She lumbers out of the bathroom and heads downstairs, with me close behind. Jerome's door stands open but he's still nowhere in sight. His prick-mobile rests on the curb in front of the house.

Phoebe saunters into his room. She sniffs beneath his bed and pulls out a box of beef jerky.

"No you don't," I say. Phoebe twists her head out of reach and quickly gulps one down whole in its wrapper. I shove her away from the box and have trouble forcing it back to its resting place. I kick the meaty treasure trove and stub my toe on the metal support beneath the box spring. When I hop around the room squealing in pain, Phoebe whines and lets out a sympathetic yowl.

Jerome's jacket falls off the bedrail, and I pick up the blazer. I think about going through his pockets and about tossing all the beef jerky he hides beneath the bed. The tightness in my chest returns and increases. I don't want to buy into the anger growing within and will myself to rise above the feeling. With my hand on my heart, I wait for the tension to dissipate. I hang the jacket in the closet and exit with Phoebe, worried about taking a stress test. I force myself to dial and set the appointment.

CHAPTER TWENTY

One Step Up

BARELY TEN MINUTES ELAPSE BEFORE Amy is complaining about our outing on the boardwalk. She groans dramatically. "My armpits are already wet."

I wipe at my cheeks with a tissue. "It's healthy to sweat. Cleans out your pores and cleanses your system."

Amy scoffs. "A facial is more my style. And even a high colonic doesn't sound so bad compared to all this humidity."

I don't think it's possible but she slows more.

"Can we pick up speed? You said you'd jog with me. This isn't jogging."

"I lied."

"Not funny, Amy."

"There are better ways to work up a sweat," she says. "Locked in the arms of a hot guy comes to mind."

I think about waving her off with a "Please. Not again." Instead, I smile and say, "Intimacy does make life a lot better."

Amy's mouth drops open for a second. "You're agreeing with me?" She rolls her eyes in thought. "This is more than a little un-you." She narrows her gaze. "What happened to 'I'm never getting involved again?'"

"I said intimacy, not hot sex. There's a difference."

"Not to me."

I sigh. "Listen, I've been thinking..." I hesitate. "I've decided it's time to take the reins into my hands. One of the things I can do for myself is—"

"Have sex?"

"Geez, can you listen without interrupting?"

"Oh wow. You're alive."

I am. But while Sammy's touch lit up a part of my brain I didn't know still existed, and a sexy dream woke me in the middle of the night, it's not those things that occupy front and center in my mind. It's my stress test yesterday. In spite of my apprehension I came through it fine. One more test remains.

So far, nothing serious showed up anywhere on any of the medical procedures. Other than my annoyingly high cholesterol and the occasional twinge in my chest, my medical landscape looks neat and tidy. The collapse on the boardwalk was obviously nothing to worry about. My goals now include taking up less physical space in the world and lowering my cholesterol. I want to tell Amy about my new choice of diet and fitness lifestyle, but she continues down another path with no room for a change in direction.

"Hot sex." Amy pumps a fist in the air.

A look I know well spreads over her face, making me cringe. "Oh no. Spare me. Not another Amy idea."

"Maybe we should try together."

I eye her, not sure what she means. "Together?"

"I'm game for a casual hookup if you are."

"You spend way too much time with your vibrator. I think it's turning your brain to custard."

"Hey, if we go out and hunt it'll be good for me and for you since you won't have to hear Old Reliable buzzing."

I pinch the bridge of my nose. "There's a phrase I detest—'Good for you.' Nothing fun is ever good for you." I pause. "You really named your vibrator Old Reliable?"

"Come on. Let's take a pledge to get lucky."

"Amy, luck happens. You can't make it happen. Especially

with regard to men. Besides, why would I want to do that?" No-no. Not a good idea at all.

"I disagree." Amy wiggles her shoulders and her hips in a poor attempt at being sexy. "We can set out to get lucky in bed and make it happen if we put our minds to it."

"I don't think we should manipulate life like that."

"Are you afraid?" Amy stares at me. "Men set out to get lucky all the time. Why not us? It's a great way for you to get even with Jerome."

"Can't we find a guy for you while I work on getting fit? My health's what I wanted to talk to you about, not revenge and not hooking up. I don't want to get even with Jerome. Not that way. I want to get healthy."

Amy pulls on her earlobe. "You were thinking about sex. Be honest."

"How about finding a fellow simply for companionship? I'm still married to the lump named Jerome. The bum's having supplies delivered from Peapod. He's never leaving—though he has disappeared for the past few of days. I don't need another man complicating things."

I'm reluctant to talk about Sammy and how confused he makes me. It scares the hell out of me to think there might be feelings for me on his side.

"We need to do this now, before my ass falls any farther." Amy smacks herself on the rear. "I'm gonna have a pancake back there soon." She moans. "And I've got a tummy to tend to."

"You're not the only one." I take a furtive glance at the nearly empty boardwalk. No one is nearby. I lift up my shirt and show my waistband. "I think it would make more sense to pledge to get rid of the ol' muffin-top. I'm working on exercising more."

"We can do both. Get fit and get a fella."

My intestines lurch sideways. "I'll think about it."

"Good. That's not a no. Jerome's history, hon. Get on with your life." Amy rubs her hands together. "If we're comparing waists, I think mine's far worse than yours." She lifts her top and pulls at the flesh. "I can shove my skin down and move it around. I hate this stuff." She smooths her shirt. "We need a name... What about Desperate Grandmas?"

I glare at her. "We don't need a lame name. I know you're about to be a granny, but I'm not. You're the one who had twins at twenty-three."

"And you're the one who had a child so late."

"I was thirty-seven. Lots of women have a baby at that age. And neither of us is desperate."

Amy purses her lips.

"What's making you act so strangely lately?" She wrinkles her nose. "Losing Jerome rocked your world, I understand that. Then the guy next door appears and is obviously interested in you, and it kind of freaks you out, and next you adopt the fragrant Miss Phoebe." She stops and snaps her fingers. "Oooh. The guy next door. That's why you're thinking of sex again, isn't it? And why you don't want to join in and get lucky with any old fella."

"Thank you very much, Dr. Phil." I flip her the bird. "I didn't lose Jerome. I ditched the prick."

Amy smiles, clearly glad she's irked me. "It's starting to make sense. But you definitely need practice. Like going on job interviews. You can go on sex interviews. Then you'll be ready for the real thing with Mr. Wonderful next door."

"You're being ridiculous." I can't hold back a chuckle.

"Am I? What're you going to do to get the ball rolling after Jerome?" She rolls her eyes. "For the record, he was such a gentleman all these years, wasn't he? I hate the way he treats you. Even now he's being a royal bastard. He comes and goes as he pleases. What he did to Phoebe is unforgivable. You're lucky she was there and he didn't hit you."

Amy's comments wound. I chew at my cheek and the taste of blood fills my mouth. I need to bounce something off her. The words catch in my throat. "Do you think someone like Sammy could be interested in me?"

"Hell, yes."

"He's really young."

"Stop that. You have so much to offer. You deserve someone who treats you right. I want you to be happy. And it could be Sammy who wants that too. Besides, from what you've told me he's an old soul type, so forget the age thing."

"I've been thinking about him."

"I knew it." Amy pokes my side with her elbow. "But that doesn't mean you can't have some fun with other men while you sort out where you are with him. You could look for someone more age appropriate if you want. It might pique his interest."

"You're impossible. That wouldn't be moving ahead. It'd be taking a few steps backward. It could ruin everything, if there is anything there to ruin."

"It's worth a try, Fi. I know it's not your usual way of operating. You're a lot sweeter and more loyal than I could ever be. But, honest, why not give it a whirl?"

Amy points to the public restroom. "I need to make a pit stop."

While I wait for her to return I move to the railing and watch the ocean. The lyrics to "One Step Up" crowd out other thoughts. Jerome and I continually act out the scenario of this heartbreaking, eloquent ballad. We reconcile, take a step forward, and eventually wind up further apart than ever. I hate the lines about there being fault on both sides. Bruce admits not being the man he wanted to be, but I'm having trouble being that self-aware. What I do know is I need to find a path moving to the future or wind up being relegated to playing out the same sad story over and over. Alarm bells warn me that Amy's plan of random hooking up reeks of misdirection. I might land in a place filled with even more hurt. But the thought of venturing into a serious relationship also terrifies me. Much better to work on getting fit than deal with these matters of the heart.

Amy joins me at the railing and picks up right where she left off. "I'll search for a guy but I'm not giving up Old Reliable." She grins. "I called Terri from the bathroom. She's in."

"What? But—"

"Hah. It's game on, sister."

I cannot believe she's charged ahead and committed not only me but Terri to join her. She wags her finger at me. "And don't expect me to show up on this boardwalk on a daily basis. My knee isn't predictable. I still go to physical therapy."

"You seem to move okay at the mall."

Amy lets out a good-natured hoot. She never minds when I call her out. I lengthen my stride. "Let's up the pace a bit. I need to get aerobic activity. So do you."

Amy matches my steps. For the first time in ages, I possess a plan for the future. My commitment to my health pleases me. I try not to think about Amy's challenge, but the subject refuses to be banished.

Maybe this push from Amy to find someone is what I need to break out of the stagnation that plagues me. Can I go through with her pledge? The old Tina Turner song comes to mind. "What's love got to do with it?"

Words for Amy to live by, not me.

The sad reality of my broken relationship sinks in and overwhelms me. I hear the loud cackle rise up from the dark place. Fingers claw into my gut, twisting my intestines.

We near the Paramount Theater in Asbury, and a man draws alongside. He passes us and Amy nudges me. "Would you do him?" She nods at the guy who jogs away slowly. The fabric of his grey sweatpants stretches tight across his muscled rear.

"How on earth would I know that?"

"It's a simple question. Seems to me there are two types of men in the world. The ones you'd do and the ones you'd never do. What about him?"

"I didn't see him."

"He's turning and going to come up on us again. Take a gander and tell me what you think."

My jaw drops, and I gulp air unable to hide disdain. "Amy, cut it out."

"You're thinking about jumping feet first into the relationship pool, so how about him?"

"It's like you're trying to decide whether to buy the beige or the white sweater."

Amy sniffs. "Red or purple are more my colors. And right now gray is right up there as lovely too." She cocks her head towards me.

I turn away. Amy's banter crystalizes the fact that I still view life through a romantic lens. Sure, Jerome's a jerk, but I need to believe such a thing as an emotional connection exists and can fend off the slings and arrows of existence. It jolts me when Sammy springs into my consciousness. My head swims.

The fellow in sweatpants pulls alongside, and I take a furtive glance. Late forties, decent shape. He sports a full head of gray hair and beard stubble that matches. He shoots me a wink. I blink and study the sky. He picks up his pace and swaggers past. Beside me, Amy laughs.

"I'd do him," Amy says. "He has kind eyes. Nice butt too."

I slow to a walk. "I have to know the guy or I'll feel like crap."

Her head shakes slowly from side to side, and her grin turns impish. "That's what I was afraid of. This pledge to get lucky is never going to work unless you stop thinking. Go for it." She points at me. "You need to drink more. And you should think of sex like exercising. You hop on the treadmill, right?"

Amy's quiver of metaphors about sex never empties.

She continues, "You still haven't answered the question. Would you do him?"

I sprint forward knowing Amy can't match my pace.

She calls, "I saw him first."

"Be my guest," I shout over my shoulder.

Amy turns and lopes toward the gray-haired jogger. She looks terrific in her tight, pink jogging shorts and top. In no time she and the middle-aged man talk on the side of the boardwalk.

Amazing. No wonder she makes such a successful saleswoman.

I stop running and watch my friend work her magic. He crosses his arms. More than once he lets his gaze roam across the boardwalk to the ocean. He barely listens to Amy, but he stays put. She's in full flirt mode. I definitely possess the role of tortoise in this contest.

I laugh. The tortoise manages to beat the hare in the fable, doesn't he?

CHAPTER TWENTY-ONE

Hungry Heart

AFTER MY JOG, I TURN down the path to my porch thinking of Amy's encounter with the fellow on the boardwalk. She might not come home for some time. Sweat drips down my neck. The workout leaves me exhilarated, and I hum "Hungry Heart." Like the song says, who hasn't taken wrong turns in life and love? The Boss belts encouragement to keep on going, keep on looking for a home.

I stop humming.

Jerome perches on a rocking chair, tapping furiously on an electronic gizmo. What a gadget junkie. He once paid a mailroom clerk at his office to wait in line overnight to ensure his place to acquire an iPhone. If only he'd cared as much about his marriage as his toys.

He puts down the tablet when he sees me. The color in his cheeks signals his return to health. He's clean shaven and sporting a new shirt and pants. I recognize the scowl that spreads across his face. He's definitely better.

I move to the screen door and fumble for the handle. Jerome's foot immediately blocks my entry.

"What?" I ask.

"Is this really how you want it, Sof?"

"Want what, Jerome?"

"Us. Is this how you want us to be?"

"There hasn't been an 'us' for a long time."

He sniffs and shifts his foot away. "I'm not going to plead with you."

"I'm not expecting you to."

"I'm not well, Sof." He rubs his chest. "I realize now I neglected you. When I get better, I'll make it up to you."

"Uh huh. You look pretty good to me."

He slams his fist on the bamboo coffee table, shattering fibers and leaving a deep indentation.

His outrage, like most things he does, is calculated. In the first bloom of our marriage, his fury alarmed me. I worried his fuming might spill over into greater physical violence. But he never lost control, not until the other day with Phoebe.

"You can be a real bitch, you know?"

"So you've told me."

"Major league."

"You're better, Jerome. The salt air must have helped in your healing." His neck turns a familiar scarlet.

"How can you shut it off, Sof? After all these years."

"Don't blame me."

"You're the one who's stonewalling."

"No matter what I say or do it's going to be my fault. I can live with that." I glare at him. "What are you doing here? What are we doing? Does this look like a healthy marriage to you?"

He rubs his chest and lowers his head. "You're talking nonsense."

"Maybe you want to call Doc Phelps. He might be able to help you sort out some things."

"That charlatan? What's he done for you? Nothing good that I can see. He's the one responsible for this."

"No, he's not. I am. And so are you. What the hell is wrong with you? You kicked Phoebe. You were going to hit me."

"That dog's a menace. It deserved to be kicked."

A beige car rolls down the street slowly. I study the vehicle as it approaches.

Mandy sits behind the wheel. No wonder his prick-mobile never left the street.

"You really are an asshole, Jerome."

"Hey, she's bringing me work to do."

"And that's where you've been no doubt the last couple of days. Working. Leave, Jerome. Don't come back."

I yank open the door and let it slam behind me. In spite of all my resolve, all my rationalization about how it's over between us, my hands tremble. *Oh God.* I hate myself for my reaction, hate how much I want to scream at him and throw things. Why on earth do I need to react to something so dead and gone?

Mandy calls, "Jerry? I've been waiting. Why didn't you text me?"

"I texted you. Didn't you get it?"

I roll my eyes skyward. How many times has he told me the same thing?

I climb the stairs to my room, lie down on the bed, and examine the ceiling. I count tiles and wait for Mandy's car to drive away. Eventually both doors slam, and the sound of the engine fades in the distance.

Phoebe trots in from the bathroom with a bunch of used and half-eaten tissues and some toilet paper in her mouth. A strong aroma hangs in the air. In spite of the recent bath, she smells stinkier than ever. Phoebe drops the tissues and toilet paper beside the bed and shambles away. I scoop up the mess and toss her present in the trash.

When I stand, I see the picture of Ben on the nightstand. I stroke a fingernail over his cheek. Poor little guy. At least he's not around to see what a dumbass his dad is and what a mess we've made of our marriage. Failing at anything is hard. Failing at marriage is soul-crushing. I can hear Doc Phelps asking me, "So, are you going to do anything about it?"

A familiar scent wafts toward me. Beef jerky. I turn to the doorway.

Phoebe carries three sticks of the tangy meat treat in her mouth. Drool puddles at her feet. Jerome must still have a huge supply of them. Who knows what else he hides in his room.

"Phoebe, you have the worst taste. You're a lot like me, I guess." I rub under her chin.

Phoebe rolls her head to and fro and sprays saliva in all directions. She taunts me with her treasure.

I reach for the jerky, but Phoebe avoids my grasp. With one mighty chomp she swallows her bounty, plastic-covering and all.

"Oh no, Pheebs. We're both going to regret that."

She lumbers out of the bedroom, and I follow her downstairs. Jerome's door lies open. Phoebe wanders in and collapses on the pine floor. An empty iPad box and packaging rests on the bed. No wonder he returned. Amy and I have to remember to lock all the doors.

Phoebe pulls forward on her belly, shoving her snout beneath the pin-dotted bed skirt. Her tugging rewards her with a brand new box of beef jerky and she whines with pleasure.

"No you don't."

Phoebe tears at the carton before I can grab it. She gulps down one in its wrapper. I push her away and hold the supply out of her reach. Phoebe barks at the box.

"Too bad." I shove the beef jerky in the closet. I vow to toss it later when Phoebe's not around. A strong breeze blows through the open window, scattering several slips of paper on the white computer desk to the floor.

Terrific. More mess of Jerome's to clean up.

The first is a charge receipt from the restaurant Daniel in the city. Three letter symbols are on the back. I don't know what they stand for. The next charge slip is from a florist on Park Avenue for a delivery to Miss Mandy Malone. The third is from Tiffany's stamped "Paid in Cash." An extra charge for engraving a locket *"To Mandy, a dear heart"* leaves me reeling. The last piece of paper is an itinerary that lists two people to travel to St. Bart's for the next month. My thoughts whirl. Mandy and Jerome. On a trip. And he went to Tiffany's to purchase her a gift.

I drop the papers and stumble up the stairs with Phoebe on my heels. I turn on the shower and climb in with my clothes on. The water cascades down my back. My screams and angry shouts continue until Phoebe pokes her nose beneath the shower curtain. She tosses back her head and lets out a wail of commiseration so sincere that I laugh. I stoop and comfort her. Quiet descends.

"Thanks, Pheebs." I shut off the water and wrap myself in a towel.

"Looks like I've got quite a bit of trash collecting to do. Out with all that beef jerky and everything else of his I find."

Phoebe barks and thumps her tail. I stuff three bags with Jerome's clothes and gadgets and set them aside for donation. I remove every trace of him from the bedroom and drag Phoebe's bed into the tidy space.

CHAPTER TWENTY-TWO

You're Missing

SEVERAL DAYS AFTER PURGING JEROME'S room, I return from a run and let myself inside. My watch shows more than enough time exists to take Phoebe for a short walk before I meet up with Amy and Terri for our Heavenly Bodies shopping date.

"Let's go, girl," I call. I pick up her leash and rattle it. Usually Phoebe shambles to me at the clinking of the metal links.

I whistle and move through the downstairs rooms. Jerome hasn't returned since disappearing with Mandy. I decide that bodes well for the future. He and Mandy are probably planning their trip to St. Bart's, which irritates me, but also means no more Jerome in my home.

"Come on, Phoebe. Where the heck are you?" I kneel down and press my face beneath the living room couch. Phoebe often hides under the old blue denim roll-arm. She flattens herself, pushes hard, and squeezes below it. But she doesn't appear in her usual hideaway. I spot a pair of Jerome's Nikes and pull them out, intending to add them to the growing pile of Jerome's things on the porch. The shoes have lots of chew marks along the edges. Good for Phoebe.

I stroll to the kitchen and discover pieces of beef jerky wrappers littering the floor. Breakfast no doubt. At least Phoebe left the plastic this time. How on earth did she unearth them? I thought I'd eliminated Jerome's stash. If they weren't so bad for her I'd let her have a snack of them whenever she wanted.

A breeze flutters the curtains, and I turn to shut the window before I leave. I burned toast earlier and shoved the frame up to let out the smoke. I gasp. "Oh, no." A chair rests beneath the window, and a stack of wood leans against it making a perfect ramp.

"Oh, Phoebe, you didn't."

My heart thuds in fear. Phoebe must have climbed up the pile onto the chair and gone outside. I thrust my face through the open window and look around. Pudgy Phoebe possesses enough agility to manage the short drop to the low bench on the back porch.

Panic courses through me. What if a car hits her? What if she never comes back? My front yard is open to the street. Maybe she trotted off and is already lost in Asbury Park.

"Phoebe," I call but I don't hear the jingle of her collar. I pull my head inside and rush to the rear door. I clatter down the steps and try to figure out which way she went. One of the trash cans lies on its side. Phoebe found the box of Jerome's jerky that I tossed earlier in the day. I notice fresh holes by the fence and dash to a pile of dirt. A few sticks of beef jerky poke out the mound.

"Phoebe." My voice rings shrilly in my ears. "Come here, now!" I whistle three times. The neighborhood stays quiet.

"Don't you go missing, Phoebe," I whisper. "I couldn't bear it."

Guilt wells up. My ineptitude at taking care of things leaves me in agony. The nasty cackle rises up and fills my ears, and I shake my head to stop the sound.

"Phoebe, come back, please." My words catch on a lump in my throat.

A voice from behind startles me. "Did you lose something?" Sammy has his arms wrapped around Phoebe's middle. When she sees me she pants and lets out a lengthy whine. Her long ears perk up, and her tail thumps against Sammy's thigh. He places Phoebe on the ground, and I give her a big hug.

"She was digging in my garden."

My eyes well, and I hide them in her fur. Phoebe licks at my face and squirms away.

"I'm so relieved. She managed to escape through the kitchen window."

"She had these with her." He fishes out a pair of beef jerky sticks. "And she discovered Killer's bag of dog food on the back deck and kind of helped herself to a fair amount of it as well."

"Oh gee, she eats whatever she finds. I can replace the food so Killer doesn't starve."

"Don't worry about it."

"She scared the life out of me. I never thought she'd figure out how to climb out a window."

"It's amazing what the lure of beef jerky and kibble can accomplish." He scratches Phoebe under her chin, and she closes her eyes in appreciation. She leans against his leg. Sammy's large frame doesn't waver under the weight of the dog. Phoebe makes me stumble when she rests against me like that.

"Thanks for bringing her back."

"She can come over and visit with Killer anytime. He should be here later."

Even in the harsh brightness of the late morning sun, Sammy looks handsome. He sports a sexy growth of stubble, and his hair is slightly mussed.

He yawns. "I better go get another cup of coffee. Greta had me working on inventory late last night. My brain's fried." He starts to leave but stops and faces me again. "Before I forget. Phoebe also had these with her." He digs in his pocket and withdraws a pair of cotton underwear. They've gone through so many washes that the elastic shows through the waistband.

They possess a waist.

I own the worst collection of old underwear. And now a hot young man holds my nasty cotton briefs. Can it be any worse than this?

I wail. "Oh, no." I seize the panties from Sammy.

"I think you should come over and model them someday." He

emits a roguish laugh.

I hook my fingers in Phoebe's collar. "Let's move it. You're starting a beef jerky-less diet and I'm tossing these panties in the bin."

Sammy smiles. "Ah, going commando makes a lot of sense in this heat."

I refuse to discuss underwear with him. I tug at Phoebe with all my strength, and the dog releases a sigh and stands. She shakes her large head, spraying me with drool and snot. I use the underwear to wipe at my shorts. At least the briefs come in handy.

Sammy chuckles and hits his air guitar a few times. "Brava, Phoebe. A fine performance."

Phoebe holds her nose in the air and takes off after a scent she catches, with me trotting to keep up with her.

"You're supposed to be on my side," I say to the dog's rump. "How dare you bring my underwear over to him."

Phoebe sniffs the air again, sneezes, and shuffles to the fence.

Sammy sings loudly. I pause to listen to his horrible rendition. His happy mood comes through clearly, and I finally place the song.

"'You're Missing,'" I call, remembering the words about missing someone when the lights go out, when you fall asleep, and when you wake in the morning. And how the loss you feel when someone you love disappears makes everything empty. The chasm in my chest where Ben resides widens, and I wince.

"Very clever," I say. "I was missing her terribly." I prefer not to think about the double entendres that hang in the air. I especially try to avoid dwelling on the line that mentions my bed feeling way too roomy without someone in it.

"Thought you might enjoy it," he says.

Phoebe is snapping her jaw, and I study her. She rolls her tongue and something falls from her mouth. A yellow jacket. She scurries to the stand of clematis and chomps at the air again.

"Don't do that, Phoebe. Those are wasps. They'll sting you."

But she's not to be deterred. Two more black and yellow striped wasps zoom around her. She tosses her head back and forth, sucking them in, chewing, and spitting them out. I clutch her by the collar to stop the massacre and prevent her from being harmed.

A loud buzzing near my ear stops me cold. I swat at the fast-moving thing with my underwear. Something crawls up my thigh, and I regret donning the old baggy shorts that called to me this morning. The sting on my stomach burns red hot. I drop Phoebe's collar and my underwear and slap at my stomach. The wasp still travels around.

Sammy calls. "Sofia? What's going on?"

"Wasp," I scream.

I ball the fabric at my waistband and press hard. A satisfying crunch beneath my fingers allows me to relax. But the stinging of the bite grows.

Sammy rushes over. He hovers beside me and sweeps his hand through the air. "I don't see any others. Did it get you?"

I nod, my hand on my chest.

"Come with me."

I follow Sammy into his house, and he leads me into a neat kitchen. The welcoming space strikes me as familiar even though I've never been here before. A vase on the counter holds an array of blossoms, and I draw in the calming scent of lavender.

Sammy searches in a cabinet, running his hand along a spice rack. "Come on, come on. Where did Greta put the meat tenderizer?"

"The what?"

"Ahh...got it." He charges to the shiny, stainless steel sink and opens the jar. He shakes some of the powder into a shallow bowl, adding water. An inferno rages on my stomach.

After mixing with his finger, he hands me the paste of water and meat tenderizer. "Put this on the bite. It'll digest the protein in the venom."

"It already stings a lot. Will this goo hurt?"

"Not at all. A doctor gave me this home remedy."

I push down the waistband of my shorts and suck in my tummy—which I wish was a lot less squishy and visible.

Sammy leans over. "That's a nasty bite."

I can't manage holding my waistband down and spreading the

concoction. "I don't have enough hands."

Sammy smiles and dips a finger in the mixture. He presses it gently over the swollen area, and in spite of the blazing wasp sting my nipples grow hard. I concentrate on the clutter-free kitchen to distract myself.

"It has to go on thick. I'll put some on you now, and you can take the rest home. You'll be amazed."

I already was and not only by the soothing paste. Sammy taking care of me makes him more desirable than ever. I can't believe I've advanced to this level of longing. Desiring him, however, is a far cry from trusting him or opening up to him. No way. I'd done that with Jerome and look where it got me.

Sammy steps back and admires his work. "Looks good. The swelling is receding already."

I hike up my shorts to cover the bite and take the dish from him.

"Thank you. That really helped. I'm going to have to buy some."

He sends me his crooked grin, and I send one back.

"I better see what Phoebe is up to. She's bound to get stung if she keeps chasing those yellow jacks."

Sammy points at his back screen door. "She's right here. Waiting for you."

Phoebe and I walk across the yard, and Sammy calls, "You'll be fine in half an hour."

"Thanks, again," I say.

"I think you forgot something," Sammy says, pointing.

He laughs loudly as I bend down and retrieve my underwear from the lawn. He retreats out of my line of vision.

Phoebe lumbers into the house and runs with urgency to the living room with me dashing after her.

"No, no. No more beef jerky if it's still hidden there. I'm onto your game, girl."

She reaches the denim couch and regards me with her doleful gaze. She squats and urinates on the pair Jerome's Nikes I'd meant to add to the donation pile.

"Is that what you're up to? Nice pee-mail, Pheebs."

I swear her jowls curl into a smile.

CHAPTER TWENTY-THREE

Lift Me Up

THANKS TO PHOEBE, I ARRIVE late for the Heavenly Bodies shopping spree. I spot Amy standing next to the front window display making selections from a rack of lingerie. She looks like one of the female mannequins, perfectly coifed, made-up, and neatly pressed. How she manages to put herself together so well on a consistent basis remains a mystery.

I join her, and we hug hello. Her familiar grassy scent reminds me that though I traded my baggy shorts for my newest sweatpants, I'm still wearing my morning run T-shirt and I haven't showered. I hope the post-jogging Eau de Sofia isn't too strong. I quickly back away and press my arms to my sides to hide the armpit marks I know grow second by second.

Amy grins broadly at me. The warmth of her smile is nothing compared to the blasting furnace of my back. My anxious sweat results from my misgivings about this lingerie date. Yes, I need to update my underwear wardrobe. Phoebe and the white panty caper certainly proved the inadequacy of my undergarments. However, trying on bras with Amy and Terri amounts to madness. This excursion trumps trying on bathing suits in the middle of February at the height of my vampire-like paleness. I clench my jaw. Better the lingerie devil you know than the one you don't. Besides, I'd promised Terri to visit so here I am.

From behind me Terri's voice rings out a cheery, "You made it. I can't wait to show you what's new."

"My lingerie is like my life—I don't know what to do about either of them."

Terri laces her arm through mine. "You've come to the right place to fix at least one of those problems." She sends me a sideways glance. "Any word from your ex?"

"I have no idea where he is. I can honestly say I don't care what he's up to."

"That sounds promising, hon."

I pick up a lacy bra. "So delicate. And so impractical for anyone built like me."

Terri says, "Don't say silly stuff like that."

I glance down at my full bust. The title of the tune "Lift Me Up" comes to mind, and I laugh. The song's pleading prayer about stripped bare love having the power to lift you up, has nothing to do with lingerie, but that title rings oh, so true. I need a lift for sure.

Amy and I follow Terri to the rear of the store, and I mutter, "Great." The lingerie designed for us must be so ugly Terri hides the items in the back where no one sees them. Terri immediately shoots a huge hole in that theory. She stops and points at an artful arrangement of wispy wearables on a large table.

"There are lots of options throughout the store for you. This is a new shipment that's going to be in the window next week. It's guaranteed to provide full-figured support under a sweater. It's our 'Twice Blessed' line."

"Oh Mama, now you're talkin'," Amy says.

I smooth my T-shirt. "I'll buy three if they work. Especially if they don't look like my grandma's bras. I still have nightmares about the times I helped my Nana into a long-line number. That thing had more hooks than my grandfather's fishing tackle box."

"I think you'll be pleasantly surprised," Terri says. "No long-line bras for you."

My reflection takes me back to Nana's bedroom. Nana's flesh

squashed out of the edges of the cups; the white pasty blobs terrifying me. Buttoning up her back was bad, but unhooking the thing at day's end was worse. On those help-Nana occasions I kept my eyes on the hooks or on the rose-patterned rug of the bedroom lest I came face to face with Nana's long, wrinkled breasts. I encountered the banana-shaped boobs once in a mirror hanging on the bedroom wall, and I still want to scrub my eyeballs.

We enter the fitting room area, and Terri digs into a cardboard box. "I have lots of goodies in here for you."

Amy grabs a neon pink bra and matching panty and slips inside a fitting room. She calls to us, "I can't stay long. I have a conference call from a client I have to take. I'm trying to land a big one."

"Need me?"

"Not yet, but I will. He's submitting a proposal and then you'll have to do some plans. And we should visit Terri's real estate office soon too."

"Yes," Terri calls. "I can't wait to discuss what you've come up with."

"I've already sketched out some more ideas." It's good to be working again.

Terri hands over a thin nylon piece of fabric and tosses one over the top of Amy's fitting room. "We have our own special throwaway liner so you can try everything on without your own panties."

Amy snorts. "Peds for your privates. Brilliant."

I toy with making a selection and avoid the fitting room. None of the lingerie appears sturdy enough. The thin straps and airy, light cups make me uncomfortable. A vision of my breasts as they sag and bounce flashes before me. Not a sight I want to see. Not Nana's elliptical white eggplants, but certainly not perky.

Terri coughs. "Now what's wrong?"

I dangle a lace thong in front of her. "I need fabric, big fabric to cover my rear. These thongs are horrid."

Terri places her hands on her hips. "You'd get used to it if you wore one. Guaranteed to have no panty line."

"I don't want to get used to a string up my butt. Not at this age.

Not at any age."

Terri rummages in the box. "Have it your way." She pulls out a pair of gossamer bikini panties without one smidge of white cotton. "How's this instead of a thong? It's a no panty line model too."

"Much better. And where's the bra that's going to do wonders for me under a sweater?"

Terri chuckles and pushes me to the dressing room. She hands me a blue and white silk bra, skimpy material which appears to have little support.

"This is for a twelve year old. I should know better than to believe you."

"Be quiet and try it on. I'm going to bring you a couple of the new 'Booby-traps' line too." The door shuts, and Terri's black-and-white, checked heels click away. I wonder where she discovers such interesting footwear.

I slip off my clothes and underwear and hear Amy laughing in the room next door.

"I'm glad you're amused, Amy."

"I haven't had so much fun in ages. This stuff is almost as good as my vibrator."

I avoid facing the mirror till the last possible moment. Preparing for the worst, I clench my fists and take in my reflection. I shift slightly and look at my rear, surprised at the view. How on earth does fabric make my butt so taut? I practically have those "buns of steel" the infomercials tout, instead of what I call my "buns of steel wool." Maybe the jogging is helping. I note with surprise that the wasp sting is practically gone thanks to Sammy's magic potion.

Sammy.

My insides do a flip flop.

"Would both of you come out here?" Terri calls. "You have to be dressed by now. I want to see you. Not that I don't trust your judgment." She pauses. "You're right. I don't trust your judgment. Now come on out and let's see."

I open the door to the fitting room. The blue and white bra and panty transform me, but I need to muster the courage to wear them in front of Terri. The sheer fabric of the bra exposes my nipples and the coolness of the store's air-conditioning takes immediate effect.

I step out of the dressing room and encounter not only Terri but a young man I judge to be in his late twenties sitting on one of the fabric seats in the main section of the dressing room.

"Oh." I cover my breasts with my arms and back up. Behind me the fitting room door clicks closed. My hand grips the knob and finds it locked.

Amy emerges from her dressing room and tugs at her thong. "This thing doesn't feel right." She lifts her head and takes in the young man. "Um…" Covering herself or retreating never comes to her mind.

"Relax," Terri says. "This is David."

The young fellow sports a slight smile. His tight, black T-shirt sets off his broad build. He wears dark-washed jeans, and his legs stretch out in front of him on the puffy, fabric seat. David's light brown eyes move from me to Amy and back to me. He nods and scans me up and down. I press my hands to my crotch and switch them to my breasts. My nipples stand at attention, this time not from the air conditioning.

"David's the stock clerk. He's training as a buyer. We've been letting him help with making selections for the store. That outfit you're wearing, Sofia, is one he picked out, right, D?"

"It's even better on than I imagined." He stuffs his hands into his jeans pockets and leans back against the mirror. He appears terribly comfortable as he sits and watches.

I attempt to sound composed. "Would you mind unlocking the fitting room?"

Terri stands and removes the key from the top drawer of the dresser, but she doesn't move to open the door. "That one's a keeper. Right, David?"

"Definitely. It goes great with your skin." His eyes remain riveted on my upper torso.

Amy coughs.

Terri turns to her. "The set is darling on you, hon."

"I second that." David beams at Amy.

Terri hands me another bra and panty. "Try these too. They're David's favorites." I press them to my breasts.

Terri unlocks the door to the fitting room. "I'll be back to check on you. There's a regular customer outside I can't ignore."

I know I'm not imagining it. David's eyes stay trained on me. No shocker given my state of undress. What takes me aback is my reaction to his attention. I arch my back and stand tall. I move slowly into the fitting room. Once inside, I lean against the mirror and take three deep mouthfuls of air. David possesses the most arresting eyes. My nipples remain erect. And my figure...well, the spandex definitely helps.

I don the next set of lingerie, and this time I immediately study myself in the mirror. I hear Amy shout, "Gotta go outside where there's better cell reception." The fitting room goes quiet.

Is David still out there? I listen hard. Nothing. I crack open the door.

Gone. I hear Terri talking, and her footsteps approaching rapidly. She calls to her customer, "I'll be back to help you in a minute with the right size."

The woman answers, "I'll come by tomorrow. Hold it till then."

I open the door to the dressing room and ask, "Did we scare David away?"

Terri says, "Highly unlikely. He's a doll, isn't he? Let's take your selections to the cash register. I love the way you looked in that blue duo. This set is good too."

"Honestly, Terri. Having a guy sitting out here almost gave me a heart attack. Are you out of your mind?" Terri might have a bit more of the wild woman in her than I thought.

She grins. "It's good to shake things up a little. You seemed to recover fine." She checks the clock on the wall. "I'll be at the register if you need me."

I return to the fitting room and slip on my clothes. My old bra and underwear look more pathetic than ever. I think they used to be beige. I take out my reading glasses and examine the tags on the new underthings. The price of the lingerie makes me reel. I drop the items on the fitting room rack, unable to justify the purchase, not with all the uncertainty about the future and with the bills that mount each minute. I need to conserve my funds.

At the register Terri considers my empty hands quizzically.

"I'm going to think about those sets," I say.

Terri opens her mouth to speak, and then closes it. She rings up the pile on the counter that comprises Amy's purchases and she taps her watch. "Perfect timing."

"For what?"

"We're not done. I'll meet you at the shop next door. I think Amy's already there. I'm off to ask David to close."

CHAPTER TWENTY-FOUR

Restless Nights

I SAUNTER NEXT DOOR AND PUSH open the door to the Whole Earth Shoppe. Instead of lulling me into an amiable shopping stupor, the Peruvian flute music playing over the loudspeaker unleashes a major fit of irritability. The monochromatic earth tones of the store add to my crankiness. While I wait for Amy and Terri to arrive, I study the shelves of creams and lotions. They all promise the same thing: rejuvenation and tight, wrinkle-free skin at exorbitant prices.

After fifteen minutes a breathless Amy arrives, followed a few seconds later by Terri. A handful of customers, from the young to the elderly, dot the aisles.

Terri says, "Ladies, our mission here is to shop for the fountain of youth."

I shake my head. "Hey, Ponce de Leon, didn't anyone ever tell you it doesn't exist?"

Terri hands me a brown, woven fiber basket. "I'm going to give you all the things I've found that have helped me. And I want you to do the same. Consider it to be an updated cookie swap."

"I'm done already. I still own a five-year-old bottle of multivitamins I forget to take in the morning and a blusher from twenty-odd years ago." My eyes glaze over whenever I pass a shop with signs that scream: health, beauty, and well-being are only a bottle away.

"I'm done too," Amy says. "I don't use many healthy products like these."

Undeterred, Terri says, "I'll take the lead and share." She places a bottle of Glucosamine in Amy's tan, wicker basket. "Great for your knees and joints."

"I read about that. My knees might like it." Amy arranges the bottle in the basket. "A pill is a lot nicer than jogging." She sniffs. "Too much wear and tear on the joints. I think joints are like tires. The treads wear out."

"My joints are fine." I move past the supplements section. The music plays softly here. That plus the fact that my friends are with me makes my grouchiness dissipate.

"Lucky you, you've got Michelins," Amy says.

"And a spare one around my waist."

I'm pleased when Amy and Terri laugh.

Terri meanders down the aisle. She selects bottles and tosses them into our baskets. "Fish oil capsules that don't smell for your cholesterol, vitamins to revive you, and, here you go, liquid flax seed. This is the best stuff there is for your skin, hair, nails, and connective tissue."

"You can't be serious." I examine each bottle, and when Terri faces away, I replace it on the shelves.

"We need all the help we can get. These products work. Here's a great face cream too."

I stop and read the label. "The moisturizer's a keeper. They discontinued mine."

"That's so annoying," Amy says.

"They stop making most products I get used to. Shampoo, conditioner, lipsticks. Even my favorite ravioli isn't around any longer."

"You have a favorite ravioli?" Amy asks.

I ignore her. "It's really irritating when you have to try out three or four new products. They usually cost more than the old ones. So I wind up not buying anything."

Terri delivers a sideways glance. "It's not that bad to have to investigate new ways and change. We all get stuck in ruts from old habits."

"What's so bad about ruts?" I ask. "They worked for the Roman chariots for years."

"Last I looked, Fi, we weren't living in Rome and you're no Roman." Amy holds up a bottle labeled "Get Hot Again." She clutches my arm. Her bottom lip trembles, and her eyes well unexpectedly. "Why do they make things like this? Just to fleece you of your money? It's so depressing."

"What's going on, Amy?" I ask.

"I'm never having good sex again. I know it." She rubs her cheek and stares at the floor.

"What are you talking about? You're the one pushing us to get lucky with random strangers."

"I'm going to shrivel up and be all alone. I don't want to be alone."

"Don't be silly, sweetie." Terri strokes her hand.

I wonder what led to this sudden spell of angst. A few minutes ago Amy was preening in the try-on room, now tears streak her makeup.

Terri's blue eyes flash. "There are plenty of men out there. A burger at Applebee's can be as satisfying as a steak at the Four Seasons. You won't go hungry unless you want to."

Amy sniffles. "I'm feeling like a package of outdated Costco beef."

We move to a quiet unoccupied corner and stand beneath a large sepia-toned picture of the earth. I say, "Did you take some of Terri's pills already? Maybe you're having side effects from something."

Amy waves me off. Shame crosses her face. "Sorry. That was a little panic attack. I'm okay, now. Really."

I hesitate. Amy's anguish is obvious, but once she declares a subject off limits, it's usually closed.

"You sure?"

Amy nods emphatically.

"I'm wondering if any of this stuff can help iron out my thighs and butt." I point to my chest. "Or get rid of this crepe papery substance on my boobs? Thank heavens for the low lighting in the dressing room."

Terri says, "Unfortunately we need to lift and separate even more now. You'll have to adjust the girls so they're not so crowded. And lighting definitely helps."

"What happened with Mr. Sweatpants? You never mentioned him after that day." Maybe he's the cause for her meltdown.

"We talked for a long time on the boardwalk."

Terri smiles. "Ooooh. Romance on the boardwalk."

"Talking is good. That sounds promising. It might not hurt if you took it a little slow this time," I say.

Amy squares her shoulders. "Easy for you to say. You have the next door neighbor waiting in the wings."

Terri raises her palms to the air. "What Sofia says makes a lot of sense. There might be less pain if you waited."

Amy hoots. "No pain, no gain."

I wring my hands. I might as well bang my head against the wall. Amy's seduction of men amounts to a painful addiction. The hurt stops when she ceases the activity, but she returns to the behavior time after time, unable to avoid new connections that leave her wounded. She refuses to accept the fact that a surprisingly soft center lurks beneath that hard shell.

But Amy's right about one thing. My pontificating about going slow rings untrue. I barely know Sammy yet harbor the worst schoolgirl crush on him. I'm still married. He's young and handsome. Such a pathetic pipedream. I reassure myself that unlike Amy I intend to keep things at the pipedream stage.

Terri says, "Well, it's good to know you're alive. Unfortunately, at this age lots of people assume we're dead down there. They haven't a clue. I'm jealous of both of you."

I say, "I miss cuddling and the closeness of being next to a warm body."

Amy groans. "I've never been to Planet Sofia." She faces Terri. "Sofia and I don't agree on the care and feeding of relationships."

I chew my cheek. "It's true."

Amy chuckles. "She couldn't sleep when Jerome went away on business trips. She'd call me to chat in the middle of the night."

I leave unmentioned the fact that when Jerome returned, I curled up next to him and fell into a deep slumber immediately. He joked with me about it. He boasted he was proud of his ability to put a woman to sleep.

I turn to Amy. "You and Harry got along for a long time, didn't you?"

Amy snorts at the mention of her third husband. "Harry? He was a total control freak. I don't know how I stayed with him for ten years. Actually, I do. It was the pot. His constant smoking was the mortar in the relationship."

"How many times have you been married?" Terri asks.

"Only three."

"Her first was after high school and lasted barely a year."

Amy says, "I met my second ex during college and that marriage was over before graduation."

I remember Amy telling me she was cramped, controlled, and smothered in the relationship. "After that Amy entered her serial monogamy phase."

"Then I met Harry and when we were high one night, he proposed. We married, I quit getting high, and had my twins. After I gave birth things went south fast. And when Harry quit smoking pot, we divorced."

I say, "I liked the companionship of a marriage. We used to do lots of things together in the beginning."

Amy snorts. "People have separate bedrooms, even separate wings now, and separate houses. I really do need to be on my own in my own space with my appliances."

I wrinkle my nose. "You can't hug a vibrator. I never wanted to be with anyone but Jerome. God, knowing what I know now I really needed a reality check."

"Sometimes it's easier not to face reality," Terri says. "I do like that separate houses solution. Great for business."

"I used to be so glad when Jerome came back." I remember the way he smelled of salt and earth when he leaned down to kiss me.

Amy says, "That's so Sofia. Beyond help."

"Hey, I've come to terms with all those years of denial now.

And I'm fighting my way forward as best I can."

Terri sighs. "Back in the dark ages before I met my Wally I used to believe in that type of relationship. Wally and I were more like brother and sister. I suppose I settled but we did care for one another." She takes my hand and shoots me a rueful grin. "Hon, you definitely hit the love lottery early and big. That's a problem since you'll be searching for the Holy Grail now." She points a finger. "The other problem is your wardrobe. What the heck color are those sweatpants? Fuchsia?"

I look down at my cotton sweats and top. The outfit definitely embodies a fine example of low-self-esteem wear. Pressing on my T-shirt doesn't help flatten out the wrinkles. I pull at a stray thread on the hem and use my teeth to saw it off, leaving an orange smudge on the front. At least I remembered to refresh my lipstick.

"I'm such a mess. Jerome's out of my life—but he's still in it. My heart isn't in my chest any more. It's in the pit of my stomach and it's rolling around in there."

Terri pats me on the back. "You're not married-married anymore. You're separated. It makes a difference. In a couple of months things will resolve and fall into place. You'll feel a lot better."

Terri's cell phone rings, and she extracts it from her bag. She shouts into her phone, "Birkin, don't use the Dustbuster on your sister." She covers the mouthpiece with her hand. "The babysitter's having trouble controlling the grandkids." She walks to the opposite side of the room, shouting and gesturing madly with her free hand. Two shoppers quickly move away.

I say to Amy, "Will you walk with me again tomorrow?"

"I have to work."

"Walking's good for your bones."

"Gee, wasn't it you who said you're not fond of things that are good for you?"

"How's eight o'clock sound? We can work after that."

Terri shouts from across the room, "No sweating. I'll walk and I'll talk but don't expect more."

After her call, Terri rejoins us at the natural remedies aisle. She grins and throws a box of ginger tea and another of Cran-aid tea into our baskets. "I'm a great believer in healing teas. There's nothing like them. Ginger for your tummy. And cranberry is great if you have any urinary issues."

I study the boxes. "What's wrong with my store brand tea?"

Amy wags a finger. "Nothing's wrong with it. These are improvements."

"If I spend all this time improving myself I won't have any time left to do anything else."

Amy says with uncharacteristic concern, "What about not being able to sleep at night? I'm finding it more and more difficult."

I ask, "Ambien? Unisom? Benadryl?"

Terri shakes her head. "No, no, no. The next shop is for getting a good rest."

I groan. "I can't make it through another store. I've reached my shopping limit. It's not at the mall, is it?"

From the checkout counter, the cashier chuckles. She chimes in, "Next door is The Book Nook."

Terri says, "There's nothing like a good book to get you through those long nights. Why the heck do you think women are the major buyers of books? They're the ones awake all night long."

"I'm always up for a hot romance," Amy says, "but I prefer them on my phone."

I say, "You don't listen to those when you're driving, do you?"

Amy shoots me a sheepish grin.

I count the things in my basket. Six items. A book won't break the bank. "A funny book. That's what these times call for." I pause. "So after all these years are we saying the answer to the age old question 'What do women want?' is nothing more than a good book?"

"Heavens, no. We need more than a good read," Terri says and grins. "I want a pair of shoes that are gorgeous but comfortable."

I join in the game. "A man who'll give me a foot massage would be heavenly."

Amy links her arms through ours. "A vibrator that can be used for more than fifteen minutes without the battery dying." That makes me groan.

She holds up her hand. "Seriously. True friends I can count on and who appreciate me."

I marvel at the blanket of amiability the three of us share. Our deep connection leaves me smiling the entire time the clerk rings up our purchases.

When I pull my wallet from my purse, Terri puts her hand out. "This is on me. And this is yours too." She opens her shopping tote and withdraws a small Heavenly Bodies bag. "It's the first set you tried on." Her eyes sparkle with a glacier-like luminescence.

"You didn't." I'm aware of a blush creeping across my cheeks. Gratitude fills me, not for the gift but for my caring and generous friends. Knowing I can count on them not to flake on me is priceless.

After we make selections in the bookstore we hug one another goodbye. My good mood stays with me on the drive home.

The front door creaks open, and my footsteps echo down the hallway. Other than the occasional whine from a napping Phoebe, the house sounds empty.

I push open Jerome's bedroom door, admiring the unoccupied space. The bed is unmade and rumpled, its covers in a pile courtesy of Phoebe's residency in the room.

I throw my keys and packages on the kitchen table and turn on the old radio on the counter, in need of the company of a human voice. Without thinking, my hand turns the knob to Jerome's favorite station, all-news radio. With a start I shut it off.

I bounce up the stairs and locate an iron and board in the closet. After taking off my clothes and throwing them in the laundry basket, I rummage through my closet. A pair of rumpled tan pants and a white eyelet blouse look promising. While the iron heats, I study myself in the full-length mirror. Not too bad. The reflection echoes the one in the lingerie store. I still possess female curves. More than I want with that damn muffin-top, which, though smaller, is still there. But the exercise is working and I'm managing to whip myself into reasonable shape.

The sound of off-key singing draws me to the window. I close my eyes and listen to Sammy, letting myself follow the yearning of his voice. His awkward warbling of "Restless Nights" takes me back to my own hopeful, youthful love. Flashes of Jerome and me on the beach, hand in hand. Glimpses of us with Ben, laughing and snuggling in our bed. The contrast of our fulsome then and my barren now, along with Bruce's lament of loneliness, leaves me aching for more than my faded memories.

Sammy sings loudly, and I listen hard to his phrasing and his tone to distract myself from my sadness. The man truly possesses a horrible voice. In spite of his off notes and the darkness of the lyrics, heat grows and my knees go weak.

I look at the ceiling of the master bedroom. A crack spreads slowly across the faded white paint. I cross the room and pick up the iron. My arm presses down hard on the pants, and I smile, wishing I could iron away my troubles with the same ease as flattening my slacks. Steam hisses, warmth spreads through my center, and fades.

My cell rings, and I push the talk button.

The voice at the other end of the line rings out crisp and direct.

"Sof, I want a divorce."

CHAPTER TWENTY-FIVE

Life Itself

THE NIGHT GATHERS AROUND ME when I step out into the backyard. Jerome's words repeat in my brain. I hug myself trying to keep my panic from growing.

Yes, I want a divorce. I pushed for one. Dissolving our marriage makes sense, but, in spite of my rational side understanding divorce is the right thing to do, Jerome's agreement to split fills me with apprehension and dread. I'm teetering on the edge of an abyss so dark that I fear I may never find light again if I allow myself to fall.

I scan my playlist to escape the rising laughter in my brain and to keep the gloom at bay. The title "Life Itself" makes me wince. Jerome had been my all, my life itself. Even now, with us so far apart he possesses the power to create a well of emotions. He's gone but he's ever present, a palpable entity, like the dark swirling about me. He's holding me together and pulling me apart at the same time.

Escaping Jerome's influence means entering new territory. The recent days of fighting and anger mired me in a familiar wasteland, and I'm having trouble committing to choosing a fresh path. With a jolt, I remember that he controls almost all of our assets, a large kink in any escape plan. My willing complicity in allowing him to handle all our financial matters makes me queasy.

I find the paper with the details of a lawyer Terri recommended and dial, leaving my name and number with the night service. It's way past time for sitting down and figuring out how to extract myself from our marriage.

A coil of loneliness tightens into an uncomfortable vise. A night swim might be the perfect way to stop my uncontrollable thoughts and feelings. I dash upstairs past a down-for-the count Phoebe and, once dressed in my bathing suit, shorts, and a T-shirt, I throw a towel around my neck and head to the water.

My easy jog to the beachfront without once gasping for air should be cause for celebration but is undermined by the assault of Jerome's words after his decree of wanting a divorce. He detailed a schedule of what to expect, and I tried to pay attention but failed to hear most of what he pronounced. Ideas whirled wildly, and my emotions roller-coastered from relief to fear.

I resort to Doc Phelps' breathing lesson. In my nose and out my mouth, keeping my attention on counting the breaths until my pulse slows. A few seconds later, I mount the steps to the boardwalk as the partially shrouded moon begins a ghostly rise over the ocean. The clouds part, revealing a highway of light across the water. The silvery path beckons, and for an instant my spirit soars at the incredible sight.

I climb down to the sand and jog, increasing my speed gradually until my legs move at a fast clip. My bare feet pound into the shifting sand, and the rhythm of the running blots out my mental processes. Nothing exists but me, the beach, the moon, and the ocean. I inhale deeply and enjoy the effortlessness of maintaining the speed. Things fall into place. A future lies within reach.

Up ahead, a man ambles along the shoreline. As I draw near, I recognize him. Walt Cornell. He moves a large metal detector back and forth over the surface of the sand. His face shows intense concentration at the task.

"Gorgeous night, Walt. Enjoy the hunting," I call as I pass. He fails to look up, and I assume he never hears me.

Eventually I stop running. Sweat trickles down the front of my shirt pooling between my breasts. I lean over and pull air into my lungs, forcing the breaths in my nose and out my mouth until my panting and puffing disappear.

Once I feel normal again, I strip off my T-shirt and shorts and head into the highway of light, giddy with hope. The water laps at my ankles with a balminess that I don't remember the Atlantic ever having. I dive in and swim hard past the crashing waves to the calm beyond the breakers. Lying on my back and floating allows me to regroup after the exertion. The waves crash on the shore. Other than Walt and his metal detector sweeping rhythmically along the beach, the landscape is deserted.

Music catches my ear. I listen, wondering where it comes from. The sound fades in and out when the breeze shifts. I struggle to place the song, raising my head in the air and turning it left and right, paddling to stay afloat and concentrating until the title of the song bursts into my mind.

"Darkness on the Edge of Town," I call out.

The snippets come from the direction of Asbury Park. A cover band at the Stone Pony, no doubt. I swim towards the sound, and it grows louder, buoying me up and luring me forward. Springsteen's wailing about carrying secrets through life tunnels into my soul, reminding me of how I walk around holding what happened to Ben inside. He's my secret, and no one's the wiser, but my anguish leaves me raw. Though my injury's not obvious in a physical sense, inside I harbor a deep and damaging wound. I don't want the agony I endure to be apparent. All I long for is the ability to take a breath without suffering, the power to stuff the ache into a corner and have it stay there without popping up unexpectedly and sending me spiraling off into sadness. I cling to the lyrics with their rejection of despair, hoping to attain solace in surviving.

The water grows cold beneath my legs, interrupting my reverie. I know the shift in temperature means a strong current runs below the surface, and I kick hard to return to more temperate waters. The breeze picks up suddenly and turns chilly. Whitecaps appear.

The quick change in weather alarms me. I swim towards shore, but in spite of my strong strokes, the tide drags me sideways. The current sweeps me in the opposite direction of the way I want to go, carrying me away from the beach. I scan the shoreline. A barely visible Walt still searches along the sand.

No matter how hard I swim, the ocean continues to pull me to the north until I believe I must be well into Ocean Grove waters. The sea roils and churns. A wave rolls forwards, and I duck beneath it. When I rise for air, a second wave hits me and spins me beneath the surface. I come up sputtering and spit out salty water. The shoreline's further away, and my pulse races.

I watch for another wave, chilled and tired. When I kick my feet the icy water caresses my legs and sends me back to the time I fell through the ice of the Great South Bay. I was little more than a toddler, left to the care of my older cousin, who instead of watching me as tasked while my parents prepared dinner, was off building a snow cave on the beach. My pink snowsuit filled with water. I clung to the ice while the cold numbed my legs. I hung suspended in the water and watched the ice hole close around me.

My uncle appeared on the shoreline, sent to call us home for dinner. He crawled to me on his stomach and extended his parka as a lifeline. He hauled me out of the water and threw me over his shoulder. As he carried me to shore, white spidery lines spread across the ice beneath us.

Bad things happen in the cold and in winter. The winter claimed Ben. My body feels as icy as his did that winter morning. I kick my legs in desperate fear. Numbness spreads up my calves, and freezing fingers grab at my thighs.

The moon disappears behind the clouds, and darkness envelops me. A thick fog rolls in rapidly. I no longer know which way to swim.

"Help. Which way is the shore?" I call out, spinning around in the water. Within a few seconds nothing remains visible other than the deep, spectral fog. My mouth turns to sandpaper, and I struggle to control my fear.

The wind shifts, and the music comes to me again. Springsteen's voice plaintively wails and fades. I twist my neck until I hear singing again, and I swim with all my might in the direction of the snippets of song, battling through water that pulls me one way and tugs me back. My arms ache and my legs threaten to give out, but I don't dare stop, petrified the tide will take me out even further.

The wind changes direction again, and the notes grow stronger. I concentrate on the melody that drifts over the waves. Finally the title comes to me. "Countin' on a Miracle." In spite of my predicament, I laugh, and seawater slaps into my mouth causing me to cough and gasp for air. Tightness spreads across my chest. I ignore the pressure that mounts and threatens to cascade into overwhelming agony.

Not now. I need to press forward. This isn't the time to collapse or to rest.

Voices in my head clamor for attention. One rises up over the others.

"Swim with the riptide to escape it."

My grandfather made me repeat that rule every time we visited the beach.

Another small but strong voice demands my attention.

"Swim the length of the pool. You can do it, Mom."

The memories give me strength. I tread water and fill my lungs over and over. Warmth spreads over my legs. The fog still gathers in a thick shroud and prevents me from seeing the shoreline. Without warning, the tide releases me.

An adrenaline rush sends my heartrate soaring, and I swim with more energy, towards the music. It must be the right way.

The singing grows louder. I time my strokes to the beat and lash the water until my lungs threaten to burst. I stop and tread water. The tension in my chest increases, and I fear something might snap. The sound of music ceases.

I spin, trying to find the noise again. How far out am I? Doubt grows about the location of the shoreline. Did I head the wrong way? The fog's so thick I can't see my hand in front of my face.

My arms turn to lead, and I struggle to raise them out of the water. One more stroke, I tell myself. One more. I lay back for a short rest staring up at the unseen sky.

The music starts up again, and I crawl toward the notes,

sometimes dog paddling, sometimes floating on my back. Finally the surge of the ocean pulls me along. I let the churning sea take me, and hold my breath when a wave crashes over my head.

My feet touch bottom, and I tremble with joy. I wade to the shore and collapse on the sand gasping for air. My heart pounds wildly.

Springsteen sings from a much closer spot now. "We Take Care of Our Own" he croons. The driving, catchy chorus clearly preaches hope and redemption today making my eyes well. The fog lifts slightly, and I make out the Convention Hall, nearer now, but still a distance away. I climb to my feet and stumble towards the sound.

A crowd cheers, and my pulse slows. The tightness in my chest recedes.

A towel wraps around my shoulders.

Walt Cornell rubs my back. "Are you all right? I lost track of you. Damn fog got so thick. Thank goodness it lifted. I was about to go and call for help." He holds my shorts and T-shirt.

I hug the towel tightly. "It was kind of rough out there. Too close for comfort."

He shakes his head. "It's not smart to go swimming alone at night. There aren't any life guards. The currents are bad and the weather can change rapidly at this time of year." He examines me closely. "Do you want to rest for a little while?"

"I'm okay now." To change the subject I ask, "Who's playing the music? Any idea?"

"Sounds great, doesn't it? That's coming from the Stone Pony. In Asbury."

"I kept swimming towards it, hoping it wouldn't fade. That's what kept me going." I pause. "Boy, it's loud and so is the cheering."

Walt nods. "When Bruce shows up the place goes wild."

"Bruce? We're hearing Springsteen playing at the Stone Pony?"

"There's a show on the summer stage tonight and he came in." He snaps his fingers. "Out of the blue. One of the kids told me."

"It's not a cover band?"

"Nope. The real deal."

"If I wasn't so cold and wet I'd go over there."

"Aw, to tell the truth, getting nearer isn't much different from hearing him from here."

He's exaggerating for my benefit. I listen, and each note floats to me. I say an inner thank you to Bruce for being there again when I most need him.

Walt cocks an ear towards the music. "I was in the crowd when he first played with The Big Man. Back in 1971. What a sax player he was."

"You mean when he met Clarence Clemons?"

Walt nods. "At The Student Prince, a little ways from here, not at the Stone Pony. There was a terrible storm that night and it rolled through with incredible force. Bruce was onstage and the doors got blown off their hinges. A shadowy giant of a man stood in the doorway. That was Clarence." Walt shakes his head. "It's an old story. But it's true. I miss The Big Man and that epic sax of his." He peers at the ocean. "That's the first time I met Ellie. Bruce and Clarence clicked that evening. So did Ellie and me. What a perfect night."

He tramps through the sand and I follow. "I don't mean to bore you with old war tales. Glory Days and all that."

"I liked hearing your story. I saw Bruce play with Clarence a few times."

"So you understand the loss everyone felt when he passed away. And when 'Phantom' Danny Federici died of cancer." His voice catches. " Danny's accordion and his keyboard were pure energy." He studies me. "You sure you're okay?"

"I'm good. It was a little hairy out there but I'm fine now."

We stay close to the shoreline. I turn to him and ask, "How's Ellie?"

"She and I still hit the Wonder Bar occasionally. That puts her in a better mood. That and anything Little Steven does. You ever hear his Underground Garage show? Or watch him in that show Lilyhammer?"

"For sure." I pause. "She's okay then?"

Before I can probe further he hands his metal detector to me. "Want to try?"

"That thing?"

"Hey, it's been a rather lucky night for you. Why not press it a little more?"

He tells me how to hold the arm, straps me in, and clamps his headphones onto my ears. He gives me a nudge and waves me forward. I run the metal scanner over the sand and lose myself in the whooshing and static. No buried treasure appears, but when the machine beeps I feel as though I'm given a gift on Christmas morning. Walt gleefully pockets the few pop tops that turn up.

I unstrap the scanner and tell Walt it's time for me to head back.

"I'm calling it a night. We'll walk together," he says.

We reach my place, and Walt says goodbye. In my backyard, I shake sand out of my towel. I snap it several times, enjoying the sound the terrycloth makes as it whips in the blackness. The routine action comforts me. The scent of honeysuckle permeates the air, and I draw it in, savoring the sweetness. Life itself indeed. I smooth the towel over the railing and go inside. Tail-wagging Phoebe licks the salt from every part of me she can reach. Her warm tongue tickles. She accompanies me upstairs, and I fall into bed and a grateful but restless sleep.

CHAPTER TWENTY-SIX

Be True

THE LANGOSTA LOUNGE BUZZES WITH the chatter of dozens of patrons in their quest for Friday night fun. Beside me, Amy swirls her red wine. She exhibits a rare contemplative mood, and Terri beams at the two of us across the bar top.

"What gives, girlfriend? You're way quieter than I'm used to."

Amy leans back on her barstool and faces me. "Maybe it's a sign."

"What's a sign and of what?" Terri asks.

"I meet a guy and he winds up with a broken leg and a broken wrist and is in the hospital. That must mean something."

I say to Terri, "Amy's jogger fell off his bike while training for a race. Right after they went out a second time."

Terri clinks her white wine spritzer against Amy's glass. "He'll be up and around in no time. Don't worry about it."

Amy bites her lip. "I don't know why I expected this to be different—that he was different. Maybe I'm a bad luck charm."

"You'll get to know lots about him without the drama of a heated relationship." Terri taps a finger on the marble-topped bar. "Why don't you give him a turtle when he comes home from the hospital?"

"Why would I do that?"

"My Aunt Edna says if he can take care of it, he's a keeper. If it dies you should head for the hills."

"That's insane."

"My Aunt Edna isn't insane. She knows stuff."

Amy wrinkles her nose. "Aunt Edna's advice should be flushed along with the turtle."

I stir my Jameson, stop, and hold up the swizzle stick. "If I'd ever given Jerome a turtle it would've been dead in a week."

Amy frowns. "Old news. How's it going with the neighbor?"

"Not going at all," I grumble. "I haven't seen Sammy for days." It bothers me that I haven't had the chance to tell him about my near-deadly swim or that his magic potion worked wonders for my wasp bite. I push my drink away. A couple at a high-top behind us engages in raucous banter.

Terri pipes up. "What the heck is wrong with the two of you? We're supposed to have some fun."

"Aye, aye, captain." I raise my glass and salute my friends. "The good news is my divorce is feeling like the right thing to do now. Almost drowning helped me accept that it's time to move on and to be happy for what I have. That and a long talk with the attorney you told me to call. He says I should be okay financially. Jerome can't abscond with everything."

"Almost drowning is preferable to dealing with my last divorce attorney," Amy says.

Terri pats my hand. "You're doing fine, hon."

"I'm still worried about trying to be with anyone when I'm going through this. I think I can do it and then I start to sweat."

Terri says, "No one's rushing you into anything. Take it as slow as you need. There's no schedule."

"I spent some time working at the town food pantry yesterday. I'm going back next week. It helps me keep things in perspective."

"I love that place," says Terri. "There's nothing like doing something good for someone else to get over yourself and get the old perspective back."

Amy runs her hand over her face. "I'm having such a bad streak. Such lousy sex. I don't know which time was worse, the first or the second."

"Excuse me?" I take a sip of whiskey enjoying the simple but smooth velvety taste.

"I'm surprised I was able to tell how bad it was since all I ever have lately is crappy sex. Twice with the jogger. And let's not forget David."

"The jogger? And David?" My jaw drops. Amy's been holding out on me.

Terri chimes in. "At the store. Remember when she was held up and we were waiting for her the other day? I figured it out when I found her peace pin on the floor of the stockroom."

"Ohmigod, Amy! So much for taking it slow."

"That's your idea, not mine."

"And with the jogger too? Not in the hospital, I hope."

Amy glares at me. "What if I did?"

That stings. I've been so preoccupied with my problems I've barely acknowledged hers.

"Now, now," Terri says. "The point is that dinner's on us whether it was bad or good sex. You can order three entrees if you want, Amy, in honor of your accomplishments."

Amy lifts her glass up to the light. "What happened to the pledge that we're all supposed to find a fellow? Neither of you seem to be making much of an effort. You're not quitting, are you?"

"Hell no," Terri says.

I hold up a hand. "I'm not going to be trying to meet anyone." I lift my whiskey. "May you both have many happy connections."

"I'll drink to that," Terri says.

Amy squints and gives me a disapproving frown. "You're hiding, Fi. I've seen you do this before."

"How can I be hiding? I'm right here."

"From Sammy. He's interested and you're running away like a scared kid."

"Bull."

"I'm not saying that you have to go and jump his bones. But you should give him a chance instead of shutting him out. Let yourself live."

"I'll know when it's time for me. Maybe you're pushing me

because you're not thrilled with what's happened and you want me to be miserable too."

Amy shoots me daggers.

A young man approaches and stands next to my barstool. He smiles at me. I lean in and shift away from his gaze, studying the painting of an angry ocean that hangs over the bar. The youngster orders a Fosters, and Terri nudges Amy who bats her lashes at me.

The fellow's beer arrives and he takes a long swig. He places the bottle on the bar and turns in my direction. His pale blue eyes match the color of his shirt. The young guy grins and exposes one dimple. He exhibits a killer smile that he's obviously used to flashing. I dislike the intensity in his eyes.

He says, "I don't remember seeing you here

A bad, cheesy line.

He reaches for the bowl of peanuts beside my glass and tosses a couple into his mouth, munching thoughtlessly. Though I look away, he leans toward me sending the smell of beer and nuts into my space. "I'm usually here Friday nights. You must be visiting."

Terri and Amy listen to every word. The attention of the young guy must be due to my cleavage. Amy insisted I wear an old, V-necked shirt that clings more than a little too tightly. Plus, the new bra from Terri's shop possesses a strong enough underwire that my nipples point out and not the usual down in the chill of the room.

A waiter appears and signals our table is ready. Relieved, I hop off my barstool and say, "Take care," to my admirer, training my eyes on the path ahead. We follow the server to our table, and I avoid looking back. I'm happy to trade the din of the bar for the quieter dining area where floor-to-ceiling windows provide a stunning view of the sea. The sky radiates a rosy shade of pink. I pour a glass of ice water from the carafe on the table and take a sip.

"I can't believe it," Amy says. "You're a young-man magnet."

"He must want a mother. Don't you think he's kind of fetal looking?" I glance at the bar. The boyish fellow hoists his beer to me. "He's a baby. So pink and shiny and new. He reminds me of that infant on the Gerber baby food jars."

"Don't go there," Amy says. "Stay with this, Fi."

"No, thanks. I'm working on getting used to being alone."

Amy says, "You deserve better."

I put my hands on my hips. "What about you?"

"I'm out there fighting. You don't even try."

"Do you really need another man you eventually won't have sex with in your life?"

"I like them better that way sometimes." She adds, "Incoming. Fi. It's for you."

The guy from the bar barrels towards our table. He's obviously had a few too many. He definitely reminds me of something embryonic. A fetal pig, perhaps, like the one I cut up in college biology.

He wiggles his nearly empty beer bottle over his shoulder toward the bar. "My friends and I were wondering if you ladies would like to come to a party with us?"

From the vantage of the bar, two similarly baby-faced fellows sit and stare at their buddy. None of them looks older than mid-twenties. All of them wear pastel shirts tucked into tan slacks and possess hair that parts neatly to the side, altar-boy style. They remind me of a boy group, and I expect them to burst into song at any moment.

I hold up my hand. "Is this a frat prank?"

The young man grins. "It's no joke. We'd like you all to come with us."

Amy says, "We're going to eat dinner. If you guys are still around after we've finished, we can continue this discussion in the bar."

"You're on," the pink youngster says. He nods at me and backs away.

We study our menus in silence. The song "Be True" comes over the sound system, distracting me from the food choices. Springsteen's message of the futility of clinging to pie-in-the-sky dreams about love and seduction, dreams that can never come true, that wind up leaving you broken-hearted and alone, tears me apart. My heart rises into my throat, and I swallow hard.

I place my menu on the table. "I want to go home after dinner. This isn't working for me."

"Works for me," Amy says.

Terri says, "There's no harm in talking or in trying."

"Trying what? To go somewhere and possibly sleep with one of these boys?" I take a swig of my drink. "I'm not interested in doing damage to my heart."

Amy chuckles. "Do you think the sex will be that rough?"

I glare at her. "Maybe following through on taking a pledge to get lucky has too high a price. Empty sex might harden you so much you don't feel anything. Did you ever think of that?"

"Would not being capable of feeling hurt be so bad?"

"It feels wrong on so many levels." I lift my glass and swirl the remaining liquid. "Oh, hell, I still miss my son. Not a day passes without memories of him. That hurts badly but I'm so grateful for the time I had with him I've accepted the suffering. I miss what I had with Jerome, or what I believed I had with him. I know that part of my life's over. But risking killing off everything until I'm numb isn't the way to move on."

Terri's fingers flutter on my arm for a moment. "It's okay, hon. You still believe love is sharing a life and not getting lucky one night with a stranger." Her eyes radiate kindheartedness.

"I don't want love again. I've been in love." I press my palms into the table in determination. "But I don't want this mockery either."

Terri continues, "There still can be room for another man in your life at some point. Time changes our perspective. And hearts do heal."

I'm afraid to admit that Terri might be right because it requires way too much of an emotional commitment.

"What're we going to do about our young admirers in the bar?" Amy nods towards the crowd in the other room.

"I'm sure we can disburse the three little fetal pigs later if they're still around, unless you want to take them all home, Amy." I pick up the list of specials.

"Maybe the tall one will blow my house down." Amy runs her tongue over her lips.

"Do you think they want our money?" Terri frowns. "Not that

I have much, but I wonder if it's the reason they're interested in talking to us."

"That's a good guess. I'm drawing a blank." Amy grins. "But I'm curious about what's going on in those pink skulls. And I have another challenge for you."

Terri whimpers.

"Whoever hot flashes has to buy a round of drinks."

Terri chuckles. "I'm so glad I've been taking my black cohosh. I'm barely flashing at all." She leans back in her chair and discomfort passes over her face. She fans herself. "Oh, no. The power of suggestion."

Amy signals to the waiter and points at Terri who orders another round for the table.

CHAPTER TWENTY-SEVEN

The Ties That Bind

E ACH OF US EXPERIENCES A hot flash during dinner and
buys rounds. When no one watches, I dump my Jameson
into an empty ice bucket that stands beside the table. By the
time we join the three young men in the bar, I tally that Terri and
Amy both went through four drinks to my two.

"Are you ladies up for party time?" A slight smile turns up the
corners of the mouth of the young man who spoke to me earlier.
His eyes sparkle, and my skin crawls.

I say, "What's the hurry?"

The three men look at one another. "No hurry," the second
youngster says.

"What are you drinking?" I ask.

"Corona. NFL."

I cock an eyebrow. NFL symbolizes the National Football
League to me but that doesn't seem appropriate for a Corona.

"No fucking lime." He grins.

I motion to the bartender and order a seltzer with lime for
myself, telling him to set my young companion up with a
Corona without lime.

The three young men are all friends home to attend a wedding. Mark, Alvin, and Jesse work in the financial industry. Hedge funds, mutual funds, and stocks and bonds. The one whose eyes stay glued to me is Jesse of the stocks and bonds persuasion.

The next round, I order another seltzer with lime. "I'm the designated driver," I tell Amy and Terri. "You can catch a ride with me and we'll fetch your cars tomorrow."

"Bless you." Amy crosses the air with her glass. She takes a deep swig of her drink.

"Double bless you," Terri says. "But I'm not drinking anymore either after this one. My head's going to feel awful tomorrow. I know it."

The three young men start playing a game. They bounce quarters off the bar into shot glasses and whenever one of them makes a shot, the other players drink. After a few cycles, Jesse Blue-Eyes glances at his watch, and turns his gaze to his friends.

"Are we keeping you up past your bedtime?" Amy asks.

"In a manner of speaking."

His two friends hoot.

He leans into me. "I have a question to ask you."

"So ask." I eye him. His awkwardness belies his outward posture of coolness. His brow knits, and he rolls his beer bottle between his hands.

"Let's find a little privacy."

I smile. "Anything you want to ask me, I'm sure I've been asked before. Why not spit it out in front of all of our friends?"

Jesse stands and wobbles back and forth. His face turns an odd shade of green.

"I dunno."

"Sure you do."

"Go for it, Jessboy," Mark shouts.

Jesse holds onto the bar. "I'm drunk, but I'm not wasted. Come outside with me." He smiles. "Please?" He definitely possesses intense eyes, intense blue-piggy eyes.

I hop off the barstool. "Since you're being so polite, I'll go."

Terri says, "Do you want me to come with you?"

"I can take care of myself."

Jesse stands erect with difficulty, a condition that makes

things a lot less frightening. He holds onto the bar and steadies himself.

Amy says, "You have fifteen minutes with Don Juan."

Jesse grasps my hand, and we weave our way out to the almost empty deck. Only a few stragglers from the bar stand facing the water. The chill of the evening keeps most people indoors.

"It's gorgeous out here." I relish the salt air and wrap my arms around my chest tightly. "I can't think of a time when I don't want to be by the water. Even when it's freezing it's amazing."

Jesse steadies himself on the railing and stares out to the water.

"What did you want to ask me?"

He clears his throat. "It's like this." He coughs. "Would you sleep with me?"

I laugh at the suddenness.

"Would you?"

I blink. "You're serious?"

"I am."

"How romantic."

He shrugs.

"Why do you think I'd sleep with you?" Has word of our pledge to get lucky spread around town? Terri and Amy possess more smarts than to ever tell anyone else about the bet. David? Maybe Amy told him? He's about the frat boys' age. Or maybe Amy set this whole thing up. I steam at the possibility.

"You're upset. Are you insulted I asked?"

"I don't even know you."

"Does that matter?"

"Why don't you use Tinder or Grindr like other people your age?"

"The guys like old school now and then." He slaps his thighs. "Truth is I'm getting married. Next week. It's my wedding we're out celebrating tonight."

His words jar me. "You want to sleep with a woman before you get married, and she happens to be lucky me."

"I need more experience and…it might be enjoyable for both of us."

I lean on the railing. "This is ridiculous. You have to understand what a turnoff your request is. You can't be so clueless."

His cheeks go red.

Something strikes me as tragic in his pitiful attempt to connect. Bruce talks to me again. The song "The Ties That Bind" echoes in my head with its sad tale of cheap romance and emptiness and the lesson that what matters are long-lasting connections. In spite of what Amy says, I'm certain that a one-night hookup doesn't improve my chance for happiness.

My would-be lover lets his gaze go to the horizon. "I don't know what to say."

I place my hand on his shoulder. "I'm not insulted, though I certainly think a lot of women might have slapped your face at the suggestion."

I wonder what it is about the need to attach to another human being that drives people to such sad scenarios.

He bends and kisses my hand, and the sour smell of beer wafts upward. "You're hot. I'm attracted to you." He leans in to kiss me, escalating the attack, and any trace of goodwill I harbor evaporates.

"Are you deaf? That's so not happening." I shudder and pull out of his grasp. Heat blasts up my arm in spite of my determination to send him back to little piggy land. "Your fiancé will thank me and so will you. If we slept together, we'd both regret it immediately or soon thereafter."

He hiccups. "I'm willing to risk the aftermath." The last word comes out so slurred, I'm not sure what it is at first.

I shake my head. "I've done a lot of foolish things in my life. This isn't going to be one of them."

"Damn." He grips the railing for support.

"Let's go inside and get you some coffee."

I hold the door resolutely for Jesse. Joy passes through me. Not sleeping with him leaves me more satisfied than if I'd slept with him, or with anyone else I can think of. Well, maybe not Sammy if I ever figure out what's going on with my mixed up feelings about him—and if he ever becomes interested in me after I disentangle from Jerome. I pump my fist in the air and follow behind my pink swain.

We rejoin Amy and Terri. I park myself on a stool between my friends. Jesse whispers to his buddies and within a few seconds the three young men down their drinks and leave.

"What's going on?" Amy asks.

"I wasn't into being Mrs. Robinson. Or Stifler's mom."

"Your loss," Amy says. "That fellow was cute."

But I know there's no loss involved. I did what's right for me. It's easy to go along with a plan like his. And then what? It's simply not something I want or need. I want to keep to myself and let things sit for a while. Another saying of my grandfather's nudges me: *"A murky pool of thoughts often clears provided no one constantly stirs them."*

"I'm not feeling too well." Terri clutches her stomach. "I don't usually drink more than one or two."

"Oh wow…I think the bathroom's over there." Amy points to a passageway beside the bar.

Terri claps her hand over her mouth and lurches across the room. Amy sends a concerned gaze to me. "I shouldn't have let her have so many. She told me before that she doesn't have much tolerance. We'd better follow her."

"It's not your fault. We all get carried away sometimes."

Amy grins mischievously. "If she gets sick now instead of once we're on our way, at least she won't mess up the car."

We watch over Terri in the bathroom until her stomach empties and she asks to leave.

On the way out I'm startled by the sight of Sammy at the bar. His long legs hook over the bottom rung of a stool. I take a step towards him and stop. The stunning brunette next to him strokes his arm.

The vision of the two of them smarts.

Why shouldn't he be with a beautiful young woman? I have no claim on him and I'm a lot older than she appears. Whatever is between us exists solely in my imagination.

I turn back to Amy to leave, but Sammy spots me. "Sofia. At last." He waves and pats the seat next to him.

Amy pokes me in the side. "Get over there, Fi. I'll take Terri home."

"This was fun. I love you both so much." Terri hiccups and puts her hand over her mouth.

"Are you sure you're okay to drive?"

Amy grins. "You're not the only one dumping out drinks." She hugs me. "Hey, I'm sorry for all the crap I laid on you before. I think you're doing great. I'm proud of you for sticking up for yourself."

I hang on to her and send the hug back. "I have no idea what I'm doing. I'm sorry I haven't been around much for you."

Amy whispers in my ear, "One sure bet is that handsome fellow over there likes you. So don't blow it, girlfriend."

Amy puts her arm around Terri's waist and guides her to the door. She turns back and mouths, "He's so cute."

CHAPTER TWENTY-EIGHT

You Can Look (But You Better Not Touch)

SAMMY DISENGAGES FROM THE BRUNETTE. He approaches and wraps his arms around me so tightly it takes my breath away. I sink into his chest, and my knees go weak.

Sammy whispers in my ear, "Go with this, please. I'll owe you one." He leads me to the bar with his arm in a vise around my shoulders.

"This is Helene. She's a friend of June's." He pulls me in closer. I nod and smile, not sure what to say. *You're such a moron*, I tell myself, grinning like a half-witted bimbo. This must be the Helene that June mentioned when she offered the yet-to-happen dinner at Sammy's house.

"Sofia moved here recently." Sammy rubs my arm and sparks fly. His words barely register in my preoccupied brain. .

"We've hit it off incredibly in the past few days, haven't we?"

I smile. "It's been a real joy getting to know Sammy." *Boy, that sounded lame.*

Helene's doe-like eyes move up and down, lingering on mine with a penetrating stare. Oh, no. The ol' stink-eye from a younger, well-dressed, attractive woman. June's stony assessment was bad, but this one's even worse. I do my best to tuck in my tummy and act as though I really am someone Sammy might be dating.

Sammy says, "I was wondering when you'd show up."

I fall into the role. "Sorry I'm late. It took a while to finish up at work."

He nuzzles my neck and plants a kiss at its base. I think I may erupt in pleasure right there in the bar.

"I'm glad you finally made it." He explains to Helene, "She's an interior designer. Her clients see more of her than I do." He holds me so close I feel the hardness of his ribs against me. He gives off that heady, just-showered smell I've come to recognize, and my Pavlovian puddling response kicks in.

Helene grabs her purse and stands. Even if she kicked off her stunning patent pumps I'd still be looking up at her. I detect a hint of a French accent when she says, "Thanks for the drink, Sammy. Say hi to June for me." Her light frame reminds me of the Eiffel tower. I'm doomed to be in its elegant shadow.

She makes her way through the crowd, parting it easily with her good looks; a gorgeous prophet in a sea of men. Once again I understand from afar what it is to walk in beauty.

Sammy hangs on firmly to my waist. "That was a big favor."

"What exactly is going on?"

"I'm going to pound June when I see her." He smiles at me. "You were wonderful." He sees my puzzled look.

I disengage and step back. "Care to explain?"

"June told me to meet her here for a drink and instead Helene showed up."

"She's gorgeous."

"She's okay."

"She's attractive, Sammy."

"A chimp has more brain power. All she lives for is her pedicures and manicures. She was telling me about them when you came to my rescue. How hard is it to keep nails looking good? More importantly, why should I care?" He grabs my un-manicured hands. "I like hands like yours."

"I get a manicure and pedicure now and then. Don't get all excited about these raggedy claws of mine."

He runs his thumb across the top of my hand, igniting an inferno. "You have no idea how attractive you are."

My mouth fills with cotton. How long has he been drinking? Dozens of women his age and younger surround us yet he's talking to me.

He signals for the bartender. "Want a drink?"

"I'd better not. I have to walk Phoebe and get some rest. I'm bushed."

"And I'm opening early tomorrow. I'd better get going too."

After he pays, he walks me to my car.

"Thanks, Sofia. That was fun." His eyes bore into mine. What a gorgeous green. I blink to stop myself from staring. For an instant, I think he's going to lean in and kiss me. Instead, he turns and bounces to his convertible.

Sammy's car backs up, blasting Springsteen. I recognize the refrain of "You Can Look (But You Better Not Touch)." I wonder if he intentionally chose the tune. He shoots me a crooked smile and waves goodbye.

I climb into my Camry confused, happy, and dejected.

CHAPTER TWENTY-NINE

Human Touch

A T HOME, WITH MY SKIN still tingling at the spot Sammy stroked me, I climb up the porch steps and spot a large manila envelope taped to the front door. Inside, I sit on the denim couch and tear it open. The package contains divorce papers and a lengthy separation agreement that make my head spin. My lawyer and Jerome's lawyers are engaging in paper battles. I fling the papers onto the cocktail table.

Phoebe pads into the room and nudges me. With a loud groan she manages to get her rear up onto the sofa followed by her front. She climbs into my lap and rubs her jowls on my thighs.

"You need a bath again, girl. You're beyond fragrant." A strange stench of beef jerky and sourness comes from her mouth. I sniff at her fur and gag. Her coat smells downright rotten.

"What have you been rolling around in?"

I push Phoebe off my lap and go into the kitchen. The trash can lies on its side and garbage litters the space. The remnants of the untidiness she's deemed inedible are everywhere. Catsup stains the floor, and a few pieces of rejected lettuce lie stuck to the pillow she's dragged into the room.

What a mess. I clean up the pieces of gnawed cardboard left from a box that once held a pizza and collect the plastic cups Phoebe's licked clean and chased beneath the table. I make a mental note to thoroughly mop and scrub the floor tomorrow.

"Geez, Phoebe, you need a cleaning army to keep up with you." Phoebe pants in answer and whines.

"Yeah, you do, I'm not kidding. You're as bad as Jerome."

She whines louder, and I recognize the tone. "Out? You want to go out?"

Phoebe barks and wags her tail. Her rolls of flesh jiggle with excitement.

"Of course you do. I suppose the rest of the mess can wait. Let's go, girl." I clip the leash to Phoebe's collar and lead her to the door.

"A saltwater swim is a great idea to start the process of de-smelling you."

Phoebe takes her time and halts to sniff patches of grass along the way. She sprinkles urine at each stop. When we finally descend the stairs from the boardwalk, Phoebe plops onto the sand for a rest.

"Fine. We'll wait a minute or two and then it's ocean time."

She places her chin on her paws and yawns. I sit beside her and sift sand through my fingers. Phoebe begins to snore. I pat her back and lie down to watch the moon rise over the water.

A wet, sloppy tongue licks at my neck, and I bolt upright. Killer paws at me and climbs onto my lap. I hug him, and Phoebe raises her head and thumps her tail in greeting.

Sammy crouches beside me. "You couldn't sleep either, huh?"

"Not with stinky Phoebe in the house."

"It's a beautiful night for a dog walk."

I nod without looking at him and pet Phoebe. "A dog dip in the ocean is in order for sure."

Sammy says, "Hey, are you okay?"

"Actually, no. I'm not."

"I take it it's more than that wasp bite from the other day that's on your mind?" He drops onto the sand next to me, stretching out his long legs. "Want to talk about it?"

"Not really."

He tries again. "What's bothering you?"

I clench and unclench my hands. "A lot of things. For starters, I came home to a pile of divorce papers at my door. I don't know what parts are important. It's all so complicated."

"Your lawyer should be able to help with that. If you want I can take a look. I might be able to give you a little guidance."

"Thanks. I might do that. But it's more than the papers. I know I want to do this. I feel relief that I started the process, but it's also so depressing."

He squeezes my hand, and I lose track of what I was telling him. Sammy says, "Anything else?"

"I'm worried about Amy and her random hookups. I don't want her to get hurt."

"You can't stop her from being her."

"I'm worried about our business. And I'm worried that my husband might pop up at any moment. I don't want to see him."

"That's a lot of worrying for one night."

His steady regard shows he's giving me his complete attention. I want to tell him more, but the parts left unspoken concern Ben, the darkness, and most of all Sammy's feelings toward me. A fear of rejection if I unburden myself further hangs overhead like a dark cloud, and my apprehension over becoming involved with him causes my gut to wrench. I've already said too much.

I grow quiet, and the chirp of crickets fills the night air. He stands and pulls me up by my hands. His touch sends liquid silver through my veins. He bends and kisses the inside of my wrist, and I close my eyes. I want the moment to last; I want to stay suspended in this place of tender possibility.

"I wish I could make things right for you." His fingers brush across my cheek.

"That's not your job."

"What's work got to do with anything?"

I look out to the ocean to break the spell.

He slaps his hands on his thighs. "Maybe we should say goodnight. I wouldn't want to take advantage of you."

I laugh. "My mind's reeling. I wouldn't even know it if you did take advantage of me."

"My, how flattering to me." He grins. "Come on. I'll race you to the beach."

"You're on."

I take off with Killer and Phoebe following behind. Soon Killer runs ahead. Sammy falls back a few paces. At the waterline, I collapse onto the sand. Killer licks my face, and Phoebe climbs on top of me. I gag.

"Oh my God, you got smellier after running. How's that possible?"

Sammy joins us and kneels down.

"You let me win," I say. "That's not fair."

"I enjoyed the view immensely."

I slap him on the arm.

Sammy whistles and runs towards the water. "Come on, you two."

"Oh, yes, get my stinky dog into the water."

But the ocean holds no interest for Phoebe. She plops down her rear and refuses to budge.

"Wait a sec. I have an idea." Sammy fishes in his pocket. "I found a jerky on my back porch." He unwraps the beef stick and breaks off a piece, offering it to Killer who chomps and swallows the treat. Sammy picks up Killer and grips him tightly under his arm. He approaches Phoebe and waves the remainder of the stick in her face.

"Come on, Phoebe."

Phoebe wiggles with joy, and drool forms on her jowls. She opens her mouth, and Sammy steps back a few inches. Phoebe stares at the object of her desire.

"Now you've done it. She's in a beef jerky trance."

"This could be fun."

He throws the dried meat a few feet from the shore and the tide overtakes it. "Go get it, Phoebe."

Phoebe lumbers towards the low waves. She searches the sand without luck. Finally she sees the jerky bobbing in the sea. She wades into the ocean a few yards, holding her nose above the water.

"Swim, Phoebe, swim," I call.

Phoebe paddles hard. Her powerful jaws clamp over the beef jerky, and she carries it back to the shore. She gulps down her treasure with the water lapping at her paws.

I catch up to her, cup my hands, and dump water over her back. I rub her coat and splash her. "Even wet dog smell is better than rotting garbage, Phoebe."

She trots away to drier sand, sinks down and rolls around. She's clearly enjoying her romp. She stands and runs to me with her tail wagging. I take a whiff of her coat.

"Not bad. Not pleasant, but bearable."

Sammy shouts, "Watch out."

Before I can react, Phoebe shakes violently and covers me in a spray of sand and water.

"That's the gratitude I get for making you less smelly." I shake a finger at her and wipe at my face.

Sammy laughs and helps brush away the sand on my back. The contact ignites a wildfire that passes through me and encircles my core. What a shame his young, taut, and so-full-of-life figure contrasts so starkly with my middle-aged and droopy-in-more-places-than-I-want-to-admit body.

"That was quite a show you put on at the bar," I say.

"It was easy." His eyes are mischievous, and I can't hold his gaze. Is he leading me on? I'm afraid to read anything into his words.

Phoebe shambles away and breaks the tension.

"Better get going," I say.

We stroll back up the block in a leisurely fashion. At Sammy's front walk he turns to me with a twinkle in his eyes. "I'd invite you in for a nightcap, but I don't think I could be trusted to be alone with you right now."

My insides yammer to believe him, but my fears hold me back. He hums a few bars of an immediately familiar song. I know the lyrics to "Human Touch" by heart, especially the lines about yearning to feel someone in your arms and sharing the experience of touching and exploring. Oh Bruce.

Oh Sammy.

My arousal grows again, and a tingling sensation makes its way from my stomach up my spine. The buzz wraps around my middle and shoots into my breasts with so much force that it makes me want to throw my head back and moan.

"You need to find someone your own age," I call over his humming. He's a flirt. A practiced one.

But what if he means what he says? And even if he does, he'll undoubtedly ghost me after.

He shakes his head sadly and walks Killer to his front door. He slips a key in the lock and faces me.

"'Night, Sofia."

I wave goodbye. After his porchlight dims, I continue on the path with Phoebe, aware that more than my footing leaves me unsure in the darkness.

CHAPTER THIRTY

With Every Wish

THE NEXT DAY, AMY WALKS briskly beside me on the boardwalk. "This is going to be my best art project yet."

"When do you tell me exactly what we're going to be doing?"

"Soon. Soon."

"Can you at least fill me in on what's in that paper sack you're holding?"

Amy ignores me. I resign myself to living with uncertainty and match my stride to hers.

Amy chuckles. "Boy, did Terri have a hangover today. But it was worth it."

I let out a sigh. "Too much wine, too much of many things."

"Are you going to dish on what happened with Sammy after I left you in the bar?"

I chew my lip. "I think I did something really stupid."

"Stupid good or stupid bad?"

"What the heck is stupid good?"

"Okay, okay, so you think it was stupid bad. But believe me, stupid bad easily can turn into stupid good."

"I have no idea what you're talking about. How's that possible?"

"Let's say you run out of gas. That's stupid. But if you make a connection with a guy who comes to help you out, it can turn it into stupid good." Amy eyes me. "What happened?"

"Sammy kissed me. Sort of."

Amy stops walking. She blinks twice and lets the news settle in. "Wow. At the bar?"

"There and again later."

"There was a later?"

"Let's back up. At the bar he used me as a shield."

"What?" Alarm crosses her face.

I snort. "Not a human shield. There was a woman he wanted to avoid, so he pretended to be with me."

Amy's eyes grow wide. "What kind of pretend?"

"He hugged me and kissed my neck. But I was playing a role. It was fake, not for real. It's what happened later that made me really confused."

"Go on."

We start walking again, and I spread my fingertips wide. "After the bar I took Phoebe out. I had no idea I was going to run into him. But I did and that's when things happened quickly. Oh, God, Amy, I didn't think. We were on the beach."

"Hah," Amy says. She sends Hallelujah hands to the heavens.

"He only kissed my wrist. Don't get any ideas. But I was on fire and it felt so right."

"Wait. Where on the beach?" Amy picks up her pace.

"What difference does it make where?"

"Well, it helps my imagination if I can picture the two of you."

"I don't care about your imagination."

"This is terrific. You're a MILF."

"I hate that term. What could he possibly see in me? I still worry he might think I'm too old."

"What century are you living in?"

"Maybe you're right. But if you are, what am I supposed to do?"

"Welcome to being a grownup with the same problems as the rest of us. Now you get to fantasize about more than a wrist kiss. And I'm not so sure he was pretending at the bar. If he didn't care for you he would never have used you as his so-called shield. Stay in the moment next time, Fi, and let it happen." She thrusts a paper bag at me.

"What's this?"

"It's art."

I moan.

"How encouraging and supportive," Amy says.

The fact that this art project resides inside a small bag sets my mind at rest. Small bag means small project in all likelihood and hopefully only a small dose of trouble.

I reach inside and extract a clump of tiny papers the size of the slips found in fortune cookies. I turn several of them over.

"What gives, Amy? These are blank."

"Yes, they are."

"Are we writing fortunes and sticking them in cookies later? If you knew how to bake it might not be a bad idea. Fortune cookies always taste bad."

"Maybe that's why they're free."

I shake a handful of the papers at her. "What are these?"

"They're wishes, hopes, and dreams."

"They're blank."

"Exactly right." She pulls a pen from her back pocket and parks her rear on a bench. I watch her scribble and fold the paper. Amy bends over and places the note into a crack between the boards of the boardwalk.

"Voila. My wish is out there."

"And…"

"And a person will come along and discover it and set it free."

"I'm afraid they might fine you for littering."

"It's art, not litter."

Amy scrawls again on a fresh slip of paper and she stuffs this one into another gap before offering me a pen.

I hesitate. Within a few seconds a flood of ideas flows through my mind. I fill the small pieces of paper rapidly. I wish for sunshine and for Jerome to stay away permanently. I wish for Amy to find someone who appreciates her, and I wish for Kate to be able to have many more successful Yappy Hours.

Amy laughs. "Geez, save some for tomorrow, okay?"

"How long are you going to do this?"

"As long as I need to." She picks up the paper bag. "Come on, let's get moving. I want to plant these all over the boardwalk." She reaches in her pocket and displays a batch of the papers with writing on them. "I filled these out last night while I watched over Terri."

The song "With Every Wish" plays in my head and keeps repeating. The part about how sometimes wishes come with a curse dogs me. To dislodge the tune, I study a pair of seagulls resting on top of a light post. I clear my throat. "Speaking of Terri, I wanted to mention that there's vacant space right near her realty office. You've been spending so much time traveling back and forth to Nyack. Do you think we might be able to relocate everything here? You can stay with me for as long as you want."

"Ohmigod. That's a terrific idea." Her eyes widen with excitement.

Good old Amy. She's always able to switch gears on a moment's notice.

"My apartment lease is up in two months. And I bet we could get a sublet for the design firm." Her wheels turn rapidly. "I'll call Terri when we get back. Let's head to Asbury Park, to the Paramount Theater. We can put wishes out till we get there."

"I think I've made enough wishes for today."

"Nonsense. It's good for you to dream."

Along the way, we stop and place our papers in the cracks of the boardwalk. When we turn to go back home, I notice a familiar figure. The man approaches at a slow pace.

"Look, it's Walt Cornell," I say.

He bends down and picks up a piece of paper from the boardwalk. He stuffs it into a bulging pocket. His khaki carpenter pants hang on his thin frame.

Amy studies Walt with a look of alarm on her face. "What's he doing?"

"I'd say he's doing exactly what you wanted. Setting all your wishes free."

Amy grouses, "I was hoping they'd last a couple of days. Do you think he took them all?"

"Maybe you should ask him."

Amy marches toward Walt's hunched over frame. He's tugging at one of the wishes. The paper comes free and joins the others in his pocket. He sees Amy approaching and does an about face, charging away with surprising speed for someone his age.

Amy yells to his retreating back, "Hey, wait up."

Walt ignores her.

"What are you going to do with them?" Amy calls, frustration obvious in her tone.

I catch up and drape an arm around Amy's shoulder. "It's all right. Art's in the eye of the beholder—isn't that what you always tell me?"

"But no one else will take part in this if he gathers the wishes up as soon as I put them out. Boy, he's a strange one." Amy withdraws more papers from her sack. "Maybe this bunch on the way back will last for a day or two. We'll have to put even more out."

"We're not done?"

Amy thrusts the blank slips and a pen at me. "Get wishing, girlfriend. And make them good ones."

Ahead of us Walt Cornell glances back. I think he's wearing a smile.

CHAPTER THIRTY-ONE

Two Hearts

W RITING DOWN MY WISHES INVIGORATES me. My last slips of paper were about finding the right path for my future. I also requested a steady, loyal beau for Amy several times, and a raft of house closings and lingerie sales for Terri. I steered clear of wishing for anything about Sammy, afraid of jinxing our budding relationship.

I decide to pour myself into the cleaning of the house, ready to vanquish the real cobwebs along with those of my past. Phoebe fixates on the vacuum, alternating between trying to climb aboard the canister and tangling herself in the cord. I finish my bedroom, look up and notice a white rope hanging from the ceiling in the hallway.

"How do you like that, Phoebe. We have an attic."

I tug on the thin twine, and a wooden ladder descends. The joints protest as I unfold the stairs. Once the bottom rung's steady on the floor, I turn to Phoebe.

"I'll be back in a sec." Phoebe yawns and stretches out next to the ladder.

The stairs creak and dust swirls around my head as I climb.

I stop at the top rung. Golden light pervades the small space thanks to two amber, arched windows in the eaves. I pick my way through the clutter and pull on the string of an overhead bulb.

The room must have been used as an art studio at one time. An old easel lies propped against the far wall, and several blank canvases lean against exposed beams. A stained artist's palette rests on a small bench. I step forward for a better look. The old plywood splinters sending my foot crashing through the thin flooring, pulverizing the plasterboard ceiling of the room below. White dust fills the space, choking me, and moments later I scream when my second foot joins my first. I cough and gasp for air.

I grip the joists of the attic and hang on the beams. What a disaster. I'm not sure what's below me and don't want to drop any further. My adrenaline pumps wildly.

Phoebe barks like mad, and I hear her running back and forth below. She races from my hanging legs and returns to the foot of the attic stairs—which she wisely doesn't ascend.

"Help," I call, shouting towards the attic windows.

There's no way my voice can carry outside.

Phoebe launches into her awful howl bay, and I can hardly hear myself think. Her nails click loudly as she hurries from room to room, and she regularly releases a noisy assault.

I hear her pad downstairs and reason she must be headed to the kitchen for a snack.

"Don't you dare go looking for food," I call.

Her howling turns to barking and back to howling nonstop. Finally she ceases, and I figure she's settled into the kitchen.

The doorbell rings. Phoebe unleashes her earsplitting yowling again.

"Come in, come in," I shout, but two floors above the front door I doubt anyone can hear me. Maybe it's Terri coming by to drop off Amy's latest Heavenly Bodies purchases. Or Amy, who isn't supposed to be back from a potential client meeting and shopping jaunt for hours. If she finished up early it could be her, hoping I'll open the door and help her unload the car.

My legs dangle beneath the floorboards, and my arms ache

from leaning against the rough wood. My skirt is hiked up around my waist, leaving my new blue panties on full display below.

Footsteps echo downstairs.

I yell, "Hello. I'm up here. Come upstairs. I'm in the attic. Amy, is that you?"

Sammy's voice comes at me.

"Sofia? What's going on?"

I cringe and press my legs together wanting to disappear. He calls to me from the foot of the ladder.

"Are you up there?"

"I'm stuck. I fell through the floor."

"Hang on."

Like I have any other option. Geez.

Sammy's footsteps move away, and I know where he's headed. I do my best to pull myself up out of the hole and back into the attic before he sees my exposed rear, but my arms lack that kind of power.

"I'm right below you," Sammy says. My last shred of dignity leaves, and I slump my head onto my arms. When Sammy touches my ankle, I squeeze my eyes shut in embarrassment. No. No. No. He can't be seeing half of me, the lower half of me in my new skimpy underwear.

His arms wrap around my legs, and he says, "You can let go. Let's see if I can lower you down without having to get out a saw." His embrace is warm and strong and completely upsetting.

"I've got you, Sofia."

My palms sweat. The pounding in my chest renders any attempt at calming myself useless. I try to keep myself from thinking about falling. In spite of my fear I marshal the courage to release my grip and raise my arms above my head, letting out a scream. Sammy slowly lowers me into the room below. I slide down his firm chest, and a swell of relief coupled with longing engulfs me as I draw in his familiar scent. We're so close I can feel his breath on my neck. Once my sandals land, his arms drop to his side. My skirt falls back into place. I smooth it down and look up at him aware my cheeks are burning.

"Thank you."

"Are you hurt?"

"Other than my ego? No."

He grins. "I only took a couple of pictures with my phone."

"Very funny."

Sammy scratches his cheek. "Those blue panties, they're different than the white ones. Quite nice actually."

I brush past him, head held high in spite of my embarrassment. Nope. I'm still not discussing underwear with him.

We move to the kitchen. Sammy escorts me to a chair and insists on kneeling down and examining my legs for bruises.

"You were lucky. Somehow you fell through without much more than a minor scrape." He touches my ankle, and I bite my lip as his hand slides gently up my leg.

"I'm okay. I don't think I'll be spending much time in that attic."

His fingers linger on my calf and leave me intoxicated. I want to reach out and stroke his hair. I hear Amy telling me to stay in the moment.

He says, "The flooring's old and dried out. Not hard to replace if you want to. Regardless, you'll need to have the plasterboard fixed in the ceiling. I know someone who does that." He reaches over and scratches Phoebe beneath her chin. Phoebe closes her eyes and enjoys the rubbing. I'm jealous and aware I'm competing with my dog. I bend over and pat her neck trying to distract her, but she's not interested in my petting.

Sammy says, "Phoebe has such a loud howl. I had a feeling something might be up. Luckily I stopped at home to get some papers June needs for the meeting we're having today." He glances at his watch.

"I'm so glad you came by."

The tension in the air is tangible, and we exchange an awkward silence. Sammy touches the hem of my skirt. His hands move gently up my thighs and every synapse of my being surges with electricity and anticipation. His chest presses upward, rewarding me with the weight of him between my legs. His mouth covers mine I explode into a whirling world of passion so deep I fear letting it consume me, but oh, I want it to devour me. The thrumming in my temples prevents thought, and I revel in the pure craving, driving my tongue to explore his sweet taste.

Our eyes meet, and he pulls away taking a deep breath.

"To be continued," Sammy says. Before I can argue he's up and across the room, standing in front of the back door. No chance exists to change his mind.

"Blue is my favorite color." He winks and slips outside. Disappointment fills me, and I stay seated, trying to make sense of what happened. When Phoebe licks my calf at the spot Sammy touched, I laugh and give her a big hug.

After dinner I stroll to the boardwalk to meet up with Amy and Terri for a walk before sunset. Thoughts of Sammy swirl in my head. Nothing about my surroundings cheers me. Instead, the bright blue of the sky, the cawing of the gulls, and the scent of the ocean irritate me. Even the sound of the waves fails to elicit its usual calming effect. I resort to Doc Phelps' exercise, breathing slowly and counting.

I like Sammy—that much is clear. He does seem to be trying to connect with me. The memories of his hands on my thighs, his tender kiss on my wrist, and his mouth covering mine, make me swoon and leave me yearning for much more. But something makes me uneasy.

With a start I understand it's not Sammy causing my discomfort.

It's me.

I don't know if I have it in me to trust someone again. My conveniently high emotional wall protects me from the possibility of seeing where we might travel together. But, oh, how good the ripple of passion and happiness that presses upward and grows feels when I think of him. Maybe something special could be out there.

I bend down and retrieve a small shell from a pile placed near the stairway. I scoop up a second similar shell. They're both broken, but still lovely, and not like ones I've seen on the beach before. I hold one aloft and study it in the light.

"That's part of a sand dollar."

It's Walt Cornell.

"I thought it looked familiar. But it's not white."

Walt chuckles. "They start out this way, kind of dusty and gray. You have to bleach them to make them look like the ones in the stores. Ellie does that."

"There are so many pieces here. Someone collected them."

"And none of them are whole," he says.

"They're still pretty."

"Ellie likes them too. She says, so what if they're a little broken. They're like us."

I like Ellie more and more.

Walt continues, "This time of year you can find quite a few sand dollars on the beach. You know the stories about them, don't you?" He strokes his gray, stubbled chin. His baggy, plaid shorts and white socks tucked inside black fisherman sandals remind me of the clothes my grandfather often wore to my mother's chagrin.

I shake my head.

"Most of the tales have religious overtones. They say the markings on the front and back of the shells are of the Easter lily and the Christmas poinsettia. And the holes correspond with the wounds of Christ. Oh, and if you discover a whole one and shake it you'll hear the five doves of peace in there."

"I'll have to see if I can find an intact shell."

"The truth about those so-called doves of peace is that they're what are left of the teeth of the sand dollar. You're hearing teeth rattling around when you shake one, not doves of peace." He smiles. "The religious story is a lot nicer."

"I prefer the truth."

"Me too."

He shifts from foot to foot. "I better get going. Ellie has a doctor appointment I told her I'd take her to."

"Is she ill?"

"She's fine. She faints when she gets shots and it's time for her annual flu." He laughs. "She talks tough but, boy, you should see her when she gets in that room."

Walt waves goodbye, and I watch him stride purposely down the boardwalk. I'm jealous of what he and Ellie have. They've managed to be there for each other for more years than many people have lived. The song "Two Hearts" nags at me. Ellie and Walt are living the lyrics. They go through life with their hearts entwined and they're stronger than being alone. Their two hearts together clearly *are* better than one. But me, I may be one of those people destined not to obtain that type of comfort. For me, being one of two hearts is a dream and may stay that way.

A loud "Yoo hoo" brings me back to the present. Amy and Terri approach and we exchange hugs. I realize I'm smiling.

Unlike me who still wears the same skirt and top I picked out this morning, Terri and Amy have dressed for the occasion. Terri's wearing pink workout gear and Amy's chosen designer spandex,

Terri says, "It's so nice out I'm glad to get away from the paperwork in the office."

Amy shades her eyes and scans the ocean. "Think we can take a walk by the water?"

"Why not?" I say. "How're the wishes and dreams going on the boardwalk. I thought I noticed a few missing."

"The last batch is still around. But some have disappeared. Terri's going to monitor them for me too."

I say, "I'll count them every time I run."

We kick off our sneakers, leaving them by the stairs. Terri's pink ones are half the size of my beat-up Reeboks and Amy's neon Nikes. On the sand, I wiggle my toes in the softness and Amy links her arm in mine.

"It smells great out here, doesn't it?"

"Yes, it does." I draw in the salty tang of low-tide.

Terri reaches in her pink crossbody bag and hands us flyers with the words "Big Sea Day" written in bold print at the top. A seashell border decorates the edges of the seafoam colored paper.

She says, "The end of the season clambake is almost here. You're now officially invited and you both have to come."

"I've never been to one," Amy says.

"You'll love it. The whole town pitches in and the food is delicious." Terri eyes us. "I can use some help if you're up for it."

"Why not?" I ask.

Amy sends me a sly grin. "Maybe one of those flyers should find its way into Sammy's mailbox."

"I don't think so."

"You're not the only one who has one," Amy says, shaking hers.

"Don't you dare."

"Let's see. How does putting down 'Dear Sammy, want to warm me up by the hot coals?' sound?"

"Awful." I pause. "He came by today."

"Oh, did he?" Amy is all ears and so is Terri.

"I fell through the attic and he managed to get me out."

"What?" Amy snorts with laughter. Terri displays a look of concern.

"It's an old attic. Crummy floorboards. There's an art studio up there but it's a mess. I was checking it out and next thing I knew I was through the ceiling and hanging on for dear life. Sammy heard Phoebe howling and came in." I leave out the parts about my panties being on display and the kiss.

"Geez, Fi. Some people will do anything for attention."

Terri studies me. "Did you hurt yourself?"

"Not at all."

Amy says, "You're holding back, aren't you? What exactly happened in this rescue mission?"

"Sadly, not much."

"But something, huh?"

"I felt a connection. I did." The spot Sammy touched on my leg tingles again.

Amy shakes her head. "Give it time, Fi." She studies me. "You need this. More importantly, you deserve this. Don't give up."

"You can do it, hon," Terri says.

"You two are the best," I say, happy that thanks to my friends I'm finding courage I didn't think I possessed.

CHAPTER THIRTY-TWO

The Big Muddy

THE NEXT MORNING, I TURN on my music and locate Springsteen, but the songs that play distress me. Too many pieces remind me of the trouble with Jerome. "The Big Muddy" sets my teeth on edge. Jerome becomes the poisonous snake in the song, biting and infecting me, taking me down to a dark and miserable place that lacks air. I too become a venomous viper crawling towards Sammy, wounding him, and laying him low, leaving him in a bloody state that's all my fault. My breathing becomes labored. I turn off the music and place my phone on the kitchen table, hoping a jog will dispel the deadly mood.

The beach and boardwalk lie empty at this early hour, and I note that today only a few of Amy's papers still remain between the boards. The wishes roam freely in accordance with her plan. The sun casts a tawny glow over the sand, and my run becomes enjoyable. Far out in the ocean, a lone surfer catches my attention. I slow to a stop and shade my eyes for a better view.

Rough waves crash and spray the shoreline. The boarder vanishes on the horizon. I wait and finally the figure appears again. He catches a large roller that takes him dangerously near the jetty. Sammy told me the surfers never ride close to the rocks.

The fellow loses control and tumbles into the ocean. He disappears beneath the water. His board pops up but he never emerges in the churning surf.

Alarm courses through me. Where is he?

Adrenaline fuels my legs, and I clamber down to the sand, running to the jetty at top speed. I reach the shoreline and scan the horizon but no one appears. The vanishing makes no sense. His white surfboard crashes into the jetty over and over. It tumbles and turns in the non-stop roiling, but the surfer never rises up.

I reach for my cell phone and remember it's sitting on the kitchen table. What a foolish choice.

A sound catches my ear, and I listen hard. It's a weak voice, carrying faintly to me in between the crashing of the waves.

"Help. Help me."

"Hello? Where are you?" I shout, surveying the area. Maybe my imagination is getting the better of me. "Is someone out there?"

The voice quavers. "I'm on the jetty." The rest of the words drown in the roar of the surf.

I wade into ankle-deep water and step onto rocks that lie beneath the surface at the base of the jetty. The tide surges and rolls towards the shore. Slick growth covers the stones, and my sneakers slip into the cool water. After steadying myself on the moss-covered surface, I climb gingerly.

"Raise an arm. Wave so I can see where you are," I shout.

"I can't."

The moss and algae offer poor traction, and my progress is slow. I reach the place the rocks rise out of the water and crawl on my hands and knees, cautiously moving forwards until I can clamber onto the jetty. Standing, I scan the area. The voice of the injured surfer must have come from the far point.

"I'm on the jetty," I shout.

"Hurry." His voice sounds pained. "I'm at the end."

The large gray stones form a surface flat enough for the

fishermen to set up chairs, but the footing remains treacherous. After traveling half the length of the jetty, the surfer comes into view. My spirits sink. From the shoreline he lay hidden below the sightline. But from my current vantage point I see him clearly. The rocks encase more than half of his wetsuit. A tear in the fabric exposes his chest, and blood streams from a wound. The young, slender fellow looks to be no more than twenty.

In spite of my fear, I close the gap between us and inject casualness into my voice. "There you are."

"I'm stuck." He chews his chapped lip. "I really did it this time."

I crouch beside him. "Can you move at all?"

He shakes his shaggy head. "My legs are numb. My chest really hurts." Panic spreads across his face. "The tide's coming in."

"It takes a long time for the tide to get in here. Don't worry." I want to keep him calm but know the water covers the jetty when the tide reaches full height. He needs to move up and out of harm's way well before that occurs.

The ocean washes against the rocks and retreats. I lie down on the stones and run my hand along the side of his hip. The rocks wedge him in solidly. He's not big, but he's too large for me to carry, even if I dislodge him. I slide my arm down alongside his. I tug hard, and his hand comes up with mine. He presses the arm on the stones and pushes, then collapses, unable to free himself.

I scan the shoreline for anyone taking a morning walk or jog. A few figures dot the distance.

"I'll be right back."

"Don't go." His eyes are wide with fear.

"You'll be okay. I promise not to be gone long. I have to find someone to help us."

He nods and shoots me a look that says he doesn't believe me.

"What's your name? I want to reassure him and let him know I'm not going to disappear, but he's barely listening to me. He's focused on the crashing waves.

"Your name?" I repeat.

"Leon."

I remember the time Sammy told me about Leon and his friend Mack.

"You surf here all the time, don't you?"

He nods.

"I'm Sofia. I've seen you. My friend Sammy told me about you. Where's your buddy, Mack?"

He grunts. Sorrow clouds his features. "He's no friend of mine." His face grows hard.

"Since when? You two are always out here."

"It's none of your business."

The figures on the boardwalk are growing closer. A runner moves at a fast clip towards Asbury Park. Another lopes in the opposite direction.

I point. "I'm going to see if someone has a phone."

"I'm so tired," Leon says. "I shouldn't have tried to ride the last one in. Damn, those rocks are sharp." He rests his forehead on his arm.

"Stay alert, okay? Don't fall asleep."

He nods and presses his lips together. I remain unconvinced he can do what I ask.

"I mean it. Stay awake. I'll be right back."

Leon stares into the distance. When I reach the end of the jetty, I stop myself from panicking. The water already churns several inches higher up the rocks. I jump in, and the ocean laps at my thighs as I wade to shore. The low waves roll past me, and the sea pulls at my legs. I move forward with difficulty. I estimate I have an hour or so before the tide covers the jetty and claims Leon. I put the thought of not saving him out of my mind.

By the time I reach the shoreline, a half dozen morning joggers and walkers appear on the boardwalk from both directions. Flailing my arms to attract their attention does no good. Jogger after jogger stays on course and stares straight ahead. I race to the boardwalk. The runners pass by without a glance sideways; the heads of the walkers bob to music. I yell, but the wind carries my voice back to me. I keep running and flapping my arms. A female jogger shades her eyes, pumps a fist, and keeps moving.

I shout for help. I call out again, frustrated and unsure how far my voice reaches in the stiff morning breeze. My legs grow heavy, and I force myself to keep trudging through the sand. My teeth chatter from the chill of my soaked clothes. The jetty's stones block my view of Leon; I'm worried he might slip below the water.

"Help. I need help."

A couple stops running and lifts hands to their brows. The woman raises an arm and waves.

I push myself and run harder. "Call 911. Hurry. Call 911." My legs pump violently, and my feet throw sand in all directions. I move my arms madly, trying to keep the couple from leaving. Sweat drips into my eyes and from my nose. Running in the sand with my wet, sand-laden sneakers makes my calves ache. I keep going in spite of my exhaustion.

The couple clambers down the steps towards me. When they're within a few yards, I point at the jetty. "There's an injured surfer out on the rocks."

"I'll call it in, Carlos," the woman says. She takes out her cell phone and presses buttons.

Carlos scans the water and the jetty. The couple is perhaps in their late thirties. They look fit and happy and very much in tune with one another.

Carlos says, "I don't see anyone."

"He's stuck in the jetty up to his chest. He's hurt. You can't see him from here." I turn towards the ocean and gasp. "The water's rising fast. We have to do something or he'll drown."

"Mer, did you get through?" Carlos asks.

She nods. "An ambulance is on the way, and the fire department. They're not far from here."

"I'm going back." I made a promise to Leon and I intend to keep it.

"I'll come too," Carlos says.

"Me too," Mer says.

We run towards the jetty. The wail of approaching emergency vehicles dispels the remainder of the morning quiet. The sound fails to calm me, and my pulse races riotously. A throng begins to gather on the boardwalk.

I mentally tick off what needs to happen for a successful

rescue of Leon. The EMT's have to park, have to get to the jetty, have to work quickly. They require time and almost none remains.

The realization this could result in another board-in sends a sour substance up from my gut.

"The tide…" My words catch in my throat.

We reach the shore and discover the jetty beneath a few more inches of water.

"Leon," I call. "They're coming to get you. It's going to be okay."

No answer comes back to me.

What if he slipped down into the water?

"Be careful, Carlos," Mer says. "There might be a rip current today." She points to the swirl of the water.

"We should be okay this close to shore," I say. "I was out in it and it's not that bad."

Carlos and I simultaneously step into the ocean and battle our way to the jetty. The rolling surf carries us forwards and pulls us back. The waves close to shore are larger now, and I dive under first one breaker and a second larger one. I gulp for air. Carlos follows behind me. He swims with strength and assurance, and I'm glad for the company. I'm also happy to find no cold current pulling me out to sea. After a slow slog we make it to the jetty.

"Leon, we're on our way. Hang on," I call.

Emergency personnel dot the boardwalk. Mer is waving and running towards them. The rising water buoys me up onto the flat rocks at the top of the jetty, and I scramble to safety. Carlos loses his footing on a slippery boulder. I turn and offer him a hand.

"Come this way. It's a little easier over here."

He maneuvers sideways and grabs my arm. Within a few seconds he stands beside me, barely winded.

"Leon. We're on the jetty. The rescue team's coming now." I wait. "Leon, are you there?" I pick my way along the stones, searching for a sign of him. "Leon!" I shout.

An arm waves.

Thank goodness.

"I see you. We're coming."

"Geez," Carlos says. "He's pretty far out." Wrinkles form on his brow. "Almost to the end."

We both know that the waves of the incoming tide cover that section first. Soon the water lapping at the rocks will overtake them.

"Maybe the two of us together can figure out a way to help him till the medics get here." I move tentatively towards Leon.

When I drop to my knees beside him, Leon smiles weakly. "Hey," he croaks. "I thought you'd never get back."

"What, and miss the event of the year?" I nod at my companion. "This is Carlos. He's going to help get you out."

Carlos shifts from foot to foot. "Dude, you doing okay?"

The saltwater has taken a toll, and Leon appears paler than I remember. He licks cracked and dried lips.

"Still here," he says with a wan smile.

Carlos kneels. I didn't realize how large Carlos is until he crouches beside the slight-framed Leon. Carlos possesses the broad chest and thick arms of a weight lifter. He reminds me of my Uncle Mickey and my encounter with the icy winter water. Anxiety winds through my gut, and the annoying cackle rises up from the depths of my brain, and burrows deep in my ears.

I force myself to stay in the moment and show Carlos the blood on Leon's chest.

"Are you in pain?" Carlos asks.

"Not too bad."

Carlos frowns. "I saw something like this once years ago when I was training to be a lifeguard in Belmar." He straddles Leon. "I'm going to put my arms under you and try to lift you out."

Carlos instructs me, "As he comes up grab him around the waist, and we'll see if we can free him without jarring him too much."

"Should we wait for the medics?" I doubt my strength and fear hurting Leon.

Carlos shakes his head. "I'd rather not pull him out, but there isn't much time. We have to work quickly so he's ready to be brought onto the shore. We'll let them take over once they get here."

Carlos squats and slips his muscled arms around Leon. "I'll

count to three and then lift."

A wave crashes over the point of the jetty, throwing a wall of blinding spray over us. I wipe my face and kneel behind Leon on the small shelf of rock that already holds puddles of water.

Carlos calls out, "One…two…three."

He groans, tugging at the dead weight of Leon's body.

"It's working," I say. "He moved up a little."

Carlos stands. Distress appears on his face, and he holds his hand to the small of his back. "One more time," he says.

He circles Leon with his arms again and pulls hard. Leon's torso rises a few more inches out of the rocks.

"Wow, dude. Awesome." Leon closes his eyes for a second in obvious discomfort.

Carlos hunches over and places his hands on his knees. "Damn back."

I shout and wave at the medics assembling on the shoreline. "Over here. Hurry."

Three men wade into the water with their gear over their heads. Three others load supplies into a lifeboat and push it into the water.

Leon's second arm is free now, and he raises both to the sky. Carlos grips him in a bear hug, and I encircle Leon's waist as best I can. With one more mighty tug Carlos and I pull Leon up and lay him down.

A wave crashes on the jetty and soaks all three of us. We come up for air, and Leon's eyes grow wide with concern. He grips my arm tightly.

"They're coming," I say. "It's going to be all right."

"I can't move my legs."

I need to distract him—and myself. "Tell me what happened to you and Mack."

"Why?"

"Please, tell me. I want to hear."

He blinks. "It was a big misunderstanding. That's all."

I squeeze his hand. "Whatever it is, I bet you can fix it when you get out of here. Come on. Tell me what happened."

"He'll never forgive me. The dude is so pissed."

"Why?"

"He stole my girlfriend."

"He stole your girlfriend and he's pissed at you? Shouldn't you be the one who's pissed at him?"

Carlos lets out a laugh. "Gotta admit there's logic in her reasoning, dude."

Leon says, "I've had a thing for Jasmin for over a year. Mack knew how much I liked her. When I finally got up the nerve to ask her to hang out she said no. It turns out she likes Mack."

"That sucks," Carlos says.

"I punched him in the face when he told me she called him. He wanted to take her out."

"Oh, dude, you didn't."

"Yeah, I did. Knocked out his front tooth. He's been my best friend since we were five." His bottom lip trembles.

I say, "You need to call him and apologize."

"I'm an idiot. I miss him."

"I'm sure he misses you, too. The first thing you do when you're out of here is call him, okay?"

He hesitates. "If I don't get out of this, could you do me a favor? Call Mack and tell him I'm sorry."

"I won't have to call him. You're going to tell him yourself."

The rescue team fights their way through the rough waves. The large breakers force the men back more than once. Soon three EMT's kneel beside Leon. One of them bumps fists with him, and Leon's face lights up.

"Yo, Andy, what took you so long?" Leon asks. "Were you surfing down in Point Pleasant or something?"

Andy's slender fingers wrap around Leon's wrist. He's rangy, but muscular, and he shoots Leon a comforting gaze. "I came as soon as I got the call. What did you hit, bro? Is your head okay?"

"Head's fine. I never hit it. I slammed into some rocks." He points. "The ones over there are right under the surface on medium tide. I could see the darn boulders coming at me, but couldn't avoid them. The second wave washed me right into the jetty. My legs aren't working, man."

A medic wiggles one of Leon's toes. "Feel anything?"

Leon smiles. "Yeah."

Andy says, "You'll be okay. You probably got a little numb

being stuck in that cold and cramped spot for such a long time. But we want to get that head checked out."

The EMTs and firefighters stabilize Leon's neck and make plans to move him safely to shore. They strap him to a board and climb down into the water. A strong surge near the jetty makes them unsteady for a few moments but they maintain their movement. Carlos and I follow close behind.

More firefighters and an ambulance crew wait on the boardwalk. A crowd of surfers gathers on the sand. When the stretcher comes out of the water and passes them, the surfers clap. One shouts out, "You're doing great, dude." Another, "The worst is behind you, man." Soon everyone on the boardwalk and sand claps in unison. They cheer for Leon and for the medical personnel.

The medics talk to Leon in a soothing tone.

"Can't take a deep breath, man," he says.

"Might be a rib," Andy says.

The damage to Leon's body becomes clear. The gash in his chest trickles blood. A medic touches his knee and he winces. But beyond that he appears intact.

"We're out of here," a medic says. He signals the ambulance to begin the loading process.

Carlos pumps my hand. "He's really lucky. He owes his life to you."

I shake my head. "He owes it to you and to all the medics who got here so quickly."

Mer slips into Carlos' arms and gives him a hug. "You were amazing." She smiles at me. "You too. And in the nick of time." She points at the water. "The tide's covered the jetty completely."

"Damn," Carlos says. "That was close."

My limbs grow stiff, and fatigue sets in. I want to collapse in a warm, dry place. They finish loading Leon into the ambulance, and I wave at the couple telling them, "I'm going home."

"Sounds like a wonderful idea," Carlos says.

I reach my front door and glance over at Sammy's house. His car isn't in the driveway, and the place looks deserted. It bothers me that he isn't around to hear what I've gone through. I'm aware I'm thinking about him frequently and that he's becoming a touchstone for the events of my life.

My eyes well. Saving Leon brings my failure to save Ben into gut-wrenching focus. A needle of clarity pricks me painfully. I want to tell Sammy about Leon, but I also want to tell him about Ben and more importantly I need to tell him about Ben to stop the past from holding back my future.

I move inside, shower, and change into dry clothes. To quiet the unnerving ideas that plague me, I bake three dozen scones. After the timer for the last batch goes off, I carry the tray outside to cool on the back porch. A sound nearby causes me to look over to Sammy's yard. A boy I estimate to be eight or nine years old races around in circles. Killer yaps and nips at his heels. I smile. Ben used to run around the same way, burning off excess energy. The familiar ache sets in, and I force it through me. I wait for the discomfort to pass.

June comes out into the yard.

"Hey, pumpkin, want a cupcake?"

Her legs drape over the back steps.

The boy says, "Don't call me that."

"Come give me a big hug."

The child frowns and places his arms around her neck. Want courses through me. June brings her hand from behind her back and presents the boy his treat. She plants a kiss on the top of his head and ruffles his sandy hair. A reluctant smile spreads over his face. My hurt grows deeper, but I stay riveted on the scene. June rises, and she and the boy walk into the yard. He bites into the top of the cupcake and licks at the frosting mustache that appears on his lip.

"Vanilla," June says. "Your favorite. And vanilla cake too."

June beams at him. She holds his hand, and they saunter to the rear of the yard. June names the flowers growing along the fence.

I slink back into the shadows of the porch, wanting to avoid disrupting the peaceful family yet unable to leave the scene. Sammy never mentioned that June had a son, or he had a nephew. Ben's face surfaces, and I cut off the horror that rises up and threatens to overwhelm me.

A phone rings inside Sammy's house.

"Let's see who gets there first," June says. The boy runs to the stairs, and Killer and June follow close behind. What lies beneath the tranquil Flaherty waters?

CHAPTER THIRTY-THREE

Independence Day

THE AGONIZING MEMORIES OF BEN brought on by rescuing Leon and seeing the boy in Sammy's yard refuse to leave even after my baking frenzy. I don't want to be alone. I need company, and the light pouring from the Cornells residence beckons.

I knock on the front entrance. After a few seconds I rap again, harder. The Cornells' wooden door differs markedly from the usual faded, oak specimen or modern, steel replacement of most of the homes on the block. I run my gaze over the honey-colored portal and lean in for a closer look at the surface.

Fine marks lay etched into the wood in an intricate and lyrical pattern. Diagonal lines rise from the bottom corner and shoot out across the entire surface. I balance my scones on one hip and reach out to touch the grooves. The door swings open.

Walt Cornell stares at me. "Can I help you?"

"I brought you something." I extend a decorative platter holding a dozen scones. "I baked these a little while ago. I thought you and Ellie might enjoy having some." Walt bends and sniffs. "They smell really good." His brow knits in thought.

"Ellie's not here. I don't think she'd mind if I took them."

I hand the dish to Walt and offer a small shopping bag. "Here's a pot of jam and a small jar of honey. You can see which you like better. They're actually even good without anything."

"This is really nice of you. Ellie loves sweets."

"Then these should make her happy." I smile. "I was admiring your door. It's really unusual. Did you carve the wood?"

He hesitates and nods. "Part of it. Ellie did most of the work."

"It makes me want to think about roads I've traveled and others I've passed by."

My comment strikes a sympathetic cord. Walt grins and throws the door wide, motioning me to come in. He lifts the scones to his nose and inhales deeply. "They really do smell wonderful."

When I step over the threshold, I gasp with delight. Sculptures and decorated objects line the crowded hallway. A silver vase filled with crystal flowers reaches as high as my shoulders and glints in the diffuse light of the hall. Above it, a pale green mobile made of fabric triangles and wire tinkles, stirred by the breeze let in by the open door. I stand sideways to navigate the cluttered space and move past a similarly stuffed living room.

"Are you a collector? You've got so many gorgeous things in here." The vast array of attractive and unusual items shatters my expectations. With all the piles of junk outside, I assumed the home harbored a similarly messy interior. Instead of castoff items, countless fascinating sculptures and pieces of art captivate me and make me want to stop to examine them. An urge to reach out and run my fingers over the fluid wood of two carved statues takes hold, but I keep my hands in my pockets, afraid I might upset Walt.

"I guess you could say we're collectors. Reluctant collectors. I'd like to get rid of a lot of this stuff." Walt leads me through a hallway into a den filled with art objects that differ from the ones in the living room and hall. He places the tray of scones on an end table.

"These are Ellie's special creations. They're a lot better made than the others you saw on the way in."

"She's an artist? The detail and variety is phenomenal."

"She never stops. The woman barely sleeps. I go out and find things for her and the next thing I know she's built it into something."

"She's so talented. I expect some of the pieces to move they're so lifelike." I take in a statue of a tall, thin girl with arms raised skyward. Constructed of small pieces of metal and wood, the statue shines in the sun. I recognize the metal. The girl's legs and torso consist of old pop-tops and pieces of cut-up aluminum cans. I remember using Walt's metal detector and him pocketing the pop tops on the beach.

Walt cocks his head. "The man who lives next to you, Sammy, he once told us he could sell a lot of her creations. He claims a market exists for her type of work."

"He told you about selling her work?"

Walt whispers, "I like Sammy, but Ellie doesn't trust him. She barely trusts me anymore." He hooks his thumb over his belt, the only thing holding up his baggy white painter pants. Concern crosses his face. "I'm so worried about what she's up to some nights I hardly sleep."

"Where is she now?"

"Out searching for things. Sometimes she doesn't like what I bring her, or she needs a special piece. I hate when she goes out picking and poking. That's what she calls it." He eyeballs an antique clock on the wall. "She'll be back in a few minutes. She promised she would."

I spy a small metal and wood statue of a fish in full leap with a shimmering ocean at its base. Desire overcomes me, and I let my hand run over the lifelike form. I shiver, charged with energy.

"There's so much momentum and power in her pieces. Touching this one makes me feel great." I step back. "I'm sorry. I couldn't resist. I should keep my hands to myself." I shove them in my pockets.

"It's not a problem. They're meant to be touched. That's what Ellie says. I don't know how she captures the vitality and life. Sometimes I think they're watching me. It can get a little creepy when you're alone here."

"Maybe I could talk to her about Sammy? I've seen his store

and it couldn't hurt for her to meet with him."

Walt emphatically shakes his head. "No, no, no. Ellie takes a long time to trust anyone and even longer to trust them with her work." He angles his face towards me. "Don't take this the wrong way, but if you speak to her about selling her pieces she'll go into hiding. I might not see her for a couple of days. She'll lock herself in her room or worse yet go live under the boardwalk with the cats that stay there. She's disappeared like that a couple of times."

Ellie's antisocial behavior triggers alarm bells. "That sounds a little dangerous."

Walt chuckles. "She thinks she's hiding but between us, I've developed ways of checking on her."

"I'll keep quiet about her seeing Sammy. But I can tell her how much I like her stuff, can't I?"

"Let's see how she is when she comes in." He studies me with an intense gaze. "She's interested in you. She told me she wanted to make a mold of your head. She likes the shape of it."

I let out a laugh.

"Even if she does like you, it'd be quite a task to get her to talk to Sammy about anything as long as little Billy shows up in his yard. That does tend to disturb her."

After a few seconds I figure out what Walt means.

"You mean the boy I saw in Sammy's yard? He's adorable. Why does he upset her?"

Walt runs his hand over his face. "She lost a twin brother when she was young. That little fella reminds her of him, though lately I've caught her watching Billy and not running for the hills. I wish we'd been able to have one of our own. It might have helped her some."

"I'm sorry."

"That Billy, he's a perfect clone of his dad. They should have called him Sam, Jr. instead of Billy."

My jaw drops. I struggle to find words.

Walt considers me quizzically. "You okay? Want to sit down?"

"I'm fine. Absolutely fine."

He shifts from one foot to the other. "Ellie says I'm terrible about knowing what to say and what not to say. Conversation isn't easy."

"Sometimes silence is quite nice."

He smiles.

"Does the boy visit there often?" All this time and Sammy never mentioned him to me.

"It's hard to say. When they're out in the yard or on the beach together I can see they're both happy. I guess the divorce was what they needed and now everyone seems content." He shakes his head. "I better not say any more."

Divorced. What a way to find out. I smile and hold my tongue, though I want to probe him about Sammy's situation.

Questions fill my head. How long a marriage? How much time passed since the divorce and why hasn't he told me about it? I realize that I've moved from worrying about him being too young, to worrying about trusting him to be honest in a relationship. Most importantly, this means I think there's a budding relationship, and I care about his answers to all the questions that occupy my thoughts. I want things to be right between us. I also don't see how that's possible.

Feet stomp up the front stairs and the door bangs open. "There she is. Right on time."

Walt proceeds to the front door, and I tag along. Ellie Cornell's rear enters first, her back bent over from the waist. She huffs and puffs, tugging hard at a large object. Walt hastens to her.

"Geez, Ellie, let me help you. How many times have I told you not to go trying to drag heavy stuff up the stairs by yourself?"

Ellie ignores him. She gives one last yank and pulls a large piece of driftwood through the doorway. "I thought our old wagon would collapse before I got this one home."

She gasps for air and leans over. A beat-up Radio Flyer wagon leans against the bottom step.

"You need something sturdier to carry stuff this big. I swear I'm going to toss that piece- of-junk wagon one of these days. That'd stop you collecting stuff for sure." Walt pushes the wood into the hall and drags it towards the kitchen.

Ellie slips out of her tattered hunting jacket. She falls into a chair in the living room and closes her eyes. I join her there. All color drains from her face. She calls, "You forget how strong I am. I'll carry the stuff home in my arms if I have to." She raises a wiry arm and makes a fist.

"There's no more room," Walt shouts.

I say, "Can I get you a drink of water."

Ellie's eyes pop open. She shoots me a who-the-heck-are-you-and-what-are-you-doing-in-my-house glare.

Walt enters the living room and says, "Sofia dropped by from next door. She brought us some scones. They're in your den."

Ellie sends me a wary gaze and turns to Walt. "This wood reminded me of the piece you were working on last summer."

The grooves in Walt's brow grow deeper.

"I figured you might want to try your hand with it again."

"I don't know, Ellie. I thought the carving was going great but it wasn't. I'm not sure I can face something so complex after that last time."

"Sure you can." She points at the living room pieces. "You've done all these. This is one more in the chain. I'd like to hear you banging away again."

So Walt, not Ellie, created the pieces in the living room. His craft differs from hers, but the exquisite pieces still clamor for attention.

Walt digs his hands in his pockets and stares at his feet.

"Walter Cornell, I know that stance." Ellie glares at him. "You are one stubborn old fool."

I clear my throat. "You're both incredibly talented. Have you considered doing an exhibition?" I regret the question immediately.

Walt scowls at his wife. "She's a nice woman, Ellie. She means well."

"Oh, does she?" Ellie whips her head towards me. "What would you know about art?"

The venom in her tone takes me aback. "I'm not an expert. But I know what I like."

"Then maybe you should keep your opinions to yourself."

"Ellie," Walt says.

She turns to him. "You're an old fool. Getting us mixed up with the neighbors. Will you ever learn?"

She rises from the chair and stomps off to the back of the

house. A door slams.

"I didn't mean to upset her," I say. "I do think you both have a lot of talent."

Walt holds up his hand. "She's tired. She'll be fine once I fix her a meal. And after she has one of those scones." He grins.

"I wanted to ask you something."

He studies me. "Ask."

I clear my throat. "I saw Ellie at the doctor the other day, and I was wondering how she's doing. Not ill, I hope."

Walt laughs. "Ellie's fit as can be. Me too. Did you see her lugging in that huge piece of driftwood?" He rubs the small of his back. "I'll be hurting tomorrow, but Ellie will be ready to take a five mile walk."

I wonder if he speaks the truth. Was he covering for her? Or perhaps they value their privacy. "Was she there for a checkup?"

He leans back against a console and lets out air slowly. "She probably won't want me telling you this, but Doc Sargent is one of the few people Ellie thinks understands what she's doing. She sold him another one of her creations."

"She's okay with selling?"

"Not really." He frowns. "It's only lately she's been willing to let go of any of her work." He's clearly reluctant to tell me any of this.

"That sounds like a good thing," I say.

"We've got so many bills I don't know if we'll be able to stay here." Walt runs his fingers over a statue of a young woman. "I'm not sure how much longer we can keep the tax man away."

"All you have to do is to sell a few of her pieces, or yours, and I bet you'd be fine."

"She's funny about who she allows to buy them."

"What about yours?"

He chuckles. "I do what I do to keep me from bothering Ellie. I needed to fill my days after I retired from the Bait and Tackle shop."

"I think there's a market. I've seen things similar, things that aren't as finely done, at craft fairs."

Ellie calls out, "Walt. Would you bring me my chisel?"

Walt smiles. "She's already working. I wish I had her stamina."

He addresses the rear of the house. "Coming, my sweet."

"Don't you call me that, especially if the neighbor is here. You'll give her the wrong idea. She does have a fine head, though."

He chuckles, clearly having fun.

"I'd better get going," I say.

Walt accompanies me to the door. He bends and retrieves a chisel from an umbrella stand in the shape of an elephant. "She leaves them here so they don't get lost."

Something odd about the elephant makes me focus on the surface. Small slips of paper lay one over another. I recognize the rectangular strips. Amy's wishes are lacquered over the entire exterior. The covering of words gleams.

Walt notices me staring. "I liked your pieces of paper in the boardwalk. I picked up a lot of them. They make me think. And Ellie uses them, as you can see."

"I'll tell Amy. It's her project. I help out when I can. I bet she'll approve of what you're doing with them."

He strokes the surface of the elephant stand.

I continue, "I want to say thanks for helping me out that night when I went for that swim. I'm glad you were on the beach."

"I didn't do anything. You got back in on your own." He rubs his cheek. "I was with Ellie and her brother the night he died. He left us and went out swimming alone. We were kids."

"I'm so sorry."

"Tragedies like that change things. Life loses some luster."

"You're right." I chew at my cheek to stop my chin trembling.

I step out into the sun. The wooden door sparkles, reminding me of an Italian church I stumbled upon in a tiny town far off the regular tourist path. Walt closes the door behind me, and I head home.

I shudder as Jerome's scarlet prick-mobile pulls into my driveway. The music that blares from his radio makes me want to throw something.

Springsteen? How dare he play Springsteen. He always shuts off my music with a disdainful sneer when I choose The Boss.

I recognize the song.

"Independence Day." *Geez.* The bastard.

The lyrics are all about leaving town and saying goodbye. I draw myself up to full height to ready for an attack. The song also tells of being beyond anyone's touch. That part gives me strength, and I dig deep inside to locate the place where peace lives.

Try to touch me. Bring it on, Jerome.

CHAPTER THIRTY-FOUR

Growin' Up

"YOU WANT ME TO DO what?"

I try to make sense of Jerome's words.

"You heard me."

Jerome's on my porch, opening and closing black trash bags. "Is this all of my stuff?"

"It's what I saved for the Vietnam Veterans truck."

"That sucks, Sof."

"They'll pick up in a couple of weeks, and I don't even have to be here. I also refused two deliveries of yours yesterday."

Jerome shakes his head. "I'm serious. I want you to redecorate our old place. It's what you and your buddy do, isn't it?"

My thoughts swim. "I'm not sure I'm at all savvy about love-nest décor."

"Amy has a great sense of style. I know you'll do a good job."

"Why would I ever agree to remodeling our home?"

"Why wouldn't you? It's work, Sof. You and your partner should be happy for the offer. Last I saw business was slow." He hoists two bags onto his shoulder and grabs the third. "We don't need to go to court. Do this job, and I'll pay you enough to take care of anything you need."

I despise his knowledge of my finances. While I possess enough money to live modestly for a time, I know any type of major expense or setback has the potential to wipe me out. Adding to my fears, the divorce lawyer told me to expect a long court battle since Jerome has the means to keep things from being settled for quite some time.

I tick off some of my bills. Rent comes due each month. My almost five-year-old car sounds in need of a tune-up. Car insurance and renters insurance hang over me.

Insurance. What about health insurance? Jerome's policy covers me now. After the divorce I need to purchase my own. Amy says insurance costs lots. Depending on the last of my test results, which I've avoided getting, even more medical bills may loom in the future.

I clench my jaw and swallow the bitterness that rises in my throat. "What exactly do you have in mind?"

"A complete redo, top to bottom. It's needed it for a long time, don't you think?"

I wince. "That's ridiculous."

I treasured filling our home with items of significance. For the first few years of our marriage each time we took a vacation, I brought back a memento that served a dual purpose. The object reminded me not only of the wonderful time we enjoyed on the trip but also added a unique flavor to our surroundings. The pastel poster of the rooftops in Bermuda acquired on our first anniversary and the series of photos of Cape Cod I snapped one summer come to mind. Those line the family room. An embroidered tablecloth from a tag sale in Pennsylvania Dutch country covers the dining room table.

Since Ben died, nothing new came into the home.

I bristle. How sad to toss it all out so easily.

I square my shoulders and face him. "I got the package of divorce papers."

"You're the one who was adamant we should be divorced. We can delay." He pauses. "But I've made some decisions. I'm going to move on. And I'm letting you move on too." He temples his fingers. "I've changed, Sof."

"You haven't changed, Jerome. When Ben died you were furious. You still have a lot of anger. Kicking dogs is unforgivable. You were going to hit me."

"I didn't." He shakes his head. "You've been a total drip since we lost Ben. What did you expect me to do?"

My irritation turns to sorrow. "I tried, Jerome. My heart wasn't in it but I tried to care about you. I made the effort to rise above what I was feeling."

"What about how I was feeling?"

"You took up with other women. That's horrible. You left in every way possible. Just because you're angry doesn't mean you get to trample everything in your path."

He rolls his eyes, and casts an impatient look my way. "How about your choices? You left me too, in more ways than I can count. Are we going to rehash and fight over everything?"

His accusations shake me. The fortress I've built of his one-sided responsibility is collapsing. A part of me reluctantly is coming to understand the share I've played in the demise of my marriage.

He runs his fingers through his hair. The style flatters him. Soft waves fall over his left eye. Mandy must have taken him to a new place. His hair never looked so well-kept. "Listen, babe." He catches himself. I used to joke he called me babe because that way he could never forget my real name.

"I don't want to argue about"—he waves his hands—"stuff."

I clench and unclench my hands. "I think it's an awful shame what's happened between us. But it's happened and maybe it's happened for a reason."

"How Zen of you." He lets out a long sigh. "Whatever you want or need, I'm prepared to give you. I know you don't believe me, but I'm hoping you'll understand eventually I mean it."

My anger gets the better of me. "You're asking me to redo our home. You're going to live there with her. You've never grown up, Jerome. It's all about your immediate gratification, isn't it? You truly are a prick."

"That's been established. Old news." Ire glimmers in his eyes. "You don't want to live there. It's a goddamn morgue. Has been for years."

I glance over at his car. "The duct tape on the hood is quite attractive."

"I'll get around to fixing it."

He shifts the bags on his shoulder. "My offer stands. You and Amy have carte blanche to fix up the house. Do whatever you want to do with it. The only requirement I have is it be done modern. I don't want to recognize the place."

"The opposite of what it is now." I shake my head.

"Mandy likes clean lines. I told her we could make it anything she wanted. We'll travel or stay at her place till it's done."

I purse my lips. "This will cost you. A lot."

"You'll do it then." He smirks. "The best is always worth whatever it costs."

"I'll speak to Amy." He's pushing too many buttons for me not to react. "Why do you think it took us so long? We've been on the skids for ages."

"It was easier than rocking the boat."

"In our bed, Jerome, on Ben's birthday? I'd say that capsized it."

"It seemed like a good idea at the time." He shrugs and checks his watch. He looks up, his face contorted with rage. "You still blame me, don't you?"

"Is that what you think?" I square my shoulders. "I blame myself."

He shakes his head. "It wasn't your fault. It wasn't mine. It happened."

"I could have prevented it."

"We've gone over this hundreds of times. I thought you'd come to accept you weren't to blame."

"I could've kept him home. It was cold that morning and he had a runny nose."

He drops the bags at his feet. "Sof, he was waiting for the bus. You went back to get his gloves."

"I saw the plow, Jerome. I should've figured it might hit him. If I'd stayed or kept him home that morning it wouldn't have happened."

"The plow might have killed you too." Jerome taps a foot on the porch. "No matter what I say or do you're never going to forgive yourself, are you?"

"Can you forgive yourself?"

He grows still, and his eyes well. "No, I can't. I'm sorry for so many things. Sorry we never were able to have another child; sorry I couldn't be there the way you needed." He pauses. "But the fact is I can't do anything except look back when I'm with you. It's agony."

I collapse inside.

"I'm sorry too."

The emptiness hurts. There's nothing but the past between us. Our transformation into intimate strangers is complete.

An uncomfortable silence takes hold.

A loud crash followed by a lengthy howl startles us.

Jerome says, "What was that?"

More cries come from the rear of the house.

"Phoebe," I say. "She sounds hurt." I race to the kitchen, and Jerome follows.

We find Phoebe on the floor, lying on her side and licking her front paw. Bloody paw prints cover the table and chair.

"What'd you do?" I ask her.

Jerome lifts a broken jar. "I didn't know dogs liked honey."

"She likes anything."

I kneel next to Phoebe who guards her oozing limb. "She's cut."

"She's going to be afraid to let you come near her. I can distract her."

"How do you propose to do that?"

He withdraws a beef jerky from his pocket and unwraps it. Three sticks of beef jerky later, Phoebe allows me to inspect the wound and apply an antibiotic cream.

"It's not deep," I say. "Surface only." I wrap gauze dressing around her paw. "She'll tear off the bandage in all likelihood, but at least it'll be covered for a little while." I pat Phoebe's back. "I can take you to the vet and get a cone if it isn't healing."

"And you thought that beef jerky was an object to be scorned." He ruffles Phoebe's head. She pulls away with what I think is a sullen glare.

"Out, Jerome. Now."

Jerome leaves and trots down the steps. He loads up his bags, yells into his cell phone, and hops into his car.

I close the door and rest against it. I need to tell Amy about the visit and the work ahead. What a messy turn of events. I appease myself with the thought that it's a job. The payment should keep us going for the next year if we structure everything correctly.

Make it modern.

My stomach churns. I sigh and move into the kitchen. I bake three dozen more scones. Some for Terri and some for the food pantry.

When I finish, I retreat to the backyard. I concentrate on the flowers and the bushes that run along the fence and force myself to see each one. Doc Phelps would be proud. I count the blossoms on a late blooming rose bush and bend to sniff the fragrance.

Springsteen's song "Growin' Up" plays in my head. Still growing up at almost the age of 50.

I stand and notice Sammy in his yard.

CHAPTER THIRTY-FIVE

A Good Man is Hard to Find

SAMMY STUDIES ME INTENTLY, AND I return the gaze. He makes his way down his back steps and crosses over to my yard. His strained features set my already raw nerves further on edge.

I ball my fingers into fists. "What's going on, Sammy?"

"I'm not having the best day. And from the look on your face it's not about to get any better, is it?"

"You haven't been honest with me." He doesn't meet my eyes, and my intestines wind tighter. My temples throb.

"What about you? How honest have you been? You haven't told me half of what's going on with you."

"Attacking me isn't the answer."

"Neither is attacking me." His tone softens. "You have dreams, don't you, Sofia?"

"Of course." I face him and dig my heels into the ground.

"So do I." He shoves his hands into the pockets of his khakis.

I manage to recover in spite of my rage and jumbled thoughts. "You're changing the subject." I glare at him and continue. "There's no reason not to tell me what's happening in your life.

Have enough respect for me to do that." I suppose I shouldn't be coming on this strong, but Jerome has pushed me over the edge to full-throated bansheedom. Plus, I want to straighten out what, if anything, there is between us. I'm pissed off about him not telling me about his son. Hell, I'm seizing the day instead of my usual poking it gingerly with a stick.

Ripples of unease cross his face, and he holds his eyes shut for a second.

I blurt, "You have a son. I've seen him hanging out in your backyard."

"I wanted to tell you about him." His lips compress in discomfort.

"I found out about him earlier today." I shake my head. "It wasn't pleasant hearing something like that from Walt Cornell."

"I know I should've told you about Billy."

"But you didn't."

"I was afraid to mention it. I've been divorced for three years, and in all that time I rarely tell anyone about him."

"Why not?"

He tugs at his earlobe. "I haven't wanted to let anyone into my life. I don't want to hurt Billy, so I keep him out of things as much as I can. I swore I'd stay uninvolved."

I analyze what his explanation means. My face grows hot. "How am I supposed to feel about you wanting to stay uninvolved? You haven't been acting like you want to keep me at a distance."

"I should've kept to myself."

"What did you want? A fling with a lonely older woman?"

"I'm not like that."

"I don't know what to think about you." I pause. "You said you had dreams. What kind of dreams?"

He whispers, "They're about you, Sofia."

A shock wave goes through me.

He continues, "Every night I dream about you."

My innards melt. I force myself to stay with the logical side of my brain and refute his statements instead of allowing my emotions to win the battle. "You talk a nice game," I say to fill the gap in conversation.

"This isn't a game."

I place my hands on my hips. "I'd like to meet Billy. Or is that too much involvement for you?"

Hurt and confusion consume his features and he looks away.

Alarm bells clang in my ears. He has no intention of letting me into his life except on the most superficial of levels. Meeting his son remains off-limits. I've gotten over our age difference and took a leap hoping we could move forward, but Sammy obviously has different ideas.

He says, "We need to discuss this later. Greta asked me to meet her and I'm already late. I have to see my son."

"So go."

"I'll come by. Later."

I turn and move to my rear door. I understand nothing about Sammy. No trust exists between us. In fact, nothing at all connects us. I move inside.

I quickly gather the remaining baked goods. For the next hour I drop off my supply of scones anonymously. Doing good allows my head to clear and composure to return.

When Sammy fails to show up, I take it in my stride. The man lies. A part of me expected this no-show behavior from a smooth talker like him. But another part of me clamors for attention; the part that believed what he said earlier and counted on hearing from him. The cackle rising up in the dark recesses of my brain grows uncomfortably loud, and I whip my hair and cover my ears.

I don my sweats and climb into bed, turning my attention to drawing plans for the interior of Jerome's house. Phoebe comes to the room and whines. I pull her up onto the covers and push her down by my feet.

I sing Springsteen's "A Good Man is Hard to Find" to her. "It's true, Pheebs. They're truly rare." How evanescent my dreams are and how entrenched in having them I am. All the wrong choices in the world can't stop me from tilting at romantic windmills.

Phoebe wiggles her rear towards me and arranges her head on the comforter. She closes her eyes.

"One time, Phoebe. Only this one time you can stay and sleep up here with me, girl." Her bandage is missing. I examine her foot and see the cut has healed over, though the spot is still tender when I touch it.

Phoebe spreads out over the entire foot of the bed and groans in pleasure. A foul smell wafts from her rear, and I cover my face with a pillow. I stop myself from gagging.

"Do that again and you and your injured paw will be out on the porch."

Phoebe yawns. She settles against my feet and I long to match the easy rhythm of her breathing, consciously syncing to her inhaling and exhaling. My yearning for something deeper and better with Sammy grows with each breath. I put the plans away and turn off the light, but it takes a long time for sleep to find me.

CHAPTER THIRTY-SIX

Worlds Apart

A FEW DAYS LATER, LEON HURRIES towards me on the boardwalk. In spite of a slight limp, his legs pound the splintered, gray surface with urgency. He displays a mad grin and carries a bunch of droopy flowers that look a lot like the ones growing in my backyard.

Seeing his approach, I turn off my music mid-stanza. The words to "Worlds Apart" linger and smart. I realize Sammy and I are worlds apart at this point and the truth hurts. His lack of openness and his ghosting cemented my feelings about his inability to be honest and trustworthy. I've lived with dishonesty long enough to know that without a foundation of reliability I don't want to try to build anything with Sammy.

Leon reaches me and thrusts the bouquet out with both hands. Phoebe sniffs at the hair on his legs, her tail wagging. She tugs on his board shorts, and he hikes them back up.

"Thanks for the flowers, Leon."

He grabs my arm and pumps it up and down. "No, no, don't thank me. I'm the one who can't thank you enough for what you did." His head bobs side to side, and every part of his face grins.

Phoebe licks at his toes.

"How are you feeling?"

"Not bad. Not bad at all. I've started physical therapy. My knee's better. I tore something in it, but it's not serious. The therapist says I'm a good healer."

"What about your ribs and that big gash?"

He thumps his chest. "Aw, I was sore for a couple of days. It wasn't a deep cut, just lots of scary blood. It's all good now."

"And Mack?"

He smiles. "He came to visit me in the hospital. Went all bible-thumper on me but that's okay. I can use all the help I can get. We're cool again."

He digs in his pocket and hands me two tickets. "We wanted you to have these. They're for the break contest at the Pony next month. Mack and I will be playing. And Greta's coming too. Sammy told me you met her."

I take the tickets.

"It's going to be a really awesome competition."

"You shouldn't have."

"Don't be silly. It'll be great to have someone else cheering for us. We might win and catch a lucky break. That'd be so cool." He scratches Phoebe on the head, and she nuzzles at his pocket. She shoves her muzzle inside and roots around. Leon chuckles.

"That tickles."

I pull Phoebe's nose from Leon's pocket.

"It's cool. I've got a granola bar in there she can have." He produces the unwrapped sticky treat. Phoebe drools on his flip-flops in anticipation.

"Give her half. She's on a diet."

Leon breaks the treat and tosses half to Phoebe who catches it with lightning quickness.

"I wish she moved so fast when we were walking." I hold up the bouquet. "Thanks again for the flowers."

A puzzled look crosses his face. He hits himself in the forehead. "Oh man, I forgot to tell you. Those are from Sammy." Leon's smile rivals that of the Cheshire Cat. "He asked me to drop them off yesterday. I kept them in my fridge."

No wonder they droop.

Leon continues, "He's a good guy. It's cool he likes you. They're from his yard." His brow furrows in concentration. "He had a family emergency and said he wanted me to be sure to let you know he'd be in touch soon. I totally got caught up in a discussion with Mack and didn't remember I had them till this morning." He studies the bouquet. "I should've put them in water, huh?"

Back in my kitchen I arrange the flowers in a vase. They sag woefully. What a sad commentary on the state of our budding relationship. But I'm pleased that Sammy at least did make this small gesture of good faith.

Phoebe and I move to the front porch. I approach my favorite rocking chair and notice an envelope sitting on the seat. The inscription scrawled in shaky penmanship reads, "Thought you would enjoy these." Beneath it are the initials "WC."

I open Walt's envelope. Two gleaming white sand dollars rest inside. They're perfect specimens. I stroke a finger over the front of one remembering the story Walt told me. The design does resemble an Easter lily. I flip it over and notice what looks like a poinsettia on the reverse. I hold it up to the light and see the holes that the legend says stand for the wounds of Christ. When I shake the shell something rattles inside. That must be the teeth Walt told me about.

I hesitate for a moment and snap the shell in half, tipping the contents into my hand. The small white pieces that land on my palm do resemble doves. I want the story to be true. But I know it's not. I examine the tiny teeth. They're beautiful in their own right.

I push the two halves of the broken shell together and place them next to the still whole dollar on the seat of the chair, not sure which one I like better. The pristine shell certainly catches anyone's eye. But the broken one reveals wonderful treasure.

I carry the shells inside and arrange them on the entry table. The flyer for the clambake that Terri gave me rests nearby on a pile of old mail. An impulse takes hold, and I go with it.

Snapping the paper I locate a pen. I hastily scrawl what I hope is a breezy "Hope you can make it. Sofia" on the bottom. I scurry to Sammy's mailbox and bury the note beneath the day's mail.

What do I have to lose?

CHAPTER THIRTY-SEVEN

My City of Ruins

"I'LL FINISH UP THE LAST of the painting, Amy. You drive back to the shore and we'll celebrate tonight." I wipe sweat from my forehead and take in the tidy area. After a full day, the dining room shines with our efforts. A black and white mural of silhouetted trees with gold leaves glimmers beneath the chair rail. The trim gleams a complementary golden hue. The room pops with energy.

Amy dusts off the seat of one of the chairs. "I love the fabrics you chose to recover those chairs. Making each one different really was inspired."

I cast my gaze upward. "Look how the chandelier you found sparkles and reflects off the table. And the glow-in-the-dark stars make the whole room stunning, especially at night. The best part is I don't recognize one bit of it anymore. That's such a relief."

"Are you sure I should go? I don't think you want to be here alone."

"I'm fine. This isn't my space anymore."

"Yeah, right. You should see the way you went pale when they took the furniture out."

"It's my allergies. All the dust."

"Uh huh."

Amy knows me too well. "Really, I'm fine. I'll meet you at The Wonder Bar for Yappy Hour. I'm helping Kate out tonight, and it'll be even more fun if you come too. We can celebrate there."

Amy prods her cheek with her index finger. "I have to get to the dry cleaners, so if I go now I'll be able pick up my clothes before we go for cocktails with the dogs." She checks her watch.

I continue polishing the dining room table. "I never could have done this without you."

"Glad to be here for you." She slips into a yellow cotton cardigan. "Call me if you need anything else. I can't believe we've done so much. Or that your ex hasn't shown his face."

"He'll be back soon. The good news is that we don't need another client for at least six months."

Amy high-fives me. She steps back, a look of concern crossing her face. "Any word from Sammy?"

"Nothing." I'm both irritated with him and worried. It's more than a week since Leon gave me the bouquet of droopy flowers and Sammy hasn't reached out or returned my calls.

"Don't write him off yet, Fi. Things can work out."

I nod, but I'm not at all sure I agree with her. We hug, and Amy leans back. "Geez, you're getting a six pack for abs." She eyes me. "You look terrific. Between running and whatever else you're doing you are smokin'."

"I'm hot for sure." I wipe at my face with a towel, and Amy laughs at the bad joke. Inwardly, I'm pleased at my progress in getting in shape and also glad for Amy's compliments.

"You sure you're going to be okay alone?"

"Never fear. The intrepid Phoebe is somewhere around here." Amy blows me a kiss and waltzes out of the room. Seconds later, the front door slams shut leaving silence in its wake.

I pull a chair up to the dining room table and take in the transformation. Sadness floods me. We spent a lifetime making a home, and now it's devoid of our past. Not one thing exists from our marital days. Amy and I have eliminated all traces of our history and soon every room of the home will fill with all new furniture and objects.

But Jerome's and my yesterdays still live in my head.

The last time he called, Jerome admonished me with, "Don't leave anything untouched. I don't want any of the furnishings, Sof. No mementos either. Rip out the cabinets and change the moldings. And do whatever you want with the crap you find other than the stuff in my dresser. Box that up and I'll deal with it."

I rescued the photo albums of Ben and a few of our first years together as a happy family. Something about tossing out that part of my life with everything else struck me as wrong. Now only unimportant items remain. Stuff to be sold off or carted away, stuff even I don't want any longer.

I sing a few bars of "My City of Ruins" and my throat closes. Standing amidst the vestiges of my home leaves me bereft. The lyrics about ruination and loss haunt me, and a dark chill wends its way up my back. I'm lost. Maybe Amy should've stayed.

I pray to find the strength I need to leave the darkness behind. Bruce howls in my head about rising up, and I dig deep attempting to shake off the snarling cold rising from my center. *Rise up. Yes. Rise up.*

Blinding outrage erupts.

I charge to my car, throwing open the trunk. A large can sits in a cardboard box. The can holds enough to get the job done. I run through the steps I must take to carry out my plan. Jerome's still sailing in the Caribbean on a chartered yacht with Mandy and he plans on returning with her in triumph to his newly outfitted home. A terrific welcome awaits him.

I carry the container into the house telling myself this is right. *Oh, so right.* I proceed up the stairs to the bedroom. I uncap the can and pour some of the contents out into a bowl, dipping a brush into the liquid. The Day-Glo paint stimulates me. I write every nasty phrase and word that occurs to me on the ceiling above the bed.

"Home wrecker, whore, bitch." I call them out and the strokes go on evenly. "Bastard, cheating prick, two-timing creep." I paint rapidly. My armpits dampen with the effort.

I finish the ceiling and enter the closet. I'm impressed at how many insults come readily to mind. I collapse in exhaustion on the bed. Phoebe enters and forces her muzzle onto my thigh, and I scratch her on the head.

"Hey, girl. It's you and me against the world now."

Phoebe lumbers over to a pile of boxes that hold the last of Jerome's things. Amy gathered them, sparing me the misery of cleaning out his dresser. Phoebe sniffs inside the carton at the top marked "Jerome's things" and pulls at an old checkered shirt.

I rise from the bed. "Leave that be. No treats in that pocket."

She tugs harder, and the box teeters. I lurch to catch it before it falls, but I lose my footing on the tarp on the floor and land on my rear. The box tumbles and spills its contents.I rise, rubbing my bottom and stoop to pick up the things that lay on the floor.

"Now look what you've done, Phoebe. I'm going to have to clean up this mess."

I reach for a wooden box I recognize as Jerome's valet and open it. Inside I spot my gift of cufflinks from our first anniversary. Beside them rests an old watch that no longer runs. The watch was my first present to him when we were dating.

The top of the box holds a photo of Jerome and Ben sleeping on the living room couch curled into one another. I remember taking the picture. Another photo of the three of us smiling on a vacation in Cape Cod is tucked into the right upper corner.

Tears fill my eyes and blur my vision. I wipe them away.

"Oh, Pheebs, do you believe it? Jerome kept these photos and things all these years." He used that valet box every morning. He stored it inside his dresser and asked that we not toss it. The knowledge that a part of him cared and still cares causes remorse to surge through me. Phoebe comes over and licks at my salty face.

"What have I done, girl?"

After a minute I blow my nose and locate a can of antique white. I carefully cover every inch of my fit of pique. When I finish, I take the photos and stuff them in my purse for safe-keeping.

At Yappy Hour, I discover myself smiling easily, happy that so much of the redecoration of my former home is done. Kate asks me to man the gate to prevent pooches from escaping.

"Glad to do it. I love seeing the dogs and owners arrive. Everyone's in such a great mood."

Amy says, "Heck, I'll help out too. You never know who might come through that door."

We take up our positions, and Phoebe sprawls beside me on the ground. Amy passes me a beer, and we clink bottles.

"To the future," Amy says.

"To the future," I agree.

For once what sits out on the horizon no longer scares me. I listen hard. No cackle fills my ears. The lovely light of the setting sun welcomes me and leaves me feeling as though I've returned from exile in a far-off lonely land.

CHAPTER THIRTY-EIGHT

Blood Brothers

"**M**Y FIRST HUSBAND HAD BAD cholesterol." Amy dunks a dumpling in soy sauce. "It might be what killed him. He refused to take Lipitor or any of the statins."

I ladle a bowl of tom yum soup, fill two more, and pass them to Terri and Amy. "The bad cholesterol is the LDL. The good is the HDL."

Terri shakes her head. "How do you know that?"

"I have a little mnemonic."

"Goddamned English major." Amy chuckles, reaching for the bowl of rice crackers on the table.

"Do you want to hear it?"

Terri nods sending her silver drop earring into a dangling frenzy.

"HDL stands for Happy Dick League."

Amy groans. "I can hardly wait for the LDL."

"LDL is Limp Dick League." I grin and take a sip of soup. "Oh, that's tasty."

Amy's golden eyes roll to the ceiling. "You're bad. That's bad."

"Bet you'll never forget which one's the good and which the bad. But the best news of all is that mine is almost in the normal range. Hallelujah."

"Oh good, something to celebrate." Terri adjusts the turned-up collar of her green seersucker shirt and reaches for her chardonnay.

"Here's to my physical and economic health. We've almost finished up Jerome's big job."

We clink our glasses and drink. The restaurant is sleepy today. A couple occupies a table across the room, and a lone fellow drinks at the bar.

Amy asks, "Did you tell Jerome how much we were charging?"

"Nope."

"He doesn't care, so why bother, huh?"

"He claims he never balances his checkbook or worries about money. We're spending a reasonable amount so we should be fine." I grin and gesture with my chopstick. "I think our guest has arrived."

Amy looks in the direction of the chopstick. "Oh, yes. There's Allan." She wiggles her fingers above her head, and Allan Vander of the Allan Vander Galleries replies with a confident tip of his Panama hat. His form-fitting, plaid, untucked shirt and tight, black jeans with matching Hubbard shoes telegraph his hipster vibe.

I say, "I recognize him from his website photo." Amy had suggested we contact him. She knows him from a few conferences she attended for art professionals."

"He's cute," Terri says. "Maybe I should start collecting art."

"He's married-married," Amy says.

Terri has no trouble switching gears. "Maybe he'd like a shore place? I bet he could afford one."

"Let's stay focused on why we're here," I say. "Him taking on the Cornells as clients would be such a help to them. You're up, Amy." I agreed to come along to the meeting for moral support and intend to make myself scarce once Amy agrees to let me return home.

In a few long strides Allan reaches our table. Amy rises and exchanges cheek pecks with him. She introduces him to me and

Terri, and he folds his lanky frame into a chair.

"Sorry, I'm late. Mad-house traffic out there." He reaches for a bowl and ladles soup into it, quickly slurping up several large spoonfuls. "I'm famished."

"Thanks for making the trip from the city."

He flashes Amy a smile. "The pictures you sent rock. Those are some of the finest found art pieces I've seen in years."

"They're even better in real life. Ellie Cornell is truly gifted." Amy doesn't mention that Ellie is barely on board with the idea. While Walt immediately agreed to a meeting with an art dealer, Ellie stormed off in anger both times she mentioned the concept. That's when Walt came up with a plan.

"The artist, Ellie, will be constructing a tower in town near the Town Hall on Main Street," Amy says.

"Excellent idea for PR purposes." Allan drains his bowl.

Amy continues, "You have her husband to thank for this. He's agreed to help with her tower as long as she meets with you. She's wanted to do a large scale public art piece for a long time. She's itching to get started."

"I assume they have the permission of the elected officials?"

"The whole town's wild about the project. The mayor, the residents, the small businesses all want this to happen." She nods at Terri. "Terri's found some vacant space to construct the first model."

Terri beams. "It's perfect. An old garage with soaring ceilings."

"So meeting with me is a roadblock she has to overcome. I can live with that. What's the tower going to be?"

Amy smiles. "A wishing and dreaming tower. I've been working on the wishing and dreaming part." Amy taps her watch. "We have to be at the Cornells in about an hour. Let's enjoy lunch."

"Terrific."

"Please don't worry if Ellie seems a little distant or angry," I say. "I'm betting she'll come around and be happy to have you take her on as a client."

The art dealer waves a hand. "I've been coddling artistic temperaments for more years than I'd like to admit. As long as she doesn't come at me with a baseball bat I'm fine." He pauses.

"And even if she does come at me with one I'll probably be fine."

The waiter brings three heaping platters of food to the table, and Allan's face lights up. I can't believe how much food he packs into his thin frame. Not much later, he scrapes the last of the Pad Thai onto his plate and devours the dish with gusto. He leans back and pats his stomach. His cell rings, and he excuses himself to take the call.

Amy taps me on the hand and nods in the direction of the entry way. An exiting Allan Vander brushes by Jerome.

Amy leans in. "Were you expecting you know who?"

Jerome's wearing a dark scowl. His crossness unleashes my anxiety. "He texted earlier that he was coming down. I told him we'd be here or I'd be home later on in the day. I'm not sure what's so urgent. Maybe Mandy still wants more pink and red in the bedroom."

Amy purses her lips, "He doesn't look happy."

Jerome spots us and charges in my direction.

He stands far too close to my chair. "You have nerve, Sofia." The heads of the lone couple swivel in the direction of Jerome's angry tone.

"Let's go outside."

"Don't tell me what to do."

Terri looks confused.

I turn to Amy. "You take Terri and Allan over to the bakery."

Amy shoots me an are-you-sure-you-want-me-to-go look.

"Go find Allan. I need to catch up with Jerome."

Terri and Amy scrape their chairs back from the table. I wait for Terri's yellow strappy sandals to exit through the door before I address Jerome.

"Are you upset about the money? I didn't take that much from the account."

He slams his hand on the table. "Don't act so innocent. What childish revenge game are you up to?"

"Jerome, you're going to have to be clearer." The couple buries their faces in their dessert menus. The fellow at the bar stares for a moment and returns to his cocktail.

"The painted words, Sof. On the ceiling, in the walk-in closet.

They glow. They really glow."

Oh, no. The closet. I forgot the closet.

"I didn't mean for you to find that."

"No, you wanted Mandy to find it." He shakes his head in disgust.

"It was a mistake. I thought I'd covered up all of them."

"There were more?"

I sink into my seat. "I was angry. You were screwing around in our house. In our bed, Jerome, on our son's birthday."

Jerome hisses, "I'm glad we're through. I don't know why I've tried keeping this going."

"You haven't tried, Jerome. The only thing you've cared about is your work."

"I did what I could." His eyes blaze.

"No you didn't. And neither did I." My stomach sinks with the admission.

The air charges with silence. He crumples a little and recovers. I fish in my bag and withdraw an envelope.

"I thought you might want to have these."

Jerome reaches inside and pulls out the two photographs I rescued. He wipes at his eyes. I blink and dab my cheeks with a napkin.

Jerome stands tall. "My lawyer will be in touch. I'll put the house on the market. I need this to be over."

My stomach twists in shock. "You're selling the house?"

"It's the best thing to do. I can't face being inside those four walls any longer. I was a fool to think I could live there."

"But you planned to move in with Mandy."

"Not any more. Let someone else live in that tomb." He stomps away and the door closes behind him. I press my hands together and rub them to loosen the cold, stiff joints. They shake violently and refuse to work the buttons on my sweater. My pulse races, and discomfort pervades my chest.

The song "Blood Brothers" plays in my head, the lyrics ripping into my gut. Like the blood brothers in the song, Jerome and I made many promises to always be there for one another. We dreamed and planned. But time wore on and the hardness of life eroded everything until we arrived here, unable to connect with one another. I'm as much to blame for our fallout as he is, and now we're both traveling alone. The dark descends, and I fall into an abyss with nothing left in my heart.

Someone shakes my shoulder.

"Fi? Are you okay?"

I look up. Amy exhibits a concerned look.

"Don't look at me that way. You're scaring me."

"Sorry 'bout Jerome. I guess it didn't go too well."

"He's selling the place."

"Oh, no. After all that work we did. Well, someone will be happy to have it." She shakes her head.

I study her. "You don't have bad news for me, do you? Allan Vander hasn't changed his mind?"

She smiles. "Not at all. Let's join them at the bakery cafe."

CHAPTER THIRTY-NINE

This Life

A FTER A CELEBRATORY GELATO, I pass up the opportunity to meet with the Cornells, pleading a headache. In truth, the drama of my encounter with Jerome drained me of the ability to show good cheer. I know this art project is in Amy's wheelhouse and she can handle the details.

I drive home and rouse Phoebe for a walk. On our return, I come upon Sammy sitting on my porch. My heart soars and then sinks. I don't understand what feelings lie beneath the troubled expression I glimpse on his face before he looks away. Dark-rims around his eyes signal his lack of sleep.

He scratches his unshaven face. "I need to talk to you about some things."

My chest constricts, and a lump rises in my throat. A number of possibilities of what he's about to reveal race through my brain, none of them positive. When men tell women they have something they want to talk about, the conversations usually don't end well.

I sit on the rocker opposite him and grip the seat. A pitcher of water from earlier in the day rests on the bamboo coffee table, and I reach for it and pour a glass. Phoebe takes up residence at my feet.

"Go on." I barely hear my voice above my thudding pulse.

Sammy leans back in his chair. "The other day, my ex overdosed on some sleeping pills. Billy found her and called 911. He ran next door and the neighbor called me. That's where I've been. With Ronnie at the hospital and at Greta's or June's with Billy."

His anguish is evident, and a small part of me selfishly relaxes. I'm relieved worry about Billy causes his discomfort, not distress due to something between us.

"She was more off than usual. I should never have left him with her."

"Kids are resilient. He can bounce back."

He studies the floorboards and then raises his eyes to meet mine. "I've never told Billy why I left his mother."

My breath hitches. "Why is that?"

"He's not ready. I don't know if he'll ever be ready." He lets air out slowly, and I can't bring myself to exhale.

"Ronnie's been on edge for the past couple of weeks. She told me she heard I was seeing someone. I can manage her fine. I've gotten her through this type of attempt before."

"This is really a difficult situation for your son."

"Ronnie hasn't been well for a long time. There were signs years ago when we were dating and I chose to ignore them." He clasps and unclasps his hands.

"You're getting her help now. You're taking care of her and making sure she gets treated." Phoebe stretches and sniffs my foot. I reach down and scratch her under the chin. Her collar tags clink gently, and she leans against me. The heft of her side on my calf helps me to focus and stay in the moment.

"Ronnie was always ill, but there's more…" He pulls at a piece of loose bamboo on the table. "I didn't leave her. She threw me out, Sofia."

I steel myself and ignore the loud cackle that crams my ears. Phoebe lumbers to her feet and plops her wet jowls on my thigh.

"Billy was a mistake. I married Ronnie out of guilt after I got her pregnant." He presses his fingers to the bridge of his nose.

"After we had him, I fell in with a bad crowd. There were a lot of drugs. Many nights I didn't make it home. I wasn't faithful. Neither was she."

I rub Phoebe behind the ears, and she closes her eyes in appreciation. She laps at my arm when I stop. I don't know what to say.

"After we divorced, Ronnie started acting strangely. She cut my head out of the pictures of us and pasted in the faces of men from magazines. She broke into my place and stole things, little things. She rearranged my stuff so I'd know she'd visited. She left things in my cabinets and drawers."

"What did you do?"

"I told myself I deserved to be treated badly, to be punished. I hated myself for leaving her and Billy. So I put up with it."

"That's a harsh punishment. Everyone makes mistakes, Sammy."

"I married her because I believed I could save her. I owed it to her to fix what I had broken—I couldn't do it."

"Being a savior isn't a sound basis for a relationship. Neither is guilt."

"I let them down."

"You took the high road. You wanted to be a hero. But that's not always possible." Phoebe tries to climb into my lap. I push her rump down and point to the floor. She grunts and plops onto my feet.

"I don't understand how I let things get so bad. I was supposed to be strong enough to take care of her and make everything turn out right."

"Stop right now."

"I care about you, Sofia. I don't want to mess up your life."

"You've got to be kidding. Have you taken notice of what's going on with me? A tornado could land here right now, and it wouldn't make my life messier than it already is. It's enough to make most people run for the hills." I pause. My chest thumps wildly. "I have important things to tell you too."

"I'm glad you're finally willing to let me know what's going on up there." He taps my forehead gently.

I lean back and blink hard. A tear makes its way down my

cheek, and I fight to force out the words. "I lost a son. He was eight when he died."

A flash of light sears the back of my eyelids, and my stomach aches. A red mist forms. I breathe the way Doc Phelps told me—in my nose and out my mouth, counting each one. I don't want to relive the last moments with Ben. I can see his tiny, white coffin clearly.

"Sofia? What's going on?"

His voice brings me back to the present.

"I have trouble talking about this. He was so young, and I feel so guilty about losing him. I spiraled down into a bad place. It took years for me to feel better. Years and lots of meds that I don't need anymore."

"You don't have to tell me the details."

I take a sip of water, focusing on the wetness. "I want to, Sammy. I need to. I'll never stop grieving. You have to know that."

He pulls me to my feet and wraps his arms around me. The protective embrace gives me strength.

"Thanks." My voice cracks, and I choke back my sobs.

Everything comes back in a rush. I spill the story of Ben's death. Sammy's eyes fill before I'm half done. It's cathartic to speak the horrors aloud to him.

The rumble of the plow, the anguished screams, and the deathly silence afterward, followed by my unstoppable cries. The pool of red surrounding Ben's limp body. The softness of his cold cheek. The silk-lined coffin, so small only two pall-bearers flanked it. The deep chill of winter, and the emptiness after the loss with the great darkness that overtook me for such a long time.

I press into his chest and draw in his scent. Being with Sammy is like being on a sandbar in the midst of a roiling ocean. The waters may surround us but together I believe we can eventually make our way to the shore.

Sammy kisses me deeply. He scoops me up in his arms and kisses me again. Hunger spreads from the tips of my toes, cascading through my center.

The sound of the ocean floats to me. Sammy's hands run over

my body, and we cling together.

"I want you," I whisper, unable to endure any further anticipation. Reaching down I cup his hardness. Burning, burning, white hot.

He takes a deep breath. "Not now. Not like this."

Empty space opens between us and we disengage. The incandescent light in my skull dims.

We laugh hysterically when we spy Phoebe with her face buried beneath her paws.

"There's someone I want you to meet," Sammy says, brushing my fingertips with his lips. "We'll pick you up tomorrow morning."

CHAPTER FORTY

Trouble River

THE NEXT DAY, I JOIN Sammy on my front porch. I shoulder my overstuffed tote. "I took an extra cover-up for Billy in case the wind picks up. And I've got my swimsuit and some sandwiches and drinks too."

Sammy says, "Maybe we'll get lucky and it'll be really warm."

We bounce down the steps and find Billy leaning against Sammy's car with his hands stuffed in his pockets. He stares out at the road, a sullen pout marring his features.

I ask Sammy, "Did you check the tide chart?"

"Low tide by the time we get there. Perfect for clamming."

Sammy's hair is slicked back and combed neatly. He hasn't shaved and the stubble results in a rakish air. I'm happy to be going out with him and Billy at last, but worry nags me. Since Ben died my contact with children has been practically nonexistent. I'm not sure what to say to Billy or how to act. Plus, Sammy called me early this morning to warn me that Billy might be in a funk. Because of Sammy's erratic business hours and evening meetings, Billy's been sleeping at June's or Greta's since his mom went into the hospital and the illness and change in routine has made him distant and morose. I know Sammy wants desperately to connect with his son.

Sammy introduces us and Billy sends me a perfunctory nod.

"Come on, Billy Boy. Time's a wastin'," Sammy says. He hops into the driver's seat.

"You can ride shotgun," I say. Billy ignores me. He opens the rear door and climbs in behind Sammy so I slip into the passenger seat.

We drive in awkward silence. Billy spends time playing his iPad, a recent gift from Sammy, or playing with a fidget spinner. I pick at my nails.

"There's our mother ship," Sammy says when we arrive at the marina. He points to a nearby dock. We hurry to the changing room and don our swimsuits. After a few minutes, we board a small rental skiff and arrange our belongings in the bow.

"There's a good spot out on Barnegat Bay that should be perfect. Finley Cove."

The name's not familiar but the landscape resonates in my memory. "I think I took a trip this way a long time ago with my grandfather."

Sammy increases the speed of the skiff, and the sound of the engine drowns out any further conversation. He lets Billy take over the outboard for a time. I can see Billy's dark mood dissolving. At Finley Cove, Sammy takes over again, slowing us down and dropping the anchor into the water.

Billy's pallor has lifted some. His cheeks glow with a slight tinge of pink, and his face is relaxed. Sammy punches him in the arm playfully. The pout recedes completely.

"Are you ready?" Sammy asks. "Shoes off." He slips out of his sandals.

Billy rolls his eyes and removes his sneakers.

I point to my toes. "No rake? We're using our feet, huh?"

"Yep. We're going old school."

I kick off my flip-flops. "Feet might not be high tech, but I remember they worked perfectly."

Sammy lowers his hand into the water and tests the temperature. "Not bad at all." He stands. "Okay kiddies, all together on the count of three."

On three we jump into the waist-high water together.

Billy yelps. "It's freezing, Dad. You lied."

I whimper and move my arms and legs rapidly.

Sammy says, "You'll get used to it in a few seconds."

After a few groans the icy shock recedes and we set to work.

I say, "My grandfather used a clam rake. It was always a lot easier for him to get a bunch of clams than it was for me and my poor feet." A pair of seagulls swoops down, ready to snap up any castoffs.

Sammy wades in the opposite direction. "They've got to be out here. Leon told me he got a bushel's worth the other day."

"Leon told you to come here?" I'm not so sure he's the kind of person who's capable of sending someone to the right spot for clams.

"I made him tell me three times where he anchored." Sammy imitates Leon's voice. "Dude, I swear you can't miss it if you line up with the old bridge."

"You sound exactly like him."

"This has to be the right spot." He points a finger.

The bridge that Sammy indicates now serves as a fishing pier. A larger and newer concrete bridge looms over the pier, sending sounds of traffic to us in intermittent waves. Crabs prize the rotting pilings of the old bridge, and several boats housing fishermen who tend lines and traps sit anchored close by the structure.

"What do we do now?" Billy asks. His sandy hair hangs over his right eye in much the same fashion Sammy's does, and his eyes gleam like emeralds in the strong sun. Walt's right. He's a perfect clone of his father. In a year or two he'll be more than one teenage girl's fantasy.

Sammy says, "We have to poke around with our feet to find a bed."

I run my toes along the soft bottom of Finley Cove and feel for the edge of a clam. The squishy muck yields nothing. The gentle sucking action of the mud is familiar and frightens me a little today. Years ago I clammed fear free. I jumped in with both feet without a thought about what might be waiting below.

Billy whines. "How long do we have to do this?"

Sammy ignores him.

I point to the shore. "Why don't we head over that way? It'll be a little easier to wade closer in."

We walk slowly side by side towards a sandy beach, sliding our feet along the bottom.

"Any luck yet, Dad?"

My foot glides over a recognizable surface, and I pause. I run my toes over the hard edge again.

"I've got one."

"Really?" Billy asks.

"Come here. You can dig it up."

Billy wades over, and I tell him to put his leg next to mine. "Follow my foot with yours."

He grins, and I feel his toes bump along my arch.

"Feel that?" His foot moves over the clam. He dips beneath the surface and comes up with not one, but two littlenecks in his hand.

"I think there're more down there." His elation is unmistakable.

Billy bends again and again into the water. A wide smile erupts on his face each time he rises from the bed. Sammy places each mollusk into a bucket tied inside an old inner tube. Soon the water around Billy fills with mud stirred up from the bottom. The three of us become splotched with sandy and murky water, and I'm aware of grains of mud in my ears and hair. At one point I wipe at my face and Billy laughs and points at me.

"It looks like war paint. Lopsided war paint."

"I wouldn't talk." I slap my hand on the water and send a spray onto his chest.

Sammy smiles. "Behave children."

Billy exchanges a glance with me and in unison the two of us send a large splash of water Sammy's way. He hangs onto the basket and laughs.

We roam the area and mine for clams for almost an hour, and my feet grow tired and nicked. I'm grateful the bucket is three-quarters full, and I wish I'd brought along a pair of socks to tread in. I hadn't wanted to appear afraid of the bottom, but now the cuts on my feet sting.

Sammy fishes seaweed from the water and covers the clams

to keep them moist. A few moments later he declares we have more than enough for a feast, and we swim back to the skiff.

Fatigued and sun-burned, I pull myself into the boat. I dry in the sun, and my skin grows taut from the fine crust of salt left by the sea. I hand out sandwiches, and we eat them with gusto.

Billy begins to sniffle. I dig for a tissue in the pocket of my sweatshirt and pass it to him. He blows his nose loudly and hiccups. I put my hand over Billy's, uncomfortable in the role of comforter.

Billy watches the waves. "Mom used to tell me she would take me clamming." His jaw trembles. "She never did."

Distress passes over Sammy's face. He leans over and fiddles with the small outboard. Drops of seawater glisten on his tanned back.

I fill in the silence. "Your mom will be better soon and maybe you can bring her here. My grandfather always told me the saltwater heals everything. I think it might help her."

More tears erupt. "It's not right she left me. She didn't have to go." He hiccups. "It's all because of me."

Sammy says, "You're wrong, Billy."

"Before she went to the hospital, I heard you fighting. She wanted money."

I stare out to the horizon, unsure what to do or say.

"I miss her, Dad."

"It's not your fault."

"You broke up because of me."

Sammy holds his son's gaze. "I left because I had to. We weren't happy together. It had nothing to do with you."

"She's not coming back," he wails.

Sammy and I exchange glances. I tug on the thin ropes used for tying the skiff to the dock. Sammy hauls in the anchor and makes preparations to leave.

Remorse stabs my chest. I remember how when my mother died, my father kept me at a distance but what I wanted was closeness, a shoulder to cry on. He became immobilized when he lost her and he was unable to deal with me.

A shock wave jolts me.

The same thing happened with Ben's death. Jerome became

too caught up in his own grief to provide support. When I placed my head on my arm and cried, he moved to another room.

Billy needs a hug and reassurance, and I wish Sammy would reach out to him. I know Billy feels alone and Sammy's approach worsens the situation.

Sammy fiddles with the engine.

I say, "Hey, did your dad ever sing you 'Wild Billy's Circus Story?'"

He shakes his head.

"It's a great Springsteen song and tale. All about a kid named Billy, like you, and about all the doings at the circus. Clowns, aerialists, the fat lady on the midway. There's a part about how the Ferris wheel constantly turns and never stops."

"Never heard it."

"I'm not a good singer, but I'll give it a shot." I clear my throat and launch into the tune. Billy listens raptly, and the circus comes to life.

I finish and hand Billy a drink box. He wipes his nose and sips intently.

The motor's voice pierces the air and Sammy points the skiff back to the marina. I'm grateful to take a warm shower and change out of my swimsuit back to my shorts and top. I join Sammy and discover he's showered and changed to his board shorts and a crew-neck shirt. But Billy has decided that other than hosing off his feet and hair, he'll wait to clean up when he arrives home.

Billy falls asleep in the car and Sammy nudges him awake gently once we park in his driveway.

"You can shower and change. Come over to Sofia's when you're ready."

Billy slams the door shut, stomping off without looking at us or saying goodbye.

We unload the car, and Sammy carries the clams into my kitchen.

I say, "These are so fresh it's going to be a job shucking them."

"I can handle the opening."

I hand him a knife, and he expertly pries the clams apart, catching the juice with a bowl. I push the trash can toward him so he can easily toss the empty shells. "My dad used to make barbecued clams. My grandmother taught him." I pause. "I haven't thought about that for years." I wipe my hands on a towel. "I used to cook a lot. Now I want to bake all the time."

"Wow. You're a chef too?"

I leave out the fact that I need a person who appreciates my food to make the preparation fun and not a chore. I used to cook for Jerome and for Ben. But after Ben died, we stopped eating together.

Sammy reaches in the basket for another mollusk. "I wish Billy knew more about fishing. He could be a good fisherman. His mom never would let him go with me and I didn't force the issue. I should have."

I fix my eyes on his. "He'll go out with you. Spending time with him alone is the best thing you could do for him. He needs you, now more than ever. He could use a hug."

His face contorts. "I'm such a fool sometimes."

"It's never too late to learn."

Sammy cleans his hands and encircles my waist from behind. "I suppose I can teach him what I know."

"Me too, okay?" His breath is hot on my ear.

"Definitely. But it'll cost you."

I turn into him, kiss him and slip out of his arms. I hum a few bars of a song, and he nods.

"'Trouble River,' huh?"

"Yep. Like The Boss says, sometimes you can't stop yourself from crying. But it'll pass, and we can make things better."

He reaches for me, but I move away.

"Maybe I need a hug too," he says with a gleam in his eyes.

"Go sit at the table. I'm never going to get this meal made if I don't concentrate. Billy will be here any minute."

Sammy parks himself in a chair and soon the pot of clam sauce simmers on the stove.

He says, "Ellie and Walt are on cloud nine."

"It's great, isn't it? Allan's giving her a show next month in Manhattan."

"Do you think she'll go to the opening?"

"Nope." I laugh.

"Me either. But that's okay. She'll get a reputation as a recluse and enigmatic found artist. It's bound to drive up sales."

"I'm sorry he didn't want Walt's stuff too."

Sammy smiles. "I spoke to Walt about that."

"Oh, did you?"

"I'm taking some of his pieces on consignment."

"Really?"

"Don't get excited. I have no idea if there's a market but I'm willing to give it a try."

Once Billy arrives we wait for the pasta water to bubble. Sammy's attempts to engage his boy in conversation fall flat. An awkward silence fills the kitchen.

Phoebe pads in and licks Billy's sneakers and sniffs his legs. She lays her head in his lap and whines.

"She won't leave you alone until you rub behind her ears," I say.

Billy complies, and Phoebe closes her eyes in appreciation. He stops paying attention to her, and Phoebe lifts a paw to Billy's lap.

"You have to keep petting her till she says enough."

Billy grins and strokes Phoebe all over, sending her saggy flesh into a wiggling fit.

The pot reaches a rolling boil, and I toss in some salt and a pound of linguini. The yellow strands swirl around and in no time the three of us sit down to gorge ourselves on the clams and pasta.

I give Phoebe a beef jerky treat, this one found in the guest room drawer. A bottle of wine later, Sammy pushes back his chair and pats his stomach. "If I eat anymore I'm not going to be able to get up."

Billy asks to return to Sammy's house, and Sammy protests. I come up with a compromise. "How about watching a little TV in my den? Phoebe loves 'Animal Planet.' She could use the company."

I drop my dish towel and lead the way to the small room telling him, "She barks at the cats. She really likes puppies. I showed her the Puppy Bowl once, and she practically scratched a hole in the screen."

Before we leave Billy and Phoebe to the TV, Sammy reaches out and hugs him. Billy lingers for a second in his grip and then he pushes away with a smile on his face. Phoebe plops onto Billy's feet.

Sammy and I move to the front porch. Contentment passes over me. I'm happy about what I have, no longer only sad about what I've lost. The loss will never go away, but right now it's fallen into a manageable place.

"How about some tunes?" I ask.

"Only if you don't mind me singing." Sammy strums his air guitar.

I turn on my music, and we listen to song after Springsteen song.

"The man knows how to communicate. God, he's good." Sammy's voice rings out loudly and terribly. I recognize the lyrics and chuckle.

"'This Life,'" I say, trilling along with him. Truly the lonely earth Bruce sings about never looked so attractive. He has that so right.

The tang of low-tide hangs in the air. Sammy's incredibly off-key vocals make my ears ache. Once, Phoebe joins in from behind the screen door with long howls. She pads back to the den to rejoin Billy.

As the song ends Sammy says, "You mentioned you have dreams, Sofia. Care to share them?"

"I dream about leaving my mistakes and wrong turns behind for the better person I know I can be." I meet his eyes. "And I dream there's someone next to me doing the same thing."

The waves continue crashing against the shore.

What more do I possibly need?

CHAPTER FORTY-ONE

Because the Night

NIGHT IS FALLING, AND I shiver as I stoke the smoldering stones of the town's Big Sea Day end-of-summer clambake. Rocks clatter loudly at the edge of the water, causing me to stop and listen. The ocean sounds more restless than usual. The waves hit the jetty sending up huge plumes of spray. The sea rushes to the shore and retreats rapidly.

Terri joins me at the fire. "Are you sure you haven't tended a clambake before? You're a natural."

"You're brave to let me do this."

"I can't thank you enough. You didn't flinch when I said I needed help with cooking in the sand. Not many people are willing to volunteer for a task like this. It takes a lot of time and attention." Terri warms her hands over the tarp that covers the clambake.

I poke at the coals. "I was thinking about swimming here. Maybe not tonight because of the rough chop. But this cove is so pretty it makes me want to jump in."

Terri hoots. "This isn't a great beach for swimming. That's why it's a picnic and fishing area. It's a mess of rocks." She points to the ocean. "Do you hear the racket they're making? You think the jetty is slippery? The boulders here are so smooth and slick you take your life in your hands climbing over them. Especially at our age." She smiles, and the skin around her eyes crinkles pleasantly.

"We're not that old yet, Terri." I smooth my hair.

She lifts a corner of the tarp and peeks inside. "It's a little sad to come to this end-of-season clambake. We lose all the tourists and reclaim our turf, but it also means winter's on the way."

"I'm always sorry to see summer go."

Terri laughs. "Me too. Do you think anyone says, gee, what a shame winter's ending?"

A woman wearing a "Benny Go Home" shirt waves at Terri and passes by.

I say, "I've seen a few shirts like that one. What's it mean?"

"Bennys are tourists. It's a derogatory term for them."

"How so?"

Terri stands and wipes her hands on her shorts. "Most natives swear it refers to people from Bayonne, Elizabeth, Newark, and New York who descend on our beaches each summer."

"B-E-N-N-Y," I say. "The first letter of each city."

"The town has a love-hate relationship with them. Hooray for their money, boo for their attitude and mass invasion. It's only July and August that we get crowded and noisy, so I've never understood the need to pick on the tourists that way. They're simply trying to have a good time."

Terri leans over and pulls the tarp tight across the clambake and its smoldering rocks.

"Am I a Benny?"

"Depends who you ask." Terri grins and playfully slaps me on the arm. "I'm kidding. Year-round renters are in a different category. You might not be a native, but you're no Benny. Plus, once you and Amy open your new design office you'll practically be natives. Some old timers call the real natives clam diggers." She laughs.

"I'm glad that space on Main Street was available."

Terri straightens a corner of the tarp. "Amy's thrilled there's an apartment upstairs. I love the name you came up with."

"Pink Cadillac Design."

"Perfect. You'll have to pipe that song in over your loudspeakers."

I study the cheerful crowd. In spite of Terri's reassurance about my non-Benny status, the rest of the attendees at the clambake clearly belong. I, on the other hand, intrude awkwardly on an annual ritual. I envy the friendship of the group. I know that joining in more activities leads to acceptance; Doc Phelps told me to stay engaged with life, to jump in and do things outside my comfort zone. Withdrawing and avoiding involvement holds far more attraction. The turmoil of my past still makes me reluctant to forge new friendships or try anything unfamiliar.

I wipe my hands on my apron and make a mental note to force myself to volunteer for a town board or another group. Kate probably needs help at Yappy Hour again. That makes me smile.

I say, "I regret not pushing myself more and not branching out on my own more. When I was with him, everything was all about Jerome, and I never cared enough to live any other way." I push my hair back from my forehead. "I was a wimp. I wish we'd done a lot of things."

"Like what?"

I point to the ocean. "Jerome rarely wanted to go in the water. I love to swim. I should've done it more. I suppose it's never too late to start."

"Swimming's not for everyone, especially in the ocean at night. Aren't you the one who had a mean run-in recently with a riptide? And look at what happened to poor Leon." Terri scans the crowd. "He should be here any time. The surfers always show up."

"I bet he knows the best places to swim."

Terri shakes a finger at me. "They know what they're doing when they're in the water. They usually don't venture out alone and they respect the waves. Otherwise stuff like what happened to Leon happens." She smiles. "My mama always said you don't have to jump off the Brooklyn Bridge to know it's going to kill you. Be wary of the ocean and this cove in particular, okay? It's not like other places on the shore."

"Why on earth did your mama talk about the Brooklyn

Bridge?"

"Beats me. She never set foot outside Bradley Beach. But she always used the expression. I'm rather fond of it myself."

I watch the water and place another rock on the tarp. "My son adored the beach."

Terri squeezes my shoulder gently. "I'm so sorry, hon. Life really isn't fair to us at all." She adjusts a few rocks and stands. "I feel insensitive saying this, but my grandkids have arrived." A young boy and girl race past us followed by their parents who shout happily. One of the kids throws a kiss to Terri, and she blows one back. A pang of envy passes over me.

"I'm happy for you, Terri. You're lucky to have them."

"They love the bonfire. After the clambake it'll be time for s'mores. We cooking crew get to relax then."

Amy appears behind Terri's family carrying a bottle of wine and sporting a new fellow on her arm. She grins at me and points the bottle in the direction of the bonfire that rages in the center of the beach.

"Catch you later," she calls.

Greta strolls by clutching a guitar. Her free arm drapes across the shoulders of a young woman with a long, blonde ponytail. Greta sends me a big smile.

The end of summer party draws the whole town to the shore. Everyone but Sammy. I doubt he's going to show up. He's been absent from his home since our dinner with Billy and hasn't contacted me or returned my calls. His radio silence again leaves me unsettled. I rub my arm hard. The darkness closes in on me.

I untie my apron and hand it to Terri.

"Would you mind tending the fire for a while? I'm going to take a little stroll while there's a lull in the cooking. You know the drill better than I do."

Terri stops arranging salads on a checkered table cloth. She shakes a serving spoon my way. "Don't get any dumb ideas about going into the water. Even if you did get in, you'd never be able to climb out. Last summer they had to rescue a tourist who tried to swim here. His ankle got crushed between two boulders."

The moment I move away from the fire, the air grows chillier. I play tag with the waves along the shoreline, away from the laughter and lights of the clambake and bonfire. Someone turns on music.

Springsteen's "Because the Night" serenades me. The Boss preaches the truth as usual when he croons that a night like this belongs to lovers. Bruce's plaintive keening rips into my belly, reminding me of the emptiness and longing for connection in my life.

I keep hiking until the lyrics fade. The farther I move from the fire, the brighter the stars become and the more insistent the clacking of the boulders grows.

When the glow of the fire disappears and the voices grow faint, I stop and climb atop a large, black boulder near the water. I sit there for a long while and listen to the rush of the water and the conversation of the wind in the rocks, remembering happier times with Ben.

The hair at the back of my neck bristles. I'm no longer alone.

CHAPTER FORTY-TWO

Spirit in the Night

"TERRI, IF YOU'RE OUT THERE, I'm okay," I call to the dark. I chew my lip and hope that my friend appears and not a stranger. "I didn't jump in the ocean, you don't have to worry."

No answer. The gurgle of water over the boulders reaches my ears.

Someone coughs, and I strain to make out the face in the blackness. A shadow shifts off to my right, and Sammy steps forward into my field of vision.

"Hey. Guess I'm not the only one who figured this was the right place to be on such a perfect night."

The boulders clack in the rough surf, and the cool glow of a firefly blinks now and again. A part of me wants Sammy to stay, but a chasm of confusion stretches between us and my mixed emotions rise up in my gullet. I recall the time he told me he dreams about me but then he disappeared. Now here he is again. His hot and cold behavior can't be glossed over.

Sammy clears his throat. "I've been told they have this clambake every year."

"Terri says same time, same place. Haven't you ever attended?"

He shakes his head. "I'm not social, in spite of my sisters nagging. My father told me all about it though when I was a kid. My sisters used to go when they were young."

He kicks at the sand and continues, "My dad used to come to this place a lot. There's a legend in town about a ghost who hangs around the cove. It's the ghost of a man who met a girl here in his youth, but he wasn't able to persuade her to leave with him. He left and pined for her for ages. When he died his ghost came back and searched for her."

"Terri tells me no one ever leaves Bradley Beach. Apparently that applies to ghosts too." Silence fills the air. I gather my courage. "Speaking of leaving, you disappeared again. Want to tell me what's up with your ghosting?"

I can't see Sammy clearly with the moon shining so brightly behind him. I toss a shell out into the darkness.

Sammy says, "People do stay here for generations. If you visit the cemetery you'll see only ten or twelve family names."

"Answer me, Sammy."

He says nothing.

I slap my hands on my thighs. "I for one know when it's time to leave. Not leaving, well, that's not normal or healthy in a lot of situations." I stand and face him, ready to turn and march back to the clambake.

"Don't go, Sofia. It's such a pretty evening."

"Pretty isn't everything."

Sammy shifts, and I make out his looming outline in the half-dark. His aftershave wafts on the sea breeze. The air in front of me ripples. He comes into full view and want fills me. God, he's handsome. Too bad he's so incomprehensible and so wrong for me.

"How about going for a swim? It's a perfect night for it. The tide's out so we shouldn't have any trouble getting in over the rocks. What do you say?"

I eye him cautiously. "A swim? That's what you want to do? No one swims here. This isn't a swimming cove."

"That's not true. I've done it. Granted, it's not easy, but once you get away from the shore the swimming's fine. There's a sandbar out there where you can rest." He points into the distance. "Swimming's good. It clears my head. I think it might help."

"Does it loosen your tongue too?" I sigh. "I'm supposed to help out at the clambake. And Terri says it's too dangerous to swim here."

"Come on. It won't take long. Here, you can borrow this to swim in." He peels off his T-shirt and exposes his muscled chest. He points. "You can change over by the big rock. I'll be down at the shore. Please come with me." He walks away before I can reply.

I decide not to think about what's happening. I change into the T-shirt and leave my clothes in a heap by the boulder. I walk to the shore. Sammy balances precariously on one of the medium-sized boulders. In an attempt to steady himself, he flails his arms in the air.

"Didn't you say you did this before?"

He teeters on the rock. "Ssshhh. You're disturbing my concentration. It's all in the balance. You have to get the sense of each rock before you commit to it. If it doesn't feel right you have two choices. Either stay where you're standing or leap forward hoping the next one will be a little better." He lunges forward and perches atop a boulder that quickly settles under his feet.

"See. It's easy."

"Great. This is really great. I need the balance of a circus performer."

"You'll get the hang of it. Shadow me."

We move from boulder to boulder. Sammy goes first, and I follow his lead at first timidly, then more boldly. The surfaces are slick, but nowhere near as bad as the jetty. In time, I take a path of my own. Sometimes Sammy follows me. At last we arrive at the edge of the great line of rocks. Here the water drops off to a deep undersea shelf. We pause before diving together into the dark water and begin to swim.

We swim side by side. I sense his potential, strength, and comfort in the water. The moonlight glints off his taut back, and I marvel at how gracefully he stirs the water. The clattering boulders fade in the distance. My pulse throbs with exhilaration. I swim with ease and have no trouble keeping up. All the running has given me new-found strength.

Sammy treads water and faces the horizon. "Let's hit the sandbar. It's uncovered now."

We swim together and when we finally climb onto the exposed seabed, joy and accomplishment fill me. I swam the distance and never stopped. I drop on the damp sand. The waves at the rear of the sand bar lap gently behind me. I'm winded but not terribly so.

Sammy says, "I'm sorry, Sofia. I've been acting like an idiot."

"Why didn't you call?"

"It's not easy being me. I'm lousy at relationships. Everyone tells me that. Especially my sisters." He digs a hole in the sand with his toes.

"I don't understand you."

"What do you want to know?"

"For starters, tell me about your family." I draw lines in the sand with a razor clam shell. Gulls soar overhead. I figure this line of questioning is as good a soft entry as any.

"You've met my sisters."

"What about your mom and dad? You've never mentioned them. Did you spring from a rock?"

Sammy joins me on the sand. "There's really not too much to tell. Dad met Mom after he gave up on his gal from here. They moved to Rhode Island. They got married and had me and my sisters. Mom left us shortly after my birth. Dad came back to Bradley and raised us on his own. He brought me to this cove often. He passed away when Greta was in college."

I run my fingers through my wet hair and pull the curls loose. "Your dad's the ghost in the story?"

"You were listening."

"He never reunited with the girl he met here even after he came back with you kids?"

"Never," Sammy says. "She married and refused to see him. She died a few years ago. That's when someone started a rumor about the two of them getting together at last in this cove."

His eyes pierce mine, leaving me lost and found at the same

time. I look away. His hand covers mine, and I pull my fingers out from under his.

I study the sea. "Where have you been? What's going on?"

He picks up a shell and tosses it towards the water. "I wanted to come over. I wake up and want to see you."

"You're not making much sense."

"Billy was ill. I stayed up with him all night till his fever broke. I did a lot of thinking while I watched over him."

"You could have called."

"I know." He looks down at the sand. "I don't want to hurt you. You've been through so much. I don't know if I can be what you deserve."

"But you came tonight?"

"I had to."

"Why?"

"Give me a chance. I know I messed up but I can get this right. I want to try to get it right."

I unclench my fists. "You have to answer my calls and include me. I can't be on the sidelines, Sammy."

He nods and scrutinizes his feet. "I can do that."

"It would've been nice to know you were coming tonight. You can't disappear for days. I need more than that."

"I understand. Anything else?"

I shake my head.

Sammy smiles. "There is one more thing."

I wait.

"I should've done this long ago." He leans into me and presses his lips to mine. His skin is salty, his mouth soft and insistent. My loins grow warm.

I straighten up. "Are you sure you don't have someplace else to be?"

"Smartass "

He brushes my hair back and tilts my chin to the sky, exposing my throat.

A rush of passion surges through me. Every part of me is alive and to my astonishment orgasmic. Sammy kisses my neck, and I come. He runs a finger around my nipple, and I erupt again. I throw aside all my fears and all rationality. His desire matches mine; his hardness maddeningly enticing. We make love hungrily and sweetly. He's a gentle lover, and I open readily to his tender insistence. Sammy's rhythm mimics the crashing of the waves on the shore. The exquisite lovemaking differs from my early memories of the good times with Jerome, but is no less wonderful. He takes his time and holds back, bringing me to orgasm again and again and I'm lost in oblivion for a short sweet time.

"Please..." I say to him unable to stand much more.

"I don't want this to end."

Finally a difference in his tempo leaves me breathless. The intensity reaches the limit of what I can bear and I explode into a place where nothing exists but pure energy. He groans and shudders, and we collapse in a heap on the sand.

When we're spent we lay entwined on the strip of sandbar and watch the tide wash away our footprints. I cling to him for a moment longer. Off in the distance a rocket streaks across the sky.

"Fireworks," Sammy says.

"More like one firework."

"I bet there'll be another."

The sky stays dark.

"I like it better this way," I say.

"Me too."

"I'd better get back before Terri sends out a search party." I climb to my feet and locate the T-shirt, embarrassed now in spite of our coupling, and not wanting him to see me.

"Don't," he says.

"I'm not young anymore."

"You're beautiful, Sofia. I mean it."

He pulls the shirt away. I stand over him, naked in the moonlight. Sammy pushes up on his hands and takes me in. He rises and joins me.

"I've been coming to this cove a lot ever since my father died, especially after sundown. I'm not sure why. I guess it's because I know how much he loved it." His words trail off into the roaring surf.

I let my arms move to his neck and hug him close. "It's funny, isn't it, the way we stay connected to people we've lost. They're gone, but they're with us."

"Our own spirits in the night, huh?"

I laugh at the song reference and follow up with, "The lonely angels of the night are out there somewhere watching over us."

Sammy leans back. "You really do speak excellent Springsteen." He nuzzles my ear. "It's not only angels. The souls we find in real life are damn amazing to connect with too." The kiss he plants on the nape of my neck sends a shiver down my spine.

I smile. "No way will you ever leave this area."

"I don't think so." His arms wrap around me, and I'm overcome with the feeling this is right. This is a place I want to be and that I belong. Sammy kisses me on the tip of the nose. "You'll be happy to know that the natives are friendly." He grins and holds me tightly.

"And I've heard my next door neighbor really knows his Springsteen stuff."

"And my neighbor is hot stuff."

He whistles a few notes.

"Ah, 'She's the One,'" I say. "That's one of my favorites."

"I know people say that tune's about a hard-hearted unattainable woman. But to me it's about believing in someone no matter where you are or how far away you run. About wanting it to be right between two people."

I don't tell him how much I want that song to be about me. I always have. I want someone to feel that I'm his all, his everything, and that a protective bubble of love is out there and can save us from the meanness and unpredictable upsets life throws our way

I say, "Come on, lover-boy. I'll race you back to the cove."

He hugs me, and I press my body against his one last time before we pull away. He hits the water with me trailing close behind. A yearning grows. Even if he disappears again, it was glorious to be in his arms.

We swim to shore, and I change back into my clothes. I turn to give Sammy his T-shirt, but he's already gone. I hear him whistling in the distance.

I call the title into the darkness. "For You."

He whistles louder.

"I came for you," I sing softly, smiling at the different levels of meaning.

The song's powerful cry of a rejected lover and the desperate howl of intense, urgent love not being enough to save someone in dire straits, drills into my core. The Boss sings to me directly, but it's Sammy's voice I hear. So what if passion eventually evaporates or is left decimated by destructive behavior; the memory of that experience is enough to fuel you forever and drive you to future bouts of love no matter how evanescent.

An exquisite high from mainlining life and love runs through my veins. This is not an immature love, filled with illusions of a life without limitations. It's a love that's aware of the obstacles in its path, but is gloriously all-encompassing nonetheless. I brush the sand from the

T-shirt and fold it carefully, leaving it on the boulder.

I join Terri at the clambake, and we dish up plates of hot lobster and corn. Amy crouches in the glow of the fire, hugging her knees to her chest. She leans against her handsome new beau. Terri's grandchildren hover over the pit. They stoke the fire in an amiable fashion.

"My God, your hair's all wet," Terri says.

Amy catches my eye and smiles.

"I think I found my inner Amy," I say, and we all laugh.

The next morning Amy and I share a cup of coffee in the kitchen before we visit Terri to make further suggestions about her realty office and take a tour of our new office space.

Amy begs for a break in the constant stream of Springsteen. "At least till I've had my second cup of coffee," she pleads.

I tune in to news radio. I'm unable to block out the repetitive droning of the announcer, rehashing what I already know happened thanks to the updates on my smart phone.

Phoebe plops down onto my sandaled feet. She senses we're about to leave, and she's trying to keep track of me and prevent me from departing. I reach down and scratch her head. "Don't worry, girl. We won't be away for long."

Amy pinches her nostrils closed. "Whew. Phoebe is making it really easy to get out of here fast."

I reach to turn the radio to another station but bolt upright on hearing the newscaster blare a name that surprises me.

"Did you hear that?" I ask Amy.

"I thought I was imagining it."

"Jerome's company. They're talking about Jerome's firm."

I turn up the volume, and we pay attention to the broadcast.

The announcer continues, "The lengthy investigation has led to the arrest of a number of individuals for insider trading. Jerome Catherwood and personal trainer Amanda Malone have been detained prior to boarding a flight. More arrests are expected."

"Holy crap," Amy says.

I'm aware my mouth is gaping.

"Insider trading," Amy says. "That's awful."

"I had no idea. He was so closed off. And so angry and secretive." I pause. "I'm so sorry about what I did to the house. I was wrong to be so vengeful."

"Very artsy way of expressing your irritation, though. I'm surprised you were able to spell all those phrases correctly if you were that mad."

"I'm embarrassed. I'm going to go back and fix that closet."

"I'll be right there with you." Amy holds up a finger. "However, I want you to help me with another art project."

"Oh, no, here we go again."

"It's called Ruling the World. I'm making architectural replicas of famous buildings and putting a little King Kong on each of them."

"The Empire State Building?"

"Of course. Notre Dame. The Taj Mahal. The Parthenon. The places are endless. It'll be so much fun."

I smile. "Uh huh."

"You're taking this Jerome thing really well."

"I guess my grandfather was right about saltwater healing everything."

"Amen."

"But it's not only saltwater. Springsteen does a good job of mending wounds too."

Amy grins. "You're going to put him on again, aren't you?"

I crank up my music and a rocking Boss melody crams the air.

Amy joins me in song. Phoebe jumps in with loud yowling. I'm impressed. Her tone and timing are improving.

CHAPTER FORTY-THREE

Further on (up the road)

CASSIE'S KITCHEN CABINETS BRIM WITH dozens of platters and several sets of glassware. Everything needed to carry off my first night of entertaining a crowd lies within easy reach. I transfer eight bowls from the cupboard to the counter.

Steam rises from the large pot on the stove. As I lift the lid, a rolling boil greets me. I quickly add salt, and empty two boxes of linguini into the liquid and stir with a large wooden spoon.

Terri calls out from the dining room, "Are you sure we can't help? I'm not used to sitting around expecting to be served."

"Stay put and relax. It'll be ready in a few minutes."

Sammy, his sisters, Terri, Amy, and the Cornells sit in the dining room and wait for me to appear with their dinner. I sniff the second pot that bubbles gently beside the pasta and pump a fist in the air. The lobster sauce smells divine. I learned the preparation years ago from my grandmother, and tonight I assembled the dish from memory.

Sammy enters the kitchen. His eyes appear greener than usual, enhanced by the pale mint tone of his collared shirt.

"You really should've let my sisters have you over instead of inviting this horde to your place."

"It's my pleasure. You've all got plenty on your plates."

"What can I do?"

"Geez, your sisters trained you well."

He slips an arm around my waist and nuzzles my neck. "And I do dishes too."

I push him away and shake the wooden spoon at him. "No fair seducing the cook with sexy talk."

"Would you really rather I went inside and sat on my butt all night?"

"Certainly not." I push two platters toward him. "You can set these up on the table to use for the empty shells. And take a big bowl out of the cabinet so I can put the pasta in it."

"It smells great in here."

"Thanks. It's been a long time since I made this, and I'm hoping everything tastes as delicious as I remember."

Phoebe's nails click toward me, reminding me she needs a grooming. She pokes her nose into her dish.

"Someone's hungry," Sammy says.

"I didn't forget about you, girl." I peel a beef jerky and hand the stick to her. While surveying the contents of the cabinets I'd found a stash of Jerome's. "Only one in honor of the special occasion." Phoebe wolfs the meat down and barks. I fill her bowl with dry dog food. "This is your dinner. No more treats for you."

She sniffs at the kibble and sends me a sorry glance then gobbles down the food and whines.

"Maybe later, Pheebs. That was more than enough."

Sammy scratches Phoebe's ears, and she closes her eyes and drools. "It's impressive you have the Cornells here."

I take off my apron in preparation for dinner. I finished the prep work earlier in the daytime before the guests arrived, and now things are sailing along. So far no awkward silences come from the table. Ellie and Walt worry me. The only way I managed to have them agree to attend was to promise they can leave at any time. "It wasn't easy."

Sammy removes a large bowl from the cabinet and places it on the counter. "I talked to them a couple of times when I saw

Ellie working on what looked like a sculpture out in the yard. They usually run away when they hear my car coming down the block."

"You are a rather frightening person."

He chuckles. "They're an interesting couple. And Amy seems to really like them. She's been discussing all sorts of art projects with them non-stop."

"Whatever they dream up better not involve anything deadly or too dangerous, and preferably not require my assistance."

"Too late. They've already begun listing our tasks. But it's not too bad. From what I gathered, it involves the Yappy Hour crowd so that could be fun."

"I'll gladly go to Yappy Hour with them." I pause. "How's Billy today?"

"He's good." He drums on the counter. "Considering what's going on, he's doing well."

"It's got to be hard for him."

"He's sleeping over at a friend's tonight." Sammy strokes his cheek. "Can you come with me to the marina on the day after tomorrow? I'd like to take you and Billy out again if you're up for it."

"Sure thing." I send him a broad smile. "Maybe we can bring Phoebe along?"

"Why not?"

Sammy carries the empty platters out and almost immediately after that the kitchen door slams open.

Amy sends me a hungry gaze. "Are we ever going to eat? I'd have ordered a pizza if I knew it was going to take this long."

"You're so lovely when you're ravenous."

Amy wrinkles her nose. "Hey, I like what you're doing with your hair."

I laugh. "You mean nothing?"

"You have happy curls. They're really becoming."

"After that swim in the ocean at the clambake I decided to go with leaving them natural."

Amy rubs her temple. "It's not only the curls that are happy. So are you. I can feel it." She snaps her fingers. "That song. The one with I want to change my hair, my clothes, my face, that you sing." She whistles a few bars of "Dancing in the Dark." "You're you but you've changed in a good way. I guess you changed all of those things."

I touch my cheeks. "I don't think my face is different at all."

"Oh, it is, Fi. It really is."

Doctor Bartlett's number shows on my caller ID.

I grind my teeth and decide to answer.

"I see." I steady myself for the news. "Yes. I understand."

"What is it?" Amy asks.

"I'm waiting for the doctor. The night nurse says he's calling to tell me my latest results."

A few seconds later I exhale, say goodbye, and hang up.

Amy can't hide the look of concern on her face.

I send her a thumbs up. "He said everything is good."

Amy pumps a fist in the air.

"He told me not to worry about the tightness in my chest. None of the results showed anything amiss. It's probably stress related. And my cholesterol has dropped too."

"Time for a happy dance." Amy grabs me by the hands and circles me around. We hoot with glee.

Phoebe raises her nose and lets out a whine of approval. We stop whirling. "The doc said one other thing."

"What?"

"He said I should keep on doing whatever I'm doing, because it's working."

Phoebe thumps her tail against my calf.

One by one the guests crowd into the tiny kitchen. What is it about the geniality of a kitchen that draws all types of people into the room no matter how small? I decide not to try to evict them. They're comfortable in my space, and I weave my way through the group directing them to do small tasks. I'm pleased to see Ellie and Sammy talking.

After heaping platters with the lobsters and saucing the pasta in the big bowl, I shoo everyone into the dining room. I dish up plates of linguini and pass them to the guests. They dig in, swooning over the salty and sweet sauce. They slurp at the remaining liquid in their bowls and demolish every bit of the lobsters—they also finish three bottles of wine.

Ellie Cornell stretches her hand across the table and picks up an empty lobster tail.

"The color is spectacular, don't you think?" Her gray hair flows neatly to her shoulders tonight. She's wearing an old, denim skirt and white cotton blouse. A turquoise and silver necklace and matching dangling, stone earrings set off her eyes.

"Ellie..." Walt says in a tone that indicates he knows what she's thinking. He's found a pair of tan pants that almost fit his slender waist and his lavender shirt casts a healthy glow across his stubble-free chin.

Ellie waves him off. "I wonder if I could capture this glorious orange red. It's like a sunset."

He relaxes a bit. "Take a picture with your phone. Then we can toss the shells and I don't have to worry about bringing this pile home."

"Can I take one?"

"One, yes. I can deal with one."

"I can always get more if I need them."

He shakes a fist at her. "They're going to stink like mad, Ellie."

"I'll boil them."

"I think we could make incredible jewelry from the shells." Amy holds one next to her ear. Her cream-colored shift sets off her twinkling eyes. She joins me in clearing the table, and we tell the remaining diners to move to the porch and chat.

I always enjoy this time of the meal. The guests are usually a little tipsy, the main work is done, and conversation takes on a more relaxed and fun tone. Jerome used to tell bad jokes to everyone at this juncture; that often loosened things up even more.

I wash the platters, and Amy dries. She says, "I can't believe we took on redecorating your house."

"I had a lot of trouble focusing on that project." Wherever I turned another memory plagued me. The bedroom was the worst. I still can't get over the fact Jerome had the nerve to commit adultery in our bed. My cheeks burn with the remembrance of seeing him and Mandy. It wasn't like he couldn't afford a hotel room.

Amy scrapes off a dish into the trash. "I had my doubts but

we came through."

"Thanks for taking the lead so many times."

"You did fine. He's a royal bastard."

I hum a few bars from "Further on (up the road)."

Amy cocks her head. "That's too cryptic for me. What are you telling me?"

"It's a Springsteen song about rising up and taking your life into your own hands after going through the dark and cold. You might be in a bad place, but there's a sunny spot waiting for you further on up the road."

"Ah, so someone's gotten her optimism back."

"Cautious optimism," I say.

"Hmmm. Cautious optimism. That's something I might want to work on." Amy peers at the ceiling. "Nah."

Memories shoot through my mind of times when I threw caution to the wind, trusted, and wound up hurt. And recollections of the flip side, when trusting was the right choice, follow right behind. I'm ready to believe Sammy belongs in the latter category.

Amy arranges glasses and a bottle of Sambuca on a tray. "Let's get this further-on-up-the-road party started."

We join the guests on the porch. I settle onto the bamboo loveseat beside Sammy. His arm encircles my shoulders. Phoebe spreads out in front of the stairs, standing guard and blocking anyone's exit. Late blooming roses perfume the air.

Terri distributes the glasses, and Amy passes the bottle of Sambuca around.

"To the beautiful night," Sammy toasts.

"Here, here," Walt says.

Amy stands and hoists her drink. "And to friends, new and old."

We raise our glasses and sip. Walt and Ellie entwine fingers. I lean into Sammy, drawing in the remnants of his freshly-showered scent.

In the distance someone plays Springsteen. The music comes from too far away for me to make out the lyrics, but my gut tells me the song carries a message of hope and resilience.

I look up. Overhead the full moon consecrates the sky,

dispelling the darkness with its protective light. The possibilities in life are endless and, for now, bright.

The End

ACKNOWLEDGMENTS

I WANT TO SEND A BIG thank you out to the people who helped me bring this book to life.

Thank you, Tom, for always being there and giving me the space I need. Your love is priceless. Ditto for the rest of my family.

Thanks to the many members of The Rose & Thorn who helped with early drafts and encouraged me to keep going.

Thanks to Emma Wicker and Kate Foster for believing in this book, sharpening it, and bringing it to an audience.

Thanks to old friends, and gym buddies, and everyone who ever asked what I was working on and thought it was a cool idea—or at least acted as though it was!

Thank you, Bruce Springsteen and the E Street Band, for the music that has been a part of my life for decades. Whether it's to rock to when I'm happy or to contemplate when I'm sad, I'm grateful that your music is always there for me.

Thank you, Dee, for caring, listening, and encouraging me.

And most of all, thank you to wonderful YOU, my readers. You've embarked on a journey with me and I'm grateful for the company. You see, I'm not good alone in the dark. So all us losers and winners, and saints and sinners, let's hold hands and travel together.

ABOUT THE AUTHOR

BARBARA QUINN IS AN AWARD-WINNING short story writer and author of a variety of novels including *36C, The Speed of Dark, Hard Head, and Slings and Arrows.* Her travels have taken her to forty-seven states and five continents where she's encountered fascinating settings and inspiring people that populate her work.

Her many past jobs include lawyer, record shop owner, reporter, process server, lingerie sales clerk, waitress, and postal worker. She's a native New Yorker with roots in the Bronx, Long Island, and Westchester. She currently resides with her husband in Bradley Beach, NJ and Holmes Beach, FL. She enjoys spending time with her son and his family and planning her next adventure. She wants to remind everyone that when you meet her, SHE'S NOT SHOUTING, SHE'S ITALIAN.

www.ingramcontent.com/pod-product-compliance
Lightning Source LLC
Chambersburg PA
CBHW061558100726

47898CB00002B/423